D1559919

EVIL
WINDS

1351315

The views expressed in this work are those of the author and do not necessarily reflect the official policy or position of the Department of the Navy, Department of Defense, nor the US Government. This is a work of fiction. Any resemblance to persons living or dead is purely coincidental.

Copyright © 2018 by Michael Shusko

ISBN-13: 978-0-99819-595-7
ISBN-10: 0-99819-595-2

DEVELOPMENTAL EDITING: Philip Athans
COPYEDITING: Debra Manette
PROOFREADING: James Fraleigh
TEXT DESIGN AND TYPESETTING: John Reinhardt Book Design
COVER DESIGN: Ty Nowicki
PRODUCTION MANAGEMENT: Leigh Camp

To the peacekeepers and the peacemakers.

1

MATAK HAD NEVER BEEN this far away from home. He looked over the side rails of the old, bullet-riddled pickup truck. They had driven for several hours in the oppressive darkness. But now, bright lights shone in the desert ahead of them, illuminating the few barren shrubs and rock formations.

A wide gate swung open, letting in the convoy carrying what was left of the teenagers from the village. As the pickup carrying Matak screeched to a halt, the screaming started.

"Get out! Get out of the truck, you dogs! Hurry before I shoot you like I shot your fathers back in the village!" the men yelled as they yanked the boys out of the trucks.

Matak felt a strong hand on his shoulder and then he was airborne. He landed dazed on the hard-packed sand. The sudden sound of machine gun fire brought him back into reality. He looked and saw his fourteen-year-old cousin, Obie, get up and sprint through the open gate and into the darkness. Three men from within the compound followed, firing their weapons indiscriminately.

Matak glanced over his shoulder at the second truck—the one carrying the girls. It had also stopped, but no one was getting out of the cargo bed. He was sure he saw them load his twin sister, Fatima, into the truck back in the village.

"Please, please…" Matak prayed quietly, his thoughts returning to Obie. "Please let him make it."

But Matak's hopes for his cousin's safe escape were dashed when he saw the men return, dragging the young boy back as he kicked and screamed, trying to break free from their grip. They threw Obie onto the ground in front of the bright lights of the trucks. One man kicked the boy in the back, and he howled in pain. *If Obie had made it to freedom, he could have alerted others of our plight*, Matak thought. Perhaps he might have been able to find Matak's father. That would have been their only chance of surviving.

Matak had heard the stories of what happened to boys and girls who were taken by the Evil Winds.

"Anyone else want to try to escape?" growled a large man wearing camouflaged military cargo pants and a black T-shirt.

Matak looked up at the thick man standing a few feet in front of him.

He was rewarded by the man grabbing him by the back of his shirt. Matak was lifted two meters off the ground and found himself face-to-face with what could only be a *shaytan jinn*.

"Yes, take a good look, boy," the man snarled.

But Matak only turned his head to the side, his eyes closed as tightly as possible, shielding himself from the disfigured horror breathing into his face.

"I said look at me," the voice hissed again.

Matak couldn't help himself. It was part fear but he also had to know. He had never seen a *jinn*, or demon, before. If he was going to die in this horrible place tonight, he needed to know what the *jinn* looked like. He opened his eyes slowly and turned to look at the man holding him in the air. A thick gash, long healed but still horrific, ran down the right side of his face, damaging his eye and disfiguring his cruel grimace.

"Yes," the scarred man replied, a grin coming over his face. "Look closely. Soon it'll be like looking in a mirror. You will all look like me after I'm done with you," he bellowed, throwing Matak back to the ground.

It was all too much for Matak to bear. He began to vomit as he recalled the mangled face of his captor. A few short hours ago, he was playing with Fatima and Obie in his aunt and uncle's village. His mother had taken them there this morning for a visit. The adults were all dead now. He was forced to watch as they raped his mother and aunt and butchered his uncle with a machete. After the carnage was over, they had rounded up all the children and loaded them into the two trucks, one for boys and one for girls. Everyone in the once vibrant village had succumbed to the Evil Winds.

He was thankful that at least his 12-year-old sister was safe at home with their father. Because Halima was sick with fever back in their own village of Zarundi, this visit to their aunt and uncle in the nearby village of Gutaya almost hadn't happened. But the elders in Zarundi convinced their mother that it was her duty to go visit her sister, who had just recently had a baby. Her mother undertook the journey, taking Matak and his twin sister Fatima with her, only after Halima's fever broke. But their mother had insisted that their father remain in Zarundi to care for their youngest child.

While Matak desperately wished his father was here at this moment, he was relieved that young Halima was not. She would undoubtedly have been thrown into the truck with Fatima to await their horrific fate. Perhaps things would have been different if his father had been in Gutaya today. Matak peered into the darkness, searching for his father but knowing he wasn't there. No one was. There was no one to help them now.

Matak felt like crying, but there were no more tears. Behind him, he saw the glare of the taillights of the truck containing Fatima. It was pulling away, with the girls still on board, heading off to an unknown destination. He feared he would never see his twin sister again.

Staring as the guards bound Obie's hands and feet to ensure that the boy wouldn't make another escape attempt, Matak accepted that there was indeed no way out. He knew once the Evil Winds had you, you were never seen again. This was his new home. The only question that remained was, for how long?

2

INTENSE HEAT HIT ANGIE as she stepped off the plane. It was as though she'd put her head in an open oven. She reached for the railing, pulling back as she touched the hot metal. When she reached the bottom of the stairs, she could feel the heat radiating from the blistering tarmac beneath her feet. It was dry and relentless, burning her face as she picked up her pace and headed for the sanctuary of the small terminal in front of her.

When she entered the unkempt concrete terminal, the temperature immediately dropped to a cool 90 degrees Fahrenheit. Angie looked around the crowded room, trying to figure out where she should go. Most of the passengers veered to the right, where they would be herded through two immigration booths. The single booth on the left had a very short line. Angie assumed this was for VIPs and diplomats.

"Miss Angie?" said a small man with an even smaller voice.

She turned and noticed a weathered man approaching her. He had a full head of short cropped hair, but his face was dark and leathery. His eyes were a deep brown, almost black in color. Although the whites of his eyes had a yellowish tinge, his expression was bright and warm, welcoming Angie after her long, arduous flight. Angie guessed his age was about thirty or thirty-five years, with salt-and-pepper hair and a malnourished frame. Evidently the harsh life of sub-Saharan Africa had taken its toll on this wrinkly-skinned, well-dressed little man.

"Miss Angie?" he repeated.

"Hello," she answered, holding out her hand. "Yes, I'm Angie Bryant."

A broad smile came across the man's face, showing a full set of worn teeth.

"I am Ismael. Mr. Chesterfield sent me. He's waiting outside for you. I am to help you clear customs," he said.

It wasn't uncommon for government agencies and embassies to have expeditors waiting at the airport. Western governments and companies often hired locals to help their employees navigate the bureaucracies of the developing world. These expeditors also came in handy arranging hotel rooms, getting rental cars, and generally making life easier for foreigners working and living in Africa.

"Please, follow me, Miss Angie," Ismael said as he darted off towards the immigration booth on the left. She hurried behind her fragile-looking expeditor, not wanting to get lost in the bustling crowd pressing around her. Apparently, personal space was a foreign concept in Chad.

A young but stern immigration official spoke some harsh-sounding Arabic to Ismael. After a brief exchange, her passport was stamped and they were heading to the baggage claim area.

"Was there a problem with the immigration official, Ismael?" she asked, wondering about the terse exchange. "He didn't sound very happy with you."

"No, not at all. He's my wife's brother. He's upset with us for not coming to dinner last night," Ismael replied with a sheepish grin and a shrug of his gaunt shoulders. "Please, let us find your bags."

Well, now I know why you're the expeditor.

Angie stood by the old baggage carousel watching the broken boxes, taped-up bags, and the occasional suitcase glide slowly by. She was beginning to get nervous as fewer and fewer bags and boxes appeared on the worn conveyor belt. Finally, her large green bag appeared, amazingly unharmed despite the long trip from California.

"Here, this is it." Angie reached for the bag.

"No, Miss Angie. Please let me get it," Ismael insisted. She was certain her suitcase weighed at least as much as the man did, but he managed to lift it off the conveyor and use both hands to drag it to the doors leading into the main reception terminal.

"Really, I can carry it, Ismael."

"No, no. It's okay."

Feeling guilty but not wanting to insult her expeditor, Angie followed quietly behind him, hoping he wouldn't have a heart attack as he lugged her oversized bag through the airport exit.

▼ ▼ ▼

Henry Chesterfield was not at all what Angie had expected when she saw him standing by the white Toyota Land Cruiser with the big black UN logo plastered on the door. His deep voice on the phone had led her to image a tall, younger man rather than the portly, bespectacled chap in his early fifties who stood before her.

"Hello, Angie. Welcome to Chad," he said in perfect Queen's English.

"Hi. Henry?" she asked, wanting confirmation as she extended her hand.

"Yes," he said warmly. "Good to meet you. Let's get your luggage in the back, shall we? You must be exhausted after your long flight."

Ismael was already on it, swinging her bag off the curb and hoisting it into the back of the vehicle. Angie decided not to watch, fearing for Ismael's safety.

"Actually, I know I should be tired, but I'm too excited. I probably couldn't sleep right now even if I tried."

"Splendid. Why don't we get you checked in and we can sit in the hotel restaurant and have a talk? I have a press conference at the British embassy later this afternoon, but I have some time to fill you in on what's been going on here since we last spoke on the telephone," Henry replied.

"I guess being a media coordinator for the United Nations High Commission for Refugees keeps you busy," Angie said.

"To say the least. It would be nice if I had some help, but right now it's just yours truly. I'm the only UNHCR official in N'Djamena, despite the huge number of refugees on the eastern border with Sudan. To make matters worse, the Sudanese government has done a very good job of maintaining a total media blackout," Henry said. "As hard I try, I can't get the word out about the atrocities occurring in Sudan all by myself. The best I can do is help facilitate the journey for the few journalists like yourself who brave the long flight here to visit the refugee camps in eastern Chad."

While Henry rambled on in the backseat of the Land Cruiser, Angie focused on the rundown mud and concrete dwellings they passed on the back roads of the capital. Trash lined the dilapidated dirt alleys, conveying the depth of poverty in this abandoned corner of Africa. *If it was this bad in the capital city,* she wondered, *what must it be like across the border in war-torn Darfur?*

"I thought oil had been discovered in this part of Africa not long ago," she said, interrupting Henry's tirade about frequent loss of power in the hotel where she would be staying. "Where is the money going?"

"What little revenue remains after the foreign companies and the corrupt government officials in the region take their cut is used to make military purchases to fight rebels and insurgents instead of directly benefiting the people."

"What do foreign businesses have to do with the problems in Sudan?" she asked.

"There are a fair number of foreigners and private international companies that have been discreetly operating in Africa and other underdeveloped parts of the world for years. Profiteers from across the globe. Many operating here freely, probably even without the knowledge of their own governments. They pay off dishonest politicians, promise to build a cheap road or bridge as a sign of goodwill, all the while building factories, quarries, and refineries in remote areas to pillage oil and minerals from the people," Henry explained.

"That's horrible. You never hear about it in the States. Isn't the UN doing anything about it?"

"You will soon learn, my young ideological American friend, that this is Africa. No one cares much about this lost continent. The real atrocity is the complacency of the international community while all of these war crimes continue for decades."

Angie leaned back in her seat, flabbergasted. "You mentioned rebels here in Chad? So, there's war here too? I thought most of the fighting was in Sudan."

"Unfortunately, the political instability and violence in the Darfur region of Sudan has spilled over into this country. Much of the Chadian rebel activity is based out of western Sudan, near Darfur. They take advantage of the lawlessness there."

"So much fighting and suffering," Angie whispered, staring out at the mud shacks dotting the road leading up to her hotel.

"That's why I'm so glad you're here, Angie," Henry replied as they pulled up to the Meridien Hotel. "I'm afraid most media outlets in your country have forgotten about us here in Chad and across the border in the Sudan. There was some hope after the Rwandan genocide that the world would pay more attention to Africa, but, regrettably, it was only a passing phase. The violence has continued to escalate in Sudan yet the world turns a blind eye to the suffering. Perhaps it was thought that the creation of the new country of South Sudan would solve everything. Unfortunately, this was not the case.

"But, hopefully, you can tell the refugees' stories," he added with a smile as he got out of the SUV. "I have arranged a local charter to take us to the border to see the refugee camps tomorrow. There are twelve established camps currently, but many smaller makeshift camps are popping up in the desert on either side of the border. The Janjaweed have most of the camps surrounded and, despite the presence of nearly twenty thousand largely ineffective UNAMID soldiers and police sent to protect the refugees, the Janjaweed raids continue."

"Tell me about the Janjaweed," Angie said as they walked into the hotel.

Ismael had taken her bag to the check-in counter as Henry led Angie to a small table near the front desk. They sat down in front of the beautiful glass elevator in a tall, open foyer as a waiter brought them two bottles of water.

"They're ruthless Arab Bedouin from the north of Sudan. Their name is somewhat of a linguistic mystery, but it's usually translated as something like 'devil horsemen with rifles.' At least that's how they act. They're hardened nomads who have been sweeping through the Darfur region with the help of Sudanese government troops, weapons, planes, and financing. They won't stop until all of Sudan is Islamic and populated solely by Arabs. They want the non-Arab African tribes out of Darfur."

"And no one is able to do anything about it?" she asked.

"In a word," he said, his eyes displaying the deep sadness in his heart, "no. You see, Angie, years of desertification, famine, and overpopulation has turned millions of acres of fertile land in northern Sudan into a desert. I remember when I first came to the Sudan as a child. My father was an archaeologist in Egypt. It was lovely—lush and green. The summer rainy season turned the dry lands into beautiful, fertile fields, perfect for grazing cattle and growing millet, the staple food of Darfurians. But decades of drought and misuse of the land and natural resources has turned vast tracts of the Sahel into a barren desert. Those who lived there, mainly Arab Bedouin and herdsmen, found themselves venturing deeper south into Darfur, looking to exploit what farmland remained to find better grazing fields for their livestock. These incursions, however, were only the tip of the iceberg."

As Henry spoke, Angie took a small pad out of her bag and jotted down some notes. "What did the government do about it?" she asked.

"For years, the Sudanese government has been making the area less stable with its policy of ethnic cleansing. The Arab-dominated government and military were intolerant of the non-Arab African tribes that live in Darfur. The Fur is the largest of these non-Arab tribes, but there are others. Many people think that the war in Darfur is about religion. While some Christians and even animistic tribes do exist, the majority of Darfur inhabitants are Sunni Muslims, just like the Janjaweed. It's not about the religion, but rather the ethnicity of the villagers that put them in peril. With strong government backing, the Arab nomads from the north drove deeper into Darfur, slaughtering entire villages and stealing their land to create a more ethnically Arab state."

Angie let the man, obviously in pain over the atrocities that were overtaking his beloved adopted home, gather his thoughts. She wasn't sure if he was just tired or wiping away a tear as the British expatriate rubbed his eyes.

Finally, he continued. "There have been many international movements and resolutions against the Sudanese government, but they still have powerful allies. Some foreign governments have deep financial interests in the region and they've used their voice at the UN on more than one occasion to prevent us from doing more."

"Who's fighting for Darfur? For the refugees?"

"Well, you're here. We also have an American doctor from the NGO Medicine International who works at the camp," Henry added with a smile, referring to one of the many non-governmental organizations providing aid throughout Africa. "You'll meet him tomorrow."

"I just can't believe all this is happening and no one cares."

"Most nations just see Africa as a land of poverty and law-lessness. Their belief is that there's little to gain from investing economic or political resources here. The global profiteers that are here, on the other hand, see things quite differently. They're using the vast financial capital from their profitable companies to engage with African governments across the continent in an attempt to extract vital natural resources and sell them to the highest bidders. Unfortunately, many Western governments just don't see the benefit of investing in or helping Africa."

"That's just wrong."

"Right or wrong, it's the reality in which we find ourselves."

"Miss Angie, you're all checked in now, and your luggage is on its way to your room," Ismael reported, handing her the key.

"Thank you, Ismael," she said with the first smile of her trip. It was difficult to even force a smile when there was so much misery all around her.

"Well," Henry said as he stood up, "get some rest. You'll need it for tomorrow. The suffering you'll see is truly heart-wrench-ing and will wear you down quickly. I'll pick you up right here at nine o'clock in the morning. Do you have everything you need?"

"I'm good. Thanks, Henry. Thank you for giving me the chance to come out here. I hope I can do some good for you and the refugees."

"No, Angie Bryant. It is I who should be thanking you. You have a great opportunity here. Not many people outside of Africa see what you will see tomorrow. Tell the world, Angie. That's how you can help."

3

TAYEB BAROUDI sat on the couch of the small, dusty apartment in the middle of Toulon, France. A popular game show was on the TV, but he was focused on loading the 5.56 mm rounds into one of the dozen empty FAMAS G2 magazines lying on the table. Although the meeting was arranged by the *khalifah* himself, Tayeb was not about to take any chances. The man they were meeting with later that night was a fierce and ruthless killer. No doubt, such a man would be an asset to the organization, but he had not yet agreed to the *khalifah*'s generous offer to join their crusade. Tayeb had to be prepared for anything.

Footsteps down the hall caused Tayeb to cease his work. Instinctively, he placed the towel on his lap over the table full of magazines and waited. His right hand reached for the pistol underneath one of the seat cushions as he stared at the front door.

Slowly the doorknob turned. Tayeb patiently watched, his weapon ready for action. The door swung open and a familiar face appeared.

"Houda, you startled me. You weren't supposed to be home for another hour," Tayeb said. He stood up and walked over to his wife to help her with her bags.

"I left work early to help get ready for this evening," Houda said, kissing her husband as she closed the door behind her with her foot. Houda hung his navy uniform on the hook on the back of the door. "I stopped by the cleaners."

"Thanks," Tayeb replied, placing the bags on the loveseat in the crowded living room. "Listen, I've been thinking. I don't want you going today. It might be dangerous."

"Tayeb, we've been through this already," Houda sighed. "I'm a part of this movement as much as you are. And I'm much less conspicuous than you are, my big brute. You look like a terrorist."

"Is that so," he asked with a smile. Tayeb stood behind his young wife and put his long arms around her. Even at six months pregnant, he was still able to pull her close into his large frame like a bear holding her cub. "Seriously, though. No one is questioning your dedication, my love. But we have the baby to think about. If something was to happen to me..."

"Stop," she said, turning to face her husband. She strained her neck up to the sky as she often did when looking into her tall husband's eyes. "No more talking like that, Tayeb, do you hear me? Today is just a meeting. Faris said that the Janjaweed commander has expressed an interest in joining us. Why do you think something bad will happen?"

"I don't know. This just doesn't feel right," he replied. "You know, in the military, sometimes your gut just tells you something's wrong. I can't put my finger on it."

"Listen," she said, resting her head on his burly chest. "I know it's been a busy and stressful time over these past several months. The *khalifah* has asked much from us. But it's worth it. Imagine,

Tayeb, a pious world the way the Prophet envisioned it. Our baby can grow up in such a devout world, free of the immorality and debauchery that plagues and destroys the Western world. And we are playing a part in the *khalifah*'s master plan to bring it to reality."

The couple had had this conversation before. Tayeb's entire world was in his arms at this moment: his beautiful pregnant wife, Houda. Ironically, Tayeb had enjoyed his life in France. Born and raised in Toulon by politically and religiously moderate Algerian immigrants, he was, in his view, more a Frenchman than an Arab. He played football at lycée Côte d'Azur, sailed down the French coastline with his friends on weekends, and had even joined the French navy to serve his country. But all that changed when he met Houda a few years back.

"Why do I even try to argue with you?" he asked playfully.

"I keep asking myself the same thing," Houda retorted, holding her man more tightly.

"Okay. But you stay in the car with the weapons. I'll go inside with Faris to meet the *Sudani*," Tayeb replied. "That's final."

It was uncharacteristic of Tayeb to put his foot down with his wife. It may have been rare for a woman in a strict Islamic household to wield so much power, but their relationship was special. It wasn't arranged. Tayeb had fallen in love with Houda the moment he first saw her working in a perfume shop. His love had only grown since their marriage two years ago.

Houda turned her head again to look up at her husband. For a brief moment, Tayeb thought she was going to argue with his demand. But then she surprised him with her answer. "Okay, Tayeb. This time, we'll do it your way."

Pregnancy is softening her, Tayeb thought. When they first met, Tayeb knew that Houda was faithful to Islam and was strong in her beliefs. Her father had been an imam back in Morocco before they immigrated to Toulon when Houda was in secondary school. After the move, her father became a staunch supporter of Sharia law in France and an opponent of the secular French government.

Although Houda never told Tayeb how she met Faris, a local thug-turned-emir for the newly established United Islamic Caliphate fundamentalist movement, Tayeb suspected it was through her father, who had made it his mission to show lost Arabs living in Toulon the light of Islam. When Tayeb first met Houda's father, he thought the man detested him. After all, Tayeb was a sailor in the French navy. But her father embraced Tayeb. Through him, Tayeb found the lost religion of his youth. Although not as conservative as his beautiful wife, Tayeb now understood the importance of his Arab heritage and Islamic religion. For that reason, he secretly joined with Faris to support the spread of his *khalifah*'s message and growing movement.

All of a sudden, the front door of the apartment smashed open, sending splinters and shards of wood flying through the room. Masked men dressed in black with automatic weapons held high poured into the small room.

Houda broke free from her husband's embrace and lunged for the French G2 assault rifle leaning against the couch.

"Houda, no!" Tayeb screamed, realizing the deadly consequences of what his beloved wife was about to do. Whoever these men in black were, they obviously meant business and would mow down anyone who even appeared to be a threat. Tayeb turned toward the invaders and his worst fears were realized when he saw them aiming their weapons at Houda.

"No!" he repeated, stepping in between his wife and the armed men.

One of the men in black struck Tayeb on the chin with the butt of his weapon.

▼ ▼ ▼

Houda froze as she watched her husband hit the ground. In the pause, another intruder grabbed her before she reached the weapon near the couch. She struggled to free herself from the captor's strong grip, screaming Tayeb's name.

Two men were already on top of her husband, zip-tying Tayeb's hands behind his back. Houda herself was carried out of the room and down the flight of stairs. When they reached the street, the cold air stung her face. A hood was placed over her head, and everything suddenly went black as she was put in the back of a van.

"*Habibi*," she moaned as she sobbed uncontrollably. Her thoughts remained on her husband, his fate unknown as the van sped away through the Place Victor Hugo.

4

"CRATES OF FAMAS G2 ASSAULT RIFLES," Steve said to his French colleague. "And lots of them."

Barely thirty years old, Steve Connors already had considerable experience as a troubleshooter in some of the roughest parts of the world. His ability to blend into a crowd and use his deductive skills to put together pieces of intelligence was what kept this young, up-and-coming CIA operative in such high demand at Langley. Although his short-cropped sandy blond hair, blue eyes, and average yet all-American look made it difficult for him to infiltrate terrorist groups in the Middle East, Steve relied on his linguistic abilities and sheer intellect to successfully gather intelligence on America's adversaries.

"*Oui,*" replied Marcel Barbier, a special agent with the French Central Directorate of Interior Intelligence, or DCRI. "And we would never have found them if it wasn't for your tip."

For months, Marcel had been the DCRI lead investigator trying to track down weapons stolen from French military bases throughout southern France. Terrorist groups based out of the Sahel had been making bold moves in Africa, forging alliances

19

with any group showing hostility toward the West. French troops engaging Islamic extremists in Mali and other parts of North Africa were finding caches of military weapons manufactured in French factories. The CIA and INTERPOL had joined the DCRI as part of a broader investigation into illegal arms deals and weapon shipments to North Africa originating from southern Europe.

Up until this point, however, no one could figure out who was behind the weapons heists. But on his last mission in the United Arab Emirates, Steve had received an unexpected tip with the name of the European regional commander, or emir, of a new terrorist group that he had been tracking. The United Islamic Caliphate, or UIC as it was known in the West, led by a Yemeni named Abdullah al-Harbi, was rapidly emerging as an alternative to ISIS and al-Qaeda. From what Steve had been able to put together, the goal of the UIC was to form an international coalition of Islamic states to establish a unified, intercontinental Islamic empire.

"So, this is Faris Hannachi, al-Harbi's man in Europe?" asked Steve, looking at a wedding picture on the mantel.

"*Non,*" replied Marcel. "This man was in the *Marine Nationale.*"

"French navy?" Steve asked, looking up at the uniform of the elite *Fusiliers Marins* hanging on the back of the door.

"Naval infantry, to be exact," Marcel added as he continued to open drawers in a small desk near the window. "His name is Tayeb Baroudi. The woman is his wife, Houda. They are both in custody, but neither is saying much. I suspect we'll get nothing from them."

"But this apartment was supposed to be owned by Hannachi. Are Tayeb and Faris the same man?"

"I don't know. This apartment *is* registered to a Faris Hannachi, but it appears that Tayeb and his wife lived here.

Either way, Tayeb Baroudi is in a lot of trouble. These are all French navy weapons that have been reported missing from the *arsenal de Toulon*," replied Marcel, gesturing toward the crates of rifles stuffed into the tiny apartment. "Interestingly, Monsieur Baroudi was an armorer at the naval base here in Toulon."

"I guess we now know who's been behind the stolen weapons from your military bases." Steve strolled around the living room, searching for additional clues. "But we don't know how the rifles have been getting into the hands of terrorists in Africa. What do you know about Baroudi and his wife?"

"Nothing much on him," Marcel said, pacing around the small apartment. "He was born here in Toulon, but his parents emigrated from Algeria about thirty years ago. Apparently, they were well off. Even sent young Tayeb to a private American school here. They're both dead now. Car accident five years ago. Tayeb's an only child, and from what his comrades in the Fusiliers tell me, he was a patriotic Frenchman. Even served with distinction in Djibouti where he was involved in antipiracy operations."

"So why did he turn to the UIC?" Steve asked.

"So far he hasn't told us. But, like I said, there was nothing much on him, other than he worked in the armory on the naval base, which gave him access to weapons, delivery schedules, *et cetera*. His wife, however, is another story. Apparently, Houda Baroudi's father is very vocal about his anti-French and extremist beliefs. A local news outlet ran a story about him at a large fundamentalist rally calling for the implementation of Sharia law here in southern France a few months back. We'll know more after we finish questioning Madame Baroudi, but I suspect she and her father turned Petty Officer Tayeb Baroudi into a traitor."

"Okay. We have the weapons and the source but no idea where they were going or who the Baroudis' contact is. The wife's father?"

"We picked him up an hour ago. We don't have much to hold him on. Looks like he may have recruited Tayeb, but that's all we have on him thus far."

"Yeah, that's not too surprising," said Steve. He took a black-and-white photo of a Parisian street off the wall and checked the back for clues or papers hidden behind the frame. "The UIC will want to keep his recruiting activities at the mosque clean and separate from the actual terrorist operations. That way, recruitment can continue even if an op like this goes bad. I doubt you'll find much more of a link between the father and these two love-birds. Keep on it, though, he may know something."

"We will," Marcel replied, nodding.

"Any phones found?"

"A burner. All incoming and outgoing numbers were erased, probably as soon as they were answered," the Frenchman replied, pointing to the flip phone on the coffee table.

Steve walked over and picked it up. "Sounds like Tayeb is a smart and cautious man. He wouldn't risk someone stumbling across his phone and seeing the name of his contact or his UIC handler's name or number on it."

Steve put the phone down and continued looking around. From where he stood, he could see the refrigerator in the other room. Steve walked into the kitchen, followed closely by Marcel. There were many pictures and notes behind various magnets of places Steve imagined the young Arab couple had visited. One note, however, stood out. Steve removed the *Arc de Triomphe* magnet that held the slip of paper securely on the refrigerator door and read the note.

"I've taken a picture of that and sent it to a translator in my office," Marcel said, looking at the Arabic scribble on the note.

"No need. It says 'Pirate's Landing twelve o'clock,' with today's date."

Marcel looked at his watch. "It's twelve-thirty now."

"Your raid took place just before noon today and both of the Baroudis were here," Steve mused. "If the meeting was at twelve noon, chances are they would already have left the apartment to make the meeting. Tayeb went to an American school, right? We don't use twenty-four-hour time in America. We say a.m. and p.m. This isn't twelve noon, it's twelve midnight. Tonight. Where is this Pirate's Landing?"

"It's a bar here in Toulon. On the promenade. Not a very popular place, I think. I like the Italian restaurant next to it and eat there often. I don't see a lot of customers going in or out of the bar."

Steve handed his DCGI colleague the sheet of paper. "Sounds like a perfect place for a drop then, doesn't it?"

5

"ANGIE, YOUR FATHER AND I worked hard trying to shield you from the horrors of the world," Eunice Bryant told her only daughter over the international video chat. Angie had begun organizing her research after she had dinner and settled down into her room at Le Meridien. The final call to prayer sounded from the minaret outside her window just as she pulled out of her suitcase the stacks of notes, newspaper clippings, and articles that had anything to do with the decades-old conflict in Sudan. She had left a message that she arrived safely when she got to her room hours ago but decided to call her parents before delving into her research. "Your father's only concern right now is your safety."

"Mom, I'll be careful." Angie tried to be reassuring, knowing that her words would fall on deaf ears. "I need to write this story."

"I just don't understand, Angie. He spoke to Gerald who told him you volunteered to go to Chad? Why?" she asked.

"I can't ride Dad's coattails forever, Mom. I have to prove that I'm a serious journalist. Besides, this story needs to be told."

"Everyone at the *National Times* knows you're a serious journalist. You got that job on your own. If you want to build your career as a writer, you need to start here, where you have face time with the editors and work up the ladder like everyone else."

Deep down, Angie realized her parents knew what they were talking about. After all, her father was a Pulitzer Prize–winning author and her mother a renowned magazine photographer. But she was still not so sure her father hadn't pulled strings at the paper to get her hired.

"This is where the action is. I need to be here and write about it. I can handle it, Mom," the young woman replied. "Listen, I'm going to do a little more background for my story, then get some sleep. I'll call you tomorrow when I get to the camp, providing there's decent internet there."

"Well, we miss you, Angie. Just hurry and come home and be careful, okay?"

"I will, Mom. Give Dad a hug for me," she said.

The call ended and Angie jumped back into her work. She sifted through the notes and highlighted sections of her research, then began writing her story. Their story—the story of the refugees from Darfur. The story that she hoped would get her out from under the shadow of her famous literary parents.

Her background information was relatively complete, and she used it to begin her tale of sorrow and hopelessness. Since convincing Gerald, senior editor at the *National Times*, to let her go to Chad a few weeks ago, Angie had scoured every source at her disposal to gather as much information on the conflict in Darfur as possible. It had proven a difficult feat due to the Sudanese government's lack of transparency. There was an abundance of stories from within the refugee camps across the border in Chad, citing firsthand eye witnesses to the atrocities committed by the Janjaweed and their Sudanese government allies, but not as much from the villages within Darfur.

As Henry had mentioned, the current crisis between the two largest Arab nomadic tribes, the Baggara and Abbala, against the African, non-Arab Fur, Zaghawa, and Massaleit farming tribes, had started when grazing lands became scarcer due to regional desertification. But ethnic tensions had been present for centuries. Over the past several decades, pan-Arab nationalism had swept down from the Levant into North Africa, stirring movements to unite Arabs under one government. Fanned by racist rants from prominent leaders on the continent calling for Arab unity, the flames of ethnic strife and genocide spread like a wildfire across Darfur.

Her mother's words haunted her as she looked at the pictures of massacred villagers lying amid the burned-out huts in Darfur. Now that she was truly getting close to the carnage, the images stirred a new feeling inside of her: fear. Yes, she wanted to tell the stories of the suffering. She wanted to stake her claim as a serious journalist. But at what cost? Would she be safe?

Angie continued writing the introduction to her story as the evening progressed into night. She wrote about the tragic 1983 famine that left over a hundred thousand Sudanese dead and sparked the long, bitter war between the Janjaweed and the African tribes in Darfur. Backed by military and financial support from Chad's Arab government, the Janjaweed raided countless villages, decimating African families and their rebel allies in western Sudan. The lawlessness that ensued left hundreds of thousands dead and forced millions from their homes. The killing of civilians, burning of villages, abduction of children, and raping of women continued unchecked. Ethnic Darfurians left the region in droves, seeking shelter in the many refugee camps hastily established across the border in Chad. She described the fragile and uneasy peace signed in 2005 and the formation of the country of South Sudan. Both were failed attempts at ending the killings in Darfur.

It was almost eleven o'clock when she stopped typing. Angie was surprised she had worked so long. Since starting at the *National Times* last year, the 26-year-old writer had been assigned the usual mundane stories reserved for new journalists. She could finish most of those humdrum pieces in under an hour. Those filler stories would get her nowhere. Now she had a chance to stand out and show the literary world what she could do on her own.

Sitting in her pajamas, Angie leaned back on the bed and rubbed her eyes. She was physically, mentally, and emotionally exhausted. Angie felt both saddened and angry that the world continued to allow the genocide to occur. Maybe people outside of Africa just didn't understand the gravity of the situation in Sudan. Certainly the UN and member nations knew. But what about the people? Surely, if they were made fully aware of the genocide, they would force their governments to act. This was exactly the kind of news that could propel the people to act. And make the cover of the *National Times*.

For hours she slaved over syntax and sentence structure, to ensure she was conveying just the right feeling to convince her audience. And this was only the background story. She hadn't even begun the meat of her piece. That would start tomorrow after she arrived at the refugee camp on the border with Sudan. In just a few hours, she noticed, looking at the clock beside the bed. As much as she hated to pull herself away from her laptop, she knew she had to get some sleep. If Henry was correct, and she had no reason to doubt him, tomorrow was going to be a long and draining day.

6

STEVE CONNORS PUT DOWN the copy of *Le Monde* he was pretending to read and glanced out at the promenade. It was as deserted as the outdoor, open-air bar. Except for himself and the German tourist passed out at a corner table, the café was empty. Marcel, undercover as the bartender, was bagging up the bottles of rum emptied a half hour ago by a group of French sailors from the nearby base celebrating a comrade's promotion.

The only sound was the clanking of the metal pulleys on the mast lines of the myriad of sailboats moored on the other side of the promenade, just twenty feet from the bar, as a light breeze from the Mediterranean swept across the port. A few seagulls scampered along the concrete walkway, seeking a late-night dinner on discarded French fries and bread from the now-closed popular Italian restaurant located beside the bar. Other than that, the night was still. It was almost midnight, but a weekday, so Steve wasn't surprised by the lack of customers or the paucity of foot traffic on the promenade. There weren't many tourists here during the off season. Besides, from what Marcel had said earlier, this sleazy bar at the far end of the promenade was not a popular spot for tourists or, apparently, even the locals.

Steve was uncomfortable with the mission. Even though a team of highly trained French counterterrorist professionals were waiting to pounce from a van parked behind the bar on the Avenue de la République, he still felt vulnerable sitting at a corner table in the outdoor bar. As he waited for his target to arrive, his mind drifted back to his training in North Carolina and on the Farm. His paramilitary instructors had tried to prepare him for every contingency—something that was, of course, impossible.

Disguised as a fisherman, Steve sipped espresso while Marcel continued his work behind the counter. He glanced at his watch. Perhaps word of their raid on the UIC safe house earlier in the day had gotten out and the meeting had been changed or canceled. Steve stood to go over and speak to Marcel when he noticed a man walking along the promenade approaching the bar. After nodding to Marcel, Steve sat back down.

He remained cautious, sitting at an outside table far enough so his targets didn't feel threatened but close enough to maintain a visual on the rest of the tables in the open bar. Marcel had already planted listening devices under all the tables, so there was no need to risk getting too close.

Steve looked back down at his newspaper and tried to remain inconspicuous. He could tell the man who was approaching, who appeared to be of Middle Eastern or North African descent, if Steve judged his facial features correctly, was nervous. Steve wondered why.

▼ ▼ ▼

Faris entered the open-air bar and walked up to the counter as instructed.

"*Bières bouteille,*" he told the bartender, ordering a bottled beer as Abdullah had instructed. He took a sip of the alcoholic drink. After being recruited into the Islamic Caliphate by Abdullah al-Harbi himself, Faris and the other former members of his street gang were instructed to continue their life of debauchery, at least while in the public eye. It was hard enough for an Arab to blend into and be accepted by European society, even harder if one led an openly pious life as dictated by the Qur'an. "You must live with your enemies," Abdullah preached. "Go to their bars, date their sisters, work in their factories, and drink their beer. When you live in the belly of the beast, you must live as the beast. Only then, brothers, will your enemies accept you. Once you are on the inside, you can strike at their hearts."

Faris closed his eyes and let his taste buds absorb the satisfying drink. He was now a pious man, a man dedicated to his religion. But he did enjoy the taste of local beer.

Where is Tayeb? Faris wondered, looking down the promenade. He was late. Faris would have called the French sailor an hour ago to ensure he was coming, but Abdullah was adamant that electronic communications be kept to a minimum for security reasons, especially immediately before a meeting or operation. Besides, he had met with Houda that morning, and she assured him they would be there with the weapon samples in their van. But, so far, there was no sign of them or their van. What would he tell the Janjaweed commander?

From the opposite side of the promenade, a dark, tall, stocky man made his way slowly yet deliberately into the bar. As he approached, his impressive size became more evident to Faris. *What will this murderer do to me when he finds out the weapons are not yet here?*

From the description Faris had of the Janjaweed commander, there was no mistaking him. "Hussein?" Faris called out. He looked up at the man, easily six and a half feet tall, with a deep scar down the right side of his face. His right eye was eerily glossed over by a hazy film caused by the old wound. Faris, a veteran of many street battles in the murky French underground, was not easily spooked. This Janjaweed, however, with his ebony skin, imposing stature, and menacing cyclopic stare caused even this hardened French thug to take notice.

"It's okay," Faris said to the big man in Arabic, feeling his apprehension as he glanced at the other few patrons in the bar. Hussein turned and sat down at a table near the bar. "The place is clean," Faris continued, trying to put his new Janjaweed colleague at ease. "I run these ports. We're safe here."

"Don't lecture me about security, boy."

Faris was taken aback by the sharp retort. Who did this Janjaweed Bedouin from the Sahara think he was talking to? Abdullah al-Harbi, proclaimed *khalifah* of the new Islamic Caliphate, had chosen him, Faris Hannachi, to be his emir in Europe. He understood that Abdullah wanted to expand the caliphate into Africa, but Faris questioned his master's wisdom in trying to seduce this barbarian into merging his *Mahdiyya* with the Islamic Caliphate using French weapons. Surely there were more deserving soldiers of Islam in North Africa to tap as al-Harbi's newest emir in Africa than this desert raider. Faris conceded that Hussein bin Mohammed al-Fadi did have a powerful Janjaweed army at his disposal in Sudan and had already begun a crusade to purge non-Arabs from his lands. Hussein's own Islamic revisionist movement, his *Mahdiyya*, was quickly spreading across North Africa.

"I was told you could provide me with weapons for my men," the Janjaweed continued in a low voice.

"Yes," Faris answered obediently. If his esteemed *khalifah* needed his help coaxing Hussein to join their movement to unify the Islamic world under one leader, then Faris would do his best. "Weapons and so much more, as you will see the more you work with our organization."

"I need military-grade rifles that can be fired from horseback. Some crew-served weapons for my trucks. I need enough for five hundred men, and I need them quickly."

Faris, himself a native of North Africa, albeit from the bustling city of Algiers, kept abreast of news from his old homeland. He knew that the Janjaweed were expanding rapidly as word of their victories over the local African tribes in Darfur spread. Perhaps this was why Abdullah al-Harbi so desperately wanted the Janjaweed on his side. A ready-made and expanding army already in place in North Africa would be the perfect standard-bearer for the militant arm of the Islamic Caliphate in Africa.

"Yes, I can provide this. French-made. Very good weapons. Very durable for your soldiers to use in the desert," Faris replied. "Weapons. Money. Resources. Our *khalifah* can provide all of this to do Allah's work in the Sahel. Can we count on you to be our new emir in Africa?" he asked.

Faris jumped at the sound of a cell phone.

"'Alo," the Janjaweed commander said into the phone, then listened intently. His dark eyes moved to stare at Faris, then he glanced up at the bartender, who was walking back to the counter at the back of the café. Faris watched as the big man silently ended the call and put the phone back into his jacket pocket. When he pulled his hand out of the jacket, however, he now held a nine-millimeter pistol with a silencer attached.

"You were not careful," the Janjaweed hissed in his native Sudanese Arabic.

Before Faris could comprehend the meaning of the words, the Janjaweed rose from his chair with weapon raised. Faris wondered what he had done wrong as he stared down the barrel and prepared for his end, praying for Allah to be merciful. He had survived in the cutthroat world of the French underground because he was as cautious as he was ruthless. But he could see in the Janjaweed's eyes that his time as gang leader-turned-emir of the United Islamic Caliphate was about to come to an end. To his surprise, instead the big man turned his pistol on the bartender.

▼ ▼ ▼

Marcel never knew what hit him as the bullet pierced the side of his head and sent him sprawling across the small table he was wiping down, knocking it to the ground.

It took Steve a moment to realize what had happened to his colleague. *Silencer,* he said to himself as he withdrew his own Beretta and tried to get off a shot. But he was too slow. The first bullet hit Steve's right shoulder, the impact causing him to drop his weapon. He winced at the searing pain and waited for the next round to finish him off. Steve looked around and realized there would be no assistance from the French cavalry on the street, at least not within the next few seconds when he needed it the most. The silencer had muffled the sound of the gunfire enough that even the microphones hidden under the tables would barely pick up the sound.

"Embuscade!" Steve yelled in French, alerting the awaiting assault team of the ambush. It would still take for the assault team on the street a moment to realize what was happening in the bar. Steve didn't have that much time. It would only take the man speaking in Sudanese Arabic a second to pull the trigger. He had one chance to survive: to run. Steve ran as fast as he could, hoping to dodge the next bullet. But he would not succeed. The second round hit him square in his back, sending him over the edge of the promenade and into the warm Mediterranean Sea.

▼ ▼ ▼

Hussein walked calmly over to the edge of the promenade, keeping his pistol pointed at the water. Even though it was nighttime, the promenade lamps provided enough illumination for his good eye to notice the small pool of blood on the surface of the water. Satisfied that the threat had been neutralized, he returned to Faris.

"You fool. Those men were with the authorities. They were watching you. Your associates were caught with the weapons earlier today. They must have told the police about this meeting."

The phone call Hussein had just received had alerted him to the raid on the apartment at the Place Victor Hugo. For Hussein to broaden his influence in Africa, he recognized that he might have to cooperate with al-Harbi and perhaps even join his new pan-Islamic group of jihadists, but Hussein bin Mohammed of the Janjaweed trusted no one. He knew it would always be up to him to ensure his own security. Abdullah al-Harbi, the budding *khalifah* of the United Islaimc Caliphate, might not approve of what Hussein was about to do. Or would he? After all, Hussein was a soldier, forged from decades of violent conflicts, bitter feuds, and, now, ethnic cleansing. The *khalifah*, despite losing his European emir, might appreciate Hussein's ruthlessness. He was the commander of the Janjaweed and was feared by all in his domain. Was that not exactly what al-Harbi needed? The *khalifah* had built up his infrastructure for the new terrorist organization but still needed soldiers. And generals. Who better than Hussein to be the Islamic Caliphate's general leading a great and powerful Janjaweed army across North Africa under the *khalifah*'s banner? For Hussein's domain to expand, he would have to prove his ruthlessness and worth to his new master.

The hardened Janjaweed leader turned to the only other man who had seen his face. A man who, if captured alive, could lead the international authorities to him. Once more, Hussein raised his weapon.

Faris, realizing his fate was sealed, began praying in his native tongue: *"La allah illa Allah."* There is no god but Allah.

Hussein would show no mercy this evening, even on a brother soldier of Allah. Another shot from his silenced pistol ensured his face would remain unknown, and Faris dropped to the ground in midprayer.

DCGI reinforcements were, no doubt, en route and would be arriving any moment. But Hussein had one more person to kill this evening. It was not because the man had seen his face. Nor was the man with the authorities or even a threat. Hussein approached the drunk still passed out at a table, oblivious to the violent shoot-out in the bar. The Janjaweed commander placed the silencer to the back of the man's head and, purely out of enjoyment, pulled the trigger.

7

NGIE LOOKED OUT across the empty morning streets. It was Friday, the Islamic holy day, so she wasn't too surprised by the lack of traffic. Many shops were closed, and most people were at home preparing to go to the mosque for Friday prayers. A few bicycles stacked with bread and other food slowly made their way along the hardened mud streets and broken walkways.

For a moment, Angie was concerned when their driver drove past the airport entrance. She was about to say something to Henry, but then she noticed they were heading for a VIP gate. After the driver flashed a UN badge to the two young guards at the steel gate on the other side of the terminal, they were let through. Angie watched in amazement as they drove straight onto the tarmac to a twin-propeller aircraft parked on a narrow runway.

"No customs or security?" she asked.

"Not here," replied Henry. "Besides, it's our own contracted flight. I guess they figure we wouldn't want to hijack ourselves."

"Good point," she said as she got out of the car.

The blistering heat combined with the pungent stench of jet fuel almost made her vomit. She was more prepared this morning, however, wearing large sunglasses and a thin green silk scarf over her head. Though Chad was not necessarily one of the more pious Islamic countries, Angie thought the scarf was prudent. Not only would the gesture show respect for the conservative refugees, but it would keep the sun off her pale skin.

The small, double-engine plane sat proudly on the hot tarmac. Angie looked at it with increasing anxiety. Her two greatest fears were flying and enclosed spaces. The excitement of traveling to Africa coupled with the size of the jumbo jet that brought her to N'Djamena had dampened these phobias somewhat, but the plane in front of her now was no bigger than a large automobile—but one that flew. Anticipating a bumpy ride, she'd already premedicated herself with some over-the-counter air sickness pills she picked up in San Francisco. The drug helped her keep her breakfast down but did little to calm her nerves.

"Angie, this is Rick. He'll be our pilot today," said Henry.

Tall and lanky, with hair like straw poking out from under an old, weathered Springbok rugby cap, and wire-rimmed aviator sunglasses, Rick was probably thirty or thirty-five but with an edge to him. Angie hoped he had much more experience than his youthful appearance let on.

"Hello," he said in a South African accent. "Climb aboard. We're ready to take off, so get buckled up and we'll be on our way."

Angie noticed the large amount of rust on the fuselage, sprinkled with the occasional small round holes that appeared to be from bullets. The nausea returned and her knees felt weak.

Rick seemed to sense her apprehension and took her arm. "Don't worry, Miss Angie. Ol' Matilda here'll get you there in one piece," he said, patting the side of his weathered aircraft. "We've been through a lot together and she's never let me down."

Finding no comfort in his words, Angie climbed aboard, despite her fears and best judgment.

"How long's the flight?" she asked once tightly strapped into the cramped seat behind the pilot.

"It's six hundred miles to the UN airstrip at Bahai. It's way over on the other side of Chad and will take us over three hours to get there. Fortunately, there aren't any storms in the forecast, but that can change at a moment's notice. This part of Africa is notorious for sudden sandstorms."

Angie shot Henry a nervous look.

"It'll be fine," he assured her.

Rick started the engine, and the entire plane shook in rhythm as the two propellers began turning. Finally, at full RPMs, the fuselage steadied and Angie was able to dig her fingernails out of the armrest.

"We're going to one of the smaller refugee camps in Bahai. It's an older camp, built in 2004. It's just 1.2 kilometers from the Sudanese border. Because it's so near to Darfur, it's actually closing down due to security reasons," Henry explained.

"Why?" Angie asked. "What's the danger? I would think it'd be good to have it close to the border to facilitate refugees coming across."

"True, but we've had both the Janjaweed from Sudan and the rebels from Chad enter the camp and wreak havoc. It's just too dangerous for the refugees to be that close to the war zone," said Henry.

"When will the camp be moving?"

"Probably this year sometime, depending on the funding," Henry answered, looking out the window as the small plane took off. Angie got the feeling he'd sensed her fear of flying and kept talking to try to soothe her nerves. "It's one of the better camps in the area, actually. There are about twenty-eight thousand people living there right now. But we still have to find the millions of dollars needed for the relocation."

"Where does money like that come from?"

"NGOs, the UN, and a few donor nations. Some countries in the West, yours included, unfortunately, talk a good game about helping the situation in Darfur. But when it comes to giving money, supplying equipment or troops for security missions, however, these same countries are usually all talk but no action. That's why what you do is so vital to our mission here. We need the average person on the street to understand what's going on so they can pressure their governments to help. Without their help, I'm afraid, there's not much hope for Darfur."

"Has the formation of South Sudan helped much?" Angie asked, knowing there were still tensions between the new nation and its northern foe.

"Very little. In my opinion, it would have been better if the Darfur region had been given to South Sudan. But if you ask me, the new government there probably didn't want the headaches. They have enough to worry about fighting the North over mineral and oil rights and border incursions. Unfortunately, those left in Darfur are on their own while North Sudan—or just Sudan, as we call it—is backed by some big players. As I mentioned, there are wealthy investors that have an interest in keeping the corrupt regime in power in Sudan. Combine that with groups like the Janjaweed, ISIS, and other unscrupulous opportunists, and you have a recipe for disaster and lawlessness in the trans-Sahel."

"What's the trans-Sahel?"

"'Sahel' is the Arabic word for 'plains,'" Henry explained. "The region that lies just south of the Sahara is called the trans-Sahel. Really a misnomer, though. Over the past decades, urbanization and climate change has caused the Sahara to creep farther down into this once-fertile land. It's really all desert now."

"Fascinating. And something you don't hear about much back home. Well, I hope to change that. I plan on staying in the refugee camp for a few weeks, or for as long as it takes, if that's all right with you," Angie said.

"You are our guest, Angie Bryant. Please stay as long as you like. And, again, it is I who should be thanking you."

Angie smiled and looked out the window. The ground, five thousand feet below her, was the color of the California desert of her youth. How she had enjoyed playing in the dry, rocky fields outside of San Jose.

Peering through the Cessna's dirty window, every now and then she would get a bird's-eye view of a dried-up lake or river, winding through a dehydrated valley. There was no precipitation, no water springing from these parched hills, no vegetation in which to seek refuge from the hot, scorching sun burning the sand below. At least in San Jose there was some vegetation. But not here. This was the desert of deserts. In fact, she had read that the Arabic word for desert was *sahara*. This baked landscape, on the edge of the Sahara, was as close to hell on earth as it came.

She was going to again thank Henry for this great opportunity, but as she began to speak, loud, metallic sounds drowned out her words. She grabbed the armrest as her seat began to shake violently.

"Don't be alarmed," Rick said over his shoulder. "I just had to do some maneuvering."

"Maneuvering?" asked Angie, searching the skies and desert for any threat. But the sky was clear, the bluest she had ever seen. Not a cloud in the sky. "Around what?" But then she looked at the ground and saw it. Small ribbons of smoke rose from the desert below and behind the plane. They were barely visible. She only noticed it after a few more puffs of smoke emanated from atop a rock formation in the desert. "What's that?"

"Chad rebels. Janjaweed fighters. Maybe just smugglers. Who knows? We're on final approach to Bahai. Sometimes they just like to take potshots at us as we're landing," Rick answered.

"*Shots?* You mean they're firing at us?"

"Unfortunately, yes," Henry answered. "You see, Angie, the United Nations has tried to quell the ethnic cleansing. Several years ago, thousands of soldiers and police from a combined UN and African Unity force entered Sudan to provide humanitarian and security assistance in Darfur. These troops, however, were ill equipped and had little power to prevent the Janjaweed hordes from marauding through the villages, resulting in lawless frontier on both sides of the bord—"

The sharp, metallic sound of gunshots ripping through the left wing and fuselage cut off Henry's words. Angie looked out the window. Fuel was pouring out of new holes. The small plane did a steep nosedive, throwing Angie forward in her seat. Fortunately, she had kept her seat belt fastened or she would have slammed into the pilot's seat in front of her.

"What's happening?" she cried out.

From the corner of her eye, she could see the horizon was now vertical in her window, with the ground in front of them. At this speed, it would only be a matter of seconds before the plane crashed into the ground.

Angie reached for the Cessna's low ceiling with one hand while grasping the back of the pilot's seat with the other, bracing for impact. She realized this would do nothing to soften the blow, but felt compelled to do something. Outside the window, the leaking fuel was now on fire. Flames spewed from the side of the small plane. She squeezed her eyes shut and, for the first time since she was a child, Angie prayed.

A sudden jarring of the plane brought her horizontal once again. She fought the urge to vomit as she was thrown around in her seat. Opening her eyes and peering out the window, she could see land now just a dozen feet below the aircraft. But, she sighed, at least the land was *below* and not *in front of* the Cessna.

"Sorry, folks," Rick said. "That small-arms fire hit the engine. I had to do a combat landing and get us down quickly."

Angie looked out the window. The flaming jets of fuel had ceased—Rick must have shut down the damaged fuel tank.

"What's a combat landing?" Angie asked.

"Well, Miss Angie, you just experienced it," Rick answered.

"I take it you're a combat pilot?" she asked.

Rick turned his head and smiled at her as the plane touched down on the dirt runway. "Welcome to Bahai refugee camp."

"Well, that was interesting," she said, prying her fingernails out of the cheap pleather that covered the back of Rick's seat.

"Come," Henry answered as the plane came to a stop. "There's much to show you in your new home."

For the first time, Angie began to wonder if coming to this volatile region was such a good idea.

8

THE WOMEN OF THE VILLAGE, each wearing her finest and most colorful dress, danced into the center of Zarundi. They carried baskets and pots on their heads as an old man beat a drum near a stone well amid the mud huts with their distinct grass-thatched conical roofs. The men sat on the hot sand or wooden benches, clothed in a mixture of jeans, drab T-shirts, and *thobe*s, a sharp contrast with their brightly adorned wives, daughters, sisters, and mothers bringing in the meal for the wedding feast later in the day.

"*Shukran*, Mobassa," Haroun said, taking the reins of the camel, which was colorfully decorated and loaded with gifts for the bride. "Nadifa will be excited to see our traditions upheld."

Haroun had struggled the past month trying to make his daughter's wedding as perfect as possible. The meals, drums, and decorations were difficult enough to procure, but the camel was a rare commodity in Zarundi. He had even traveled to nearby villages to borrow or rent one to make this day special for his daughter, but all had been taken by the Janjaweed.

"You have a beautiful daughter, Haroun. Her wedding should be just as beautiful," Mobassa replied. In truth, even Mobassa had difficulty obtaining the camel, but Haroun was a dear friend. Besides, there wasn't much cause to celebrate in Darfur these days. The wedding feast was as much for the villagers as it was for the bride and groom and their families.

Mobassa watched Haroun take the camel to the hut where his daughter had spent the night with her new husband. Although the marriage celebration had been going on for days, it was not yet over. The women of the village had risen very early this morning to prepare a breakfast feast of porridge, customary for the morning after the consummation of a marriage. Mobassa smiled as he watched the joy on his neighbors' faces.

He rubbed his forehead and shielded his eyes from the bright light of the late-morning sun. Too much *marisa* last night, he said to himself, barely recalling most of the wedding celebration.

"*Baba!*" the young girl shouted as she ran up to Mobassa, her loud voice accentuating his already pounding headache.

"Halima, what are you doing out here? You're still not well. You should be home in bed," her father chided.

The twelve-year-old's eyes looked sunken and her color had not fully returned, but she did appear better than yesterday. Mobassa's mother along with other women in the village had taken turns caring for the child last night during the wedding.

"I feel better, Baba. I heard the music," she said, smiling from ear to ear. Halima had her eyes closed and swayed with the rhythmic change of the drum. "I'm hungry."

"Well, then, you must be feeling better," Mobassa said, hoisting up his little girl and carrying her to a long table now covered with the pots full of porridge.

"I miss Mama," she said, watching her father prepare her breakfast with one hand.

"Me too," Mobassa replied, still holding his youngest close to his side. "But don't worry, she'll be coming home from visiting your aunt later today. Your brother and sister will be returning as well. Don't you miss them, too?"

Halima's face soured. "I guess."

"You guess?" Mobassa howled. "What's that supposed to mean?"

"When Fatima's here, you spend all of your time with her. I like it when it's just you and me sometimes."

"Well, so do I, *Sukar*," he replied, using his nickname for his youngest child.

Seeing the bride and groom emerge from the hut, the women of the village began to sing a traditional Fur song for the newlyweds. Mobassa put down the bowl of porridge and set Halima on the ground. He held both of her hands and began to dance along with the rest of the villagers.

As he watched his beloved Halima sway with the rhythmic chanting of the old love song, Mobassa spotted a familiar face enter the village. His demeanor changed upon seeing the worried look on his colleague's face. Without saying a word, Mobassa let go of his daughter's hands and walked over to the man. Halima followed behind him, sensing the angst in her father.

"What is it, Fidail?" He knew the news wasn't going to be good. Fidail lived in a neighboring village and ventured out only when accompanying Mobassa on their excursions throughout Darfur.

"Hileh Tamim," Fidail said quietly, hanging his head as he named a nearby village.

"What about it?" Mobassa asked, knowing the answer even before he asked.

"The Evil Winds were there the other night."

Hearing the words 'Evil Winds' in the same sentence as the name of the village that his wife, son, and daughter had been visiting sent chills down Mobassa's spine. Though he was known throughout his village as strong and brave, Mobassa trembled thinking about what might have become of his family.

"Survivors?" he asked softly.

Fidail kept his head down, staring at the ground.

"Call the others. We leave immediately."

Fidail bowed his head slightly then disappeared between the huts.

"Baba?" Halima cried out from behind her father.

But her father didn't move.

"Baba?" she called again.

"Halima, go to your grandmother. I have to leave for a few days."

"But Baba, what's happened to Mama? And Matak and Fatima? Where are they?" Halima asked, tears forming in her eyes as she realized the answer.

Mobassa turned around and knelt in front of his daughter. "I don't know, *Sukar*," he said. "I just don't know."

Halima threw her small arms around her father's strong neck and hugged him tight as tears flowed down her cheeks.

"But I'm going to find out," he promised her. "Stay here with your grandmother. I won't be long."

Mobassa stood and walked out of the village without looking back. Halima was left standing alone beside a thick-trunked baobab tree. Music from the wedding lingered in the air, but the girl heard none of it. But her mind was far away from the festivities, thinking about her lost family.

9

NO MATTER HOW MANY PICTURES Angie had seen of the camps, the hours of footage she pored over learning about what life was like as a refugee, nothing prepared her for the misery she saw at Bahai. She walked between the rows of tents and makeshift homes, some separated by earthen walls, others left open to the harsh desert environment. Plastic water containers lined the perimeters of the dwellings and tent corners as the tarp coverings flapped in the hot breeze.

Bahai was the camp closest to Northern Darfur, just across the border in Sudan, and had originally been built as a temporary refugee facility. Because security in Darfur was still tenuous, many refugees decided to make the camp their permanent home. Wells and small farms were springing up to lessen the reliance on imported goods and bolster the resiliency of the Darfurian refugees. But as much as it appeared that life was returning to normal for the camp's inhabitants, fear of the Janjaweed always remained.

Angie noticed a pretty young woman with blond hair walking through the next row of tents, accompanied by two Western-looking men wearing safari clothing.

"Who are they?" she asked Henry.

"A New Zealand news team making a documentary about life in a Darfur refugee camp."

"How long have they been here?" she asked as they approached a larger tent near the entrance of the camp.

"Only for a couple of days. They arrived the day before I went to N'Djamena to pick you up. I believe their program is for some Australian public television."

"See, people do care," Angie replied, not sure if she was trying to convince Henry or herself.

"Don't get me wrong, I'm thrilled they're here. I'm sure it will make an impact back in New Zealand and Australia. The more media coverage, the better. I'll take it wherever and whenever I can. Like I've said, that's the only way we're ever going to solve this problem."

As they walked into the larger tent near the camp entrance, Angie was immediately struck by how bare it was. A few chairs and tables had been set up. A heavy-set black woman seated behind the table flashed Angie a beautiful smile.

"Hello, sugar! You must be Angie," she said warmly.

"Hi," Angie replied, surprised to hear the woman's strong Southern drawl.

"I'm Carey. I process the new check-ins here at the camp."

"Nice to meet you, Carey. Where are you from back home?"

"New Orleans, born and bred, honey. I've been with the UN here for about six months now."

"Carey is amazing," Henry said. "Without her, we'd have no idea who was in the camp. She singlehandedly manages to keep track of thousands of new refugees."

"Flattery will get you everywhere, Henry," Carey replied with a wave of her hand. Angie, however, did notice the slight blush that came across the woman's cheeks. "The world was so good at helping my city after Katrina, I felt coming over here for a spell would be a small way I could pay it forward."

"'Small,' nothing," Henry responded. "Don't let her modesty fool you, Angie. Carey is the *real* boss around here."

"Oh, you stop it now and go on so I can get back to work."

The tables and chairs lining the walls of the tent were all empty.

"What's this tent used for?"

"Well, we use the front part to check in new refugees," Henry answered. "They then head back here for different classes on what to expect from living in a refugee camp. We have medical classes, sanitation classes, human rights and abuse lectures, and so on."

"Where's the rest of the staff?"

"Child, there ain't much more than what you see," replied Carey. "We have two French nuns who teach the children in our makeshift school. Johann is from Sweden. He runs our generators and maintenance. Gabriela is a Peruvian nurse and works with Dr. Russo, the only other American in the camp. They're with Medicine International, the NGO that runs the camp with the UN. But we're okay, honey. We rely on the refugees to help out around the camp. We hire them to do various jobs that they would be doing in their villages back home. We also have some volunteers that are in and out from time to time. They usually spend three months or so on different projects, such as vaccination programs, job skills teaching, and the like."

Angie had learned all about NGOs while researching Darfur. These domestic and international aid groups were not affiliated with any government, which facilitated their ability to function in countries that might not be on friendly terms with other nations.

"That's amazing. I can't believe you do so much with so few resources."

"I'm afraid we have little choice," Henry explained. "UN forces provide some security for the camp, but we run things inside as best we can. The refugees are remarkably helpful to us. Many of them have taken traditional societal roles in the camp and are trying to do the most they can for their countrymen and women in this bad situation. We're on a small hill here. Let me show you a view of the camp."

"Bye-bye for now," Carey said as Angie and Henry walked to the back of the tent and he opened the flap, revealing white tents as far as she could see.

"This camp is about three kilometers wide by three kilometers long. But it houses almost ten thousand refugees. Even Carey can't tell you how many tents there are out there. Dozens more are added every day. The refugees do the best they can to lead normal lives here, but it's not their home. Many want to go back, but only if they can live in peace."

To the east, Angie could see new refugees making their way to the camp through the inhospitable desert.

"More Darfurians," Henry added, seeing her look out into the distance. "The Sudanese border is not far from here. Every day hundreds brave the harsh elements and the Janjaweed to seek sanctuary here. Many don't make it."

Angie's heart broke as she watched the incoming refugees, carrying everything they had on their heads and backs. Without speaking, she left the tent and walked down the hill and into the sea of tents. She passed emaciated women and children, many with flies swarming around them, lying on the side of the dusty paths between the tents. Angie walked on alone, Henry watching from a distance. She sensed he wanted her to experience the camp for herself.

Most of the refugees sat outside their tents, watching the light-skinned stranger walk among them. With gaunt faces and almost lifeless eyes, they followed her every movement. In their eyes, she could see that they witnessed horrors she could not even imagine. *Why?* That was the only word crossing her mind, again and again. *Why did they have to suffer so much? What would cause one people to want to completely annihilate and extinguish another people? What had they done to deserve this? What would anyone have to do to deserve such a terrible fate?*

As the wind shifted, a wretched stench filled her nostrils. Although she had never before experienced the smell, she knew what it was: the scent of death all around her. Angie reached up and wiped a tear from her eye. The despair that permeated the camp's surroundings was almost too much for her to bear.

She came across a medium-size tent and walked up to a frail little boy sitting outside the entrance flap. Although the boy couldn't have weighed more than fifty pounds, Angie was sure he was probably twelve or thirteen years old. The boy stared out at the horizon as the flies crawled all over his face and into his open mouth. His bare chest expanded and retracted with each painful breath he took. Angie sat beside the child and placed a comforting hand on his forehead. He was burning up with fever.

Angie looked to the left and right, searching for help.

"He has typhus," a man with a stethoscope dangling around his neck told her.

Tall and handsome, with wavy brown hair and piercing blue eyes, he wore a loose-fitting plain white T-shirt and tan cargo pants. The only thing that detracted from his amazing smile was the intensely sad look on his well-chiseled features, barely hidden beneath his unshaven face.

"His name's Ajou," the man said. "He's been sick for the past couple of days, but his family only just brought him to me. Even though I think they know we're here to help, many refugees still don't trust anyone outside of their families. I started Ajou on tetracycline, but it's very late in the disease. He's already pretty malnourished...emaciated, actually. It doesn't look good."

Angie looked sadly at little Ajou. He was so feeble. How could he hope to fight such a deadly disease?

"Is there anything else we can do for him?"

"Pray," he said as Angie stood up. "My name's Jason Russo. You must be the reporter from the States."

Angie shook his hand. It was strong, more callused than she imagined a doctor's hands would be. "Angie Bryant," she said with a smile.

"Do you want to see inside the medical tent?" he asked.

"Sure," she said, but after seeing Ajou, she wasn't really that certain.

"This is the camp's hospital and clinic, all rolled into one," Jason said as they entered the tent, waving a hand across the makeshift triage and ward areas. There were a dozen patients lying on cots or sitting in chairs. "There's Ajou's grandmother," he continued, pointing to a woman standing at a desk a few feet away.

The elderly Sudanese woman wore a flowing purple tent. She had a white scarf on her head.

"She was telling us what happened to the boy's mother, Taja," a tall, thin man standing behind the desk said. He looked clean cut and well dressed, by refugee camp standards.

"Yasser's my interpreter."

"Hello," Angie said, nodding. Then she returned her attention to the small Sudanese woman.

"A few months ago," Yasser started, translating Ajou's grandmother's words, "Taja went out to gather some wood. The trees are becoming scarce in Darfur. When I was a child, the land around our village was all farmland. But now it's desert. The

women in our village have to walk miles to gather enough wood to cook. Taja never came back. My husband and some others from our village found her. Her clothes were torn and there were cuts and bruises on her body."

"Was it the Janjaweed?"

"Probably," Jason answered. "Either them or Sudanese soldiers. They're just as bad. They use rape as a way of terrorizing the villagers. The women usually don't tell the tribal leaders when they're raped. They think they'll be treated differently, be shunned by their village. That's why most people outside of Sudan don't know about these atrocities. Usually the women don't even tell us when they come in. They've seen so much death, they're numb to it now."

"That's awful. Imagine living your entire lives in such fear and devastation," Angie said.

"Yasser, please take Ajou and his grandmother to the isolation ward in the next tent. I'll be there in a few minutes to start an IV and get him rehydrated."

"Yes, Doctor," Yasser answered dutifully, and led the elderly Sudanese woman out of the tent.

Crack! Crack!

"Is that gunfire?" Angie cried as they heard some screams in the distance.

Jason didn't answer, but ran outside the tent. "Damn!" he said, looking out on the horizon at a dozen refugees across the border in Sudan making their way towards Bahai. Behind them was a pickup truck filled with armed men, firing Kalashnikov rifles into the crowd.

"Janjaweed," Jason said.

"They're shooting the refugees!" Angie gasped at the horror unfolding in front of her eyes. "We need to go help them."

From the corner of the camp, the two Americans watched as a white SUV with UN markings sped off into the desert toward the carnage. But as Angie witnessed the atrocity so close to the camp, she realized the UN would be powerless to stop it. For the Janjaweed in the back of the pickup, it was like shooting fish in a barrel. Angie closed her eyes as the last refugee fell to the ground.

Seconds later, the gunfire stopped, and Angie opened her eyes. In the distance, the fleeing refugees were now lying motionless in the sandy wasteland.

"The UN troops won't go after them," Jason said, breaking the stillness of the crowd gathered near the medical tent, all facing the horrific scene. The Janjaweed truck, mission complete, had turned and sped off back toward the Sudanese border. "Attacks like this have occurred before. Sometimes the Janjaweed use it to lure the UN guards away, leaving the camp unprotected and wide open to larger-scale attacks. Besides, the border with Sudan is right over that hill. The UN has little authority over there."

They continued to watch as the UN SUV stopped at the bodies and checked for signs of life. One by one, the soldiers covered the bodies and slowly returned to their vehicles. A few moments later, two pickup trucks left Bahai. No ambulance was sent nor was one needed, Angie surmised. The Janjaweed had successfully completed their mission.

One by one, the mixture of refugees and aid workers near the medical tent began to disperse. *This was just another day for them*, thought Angie. The sound of a camera shutter caught her attention, and she turned to see the New Zealand news team. Angie realized that she should have taken some pictures, but she'd been too shocked to think about documenting the war crime. She would have to do better next time.

"Come on, Gabriela. Let's get ready to receive the casualties," Jason said to his nurse as he turned back toward the medical tent. Gabriela's somber face confirmed Angie's suspicions that she, too, thought there would be no survivors.

10

EVEN THOUGH IT WAS LATE in the season, the afternoon Parisian air was still chilly. As he walked along the bank of the Seine with his two most trusted bodyguards, Abdullah al-Harbi turned up the collar of his coat, as much to protect himself from the cold as to keep his identity hidden. Though his mission to create a pan-Islamic world, a united *ummah*, was still in its infancy, and he didn't travel outside of his well-protected enclave in eastern Yemen often, his face and reputation were becoming known to authorities around the world. He would not be traveling at all were it not for the incident in Toulon. He was in Paris to keep the peace and, perhaps, forge a mutually beneficial alliance.

When the self-proclaimed *khalifah* of the United Islamic Caliphate reached the luxurious high-rise apartment complex, two of Shao Ying's own guards stood like gargoyles at the private elevator. One opened the elevator door and accompanied the *khalifah* and his guards up to the penthouse. In a moment, the elevator doors opened into the luxurious two-story penthouse apartment.

The four men walked through the opulent foyer, lavishly decorated with crystal chandeliers, expensive carpets, and paintings and statues from around the world. He recognized a famous Tunisian painting depicting the legend of Elissa, or Dido, the Phoenician princess who is credited with building the ancient city of Carthage.

Ying's guard stopped at an entryway into a room with modern, bright furniture. Shao Ying sat signing papers behind a plain white desk. Abdullah had not met Shao Jun's daughter before. She was young and beautiful, probably in her early thirties at most. Ying's skin was porcelain white, flawless, and her jet-black hair was pulled back in a bun. Her athletic frame was accentuated by her tailored pantsuit. Abdullah noticed the blood-red fingernail polish on her hands as she continued writing despite his presence.

"Your attempt at luring one of my employees to join your Islamic crusade did not end up well in Toulon last night," she stated, still focusing her attention on the documents she was signing. Beside her, an intimidating man stood, stone-faced, staring directly at Abdullah. There was an emptiness in his eyes that made even Abdullah uncomfortable. It wasn't the detached look of a hardened combat veteran, but rather a completely blank stare. Almost robotic.

As if the man has no soul whatsoever, thought Abdullah.

"I had no way of knowing French intelligence would be there," Abdullah replied.

"Of course not. But *I* knew. As a matter of fact, were it not for my call to the Janjaweed commander to alert him of the trap, he would be in a French prison today. If that had happened, his affiliation with my operations in Sudan might have been compromised and become an embarrassment to me."

"That Janjaweed barbarian killed my best man in Europe," Abdullah said. "It was a mistake for me to think he could have had a place in my organization. Faris would never have been captured alive. Even if he had, he would not reveal the names of his accomplices to the authorities. Killing him was not necessary."

"Perhaps. But next time you arrange a meeting with one of my men, I expect you will give me the courtesy of letting me know first. After all, we are on the same side, you and I."

Abdullah al-Harbi certainly knew Shao Ying's work and reputation. Many of his former colleagues in al-Qaeda had business dealings with her. He himself had been approached by her father, Shao Jun, just a few months ago—before Jun's untimely death. Ying had served as her father's right hand for years, and now she held the reins of his empire tightly.

"Hussein bin Mohammed approached *me*," Abdullah continued. "He has dreams of leading his people in Sudan and purging the Sahel of non-Arabs. I thought he could assist me in expanding the Islamic Caliphate into Africa."

"I know all about Hussein's ambition. That's why I allowed the meeting in Toulon to take place. At least, until I found out that the DCGI had arrested your 'power couple' who had been stealing weapons for you from the French navy."

Abdullah was surprised at the depth of awareness this woman had about his operations. He himself had not yet determined how Tayeb and Houda Baroudi had been compromised. "You knew Hussein wanted to join my *ummah?*" Abdullah asked.

"Of course. I know many things. Such as how you need warriors to expand your new caliphate. Hussein bin Mohammed of the Janjaweed is about as fierce as they come. That's why my father had him in our employ for so long. Perhaps we can come to a mutually beneficial agreement."

Abdullah watched the woman turn her attention back to the papers in front of her.

"What do you want from me?" he asked.

"Your cooperation," she replied, once again looking up at the *khalifah*. "Consider Hussein a gift from me. We can share him for now, but take him into your organization. He's been a good soldier and I've profited from him. You will as well."

"Why this generosity?" Abdullah asked. A powerful ally like Shao Ying would be beneficial as the Islamic Caliphate competed with Da'ish and al-Qaeda and the vast number of other terrorist groups in operation, but he still wondered why she summoned him here today. He did have a unique plan to make his international caliphate succeed where the others had failed. Perhaps Ying recognized this. She was, after all, well versed in international affairs and seemingly omniscient—just like her father.

"Let's just say that I believe we should work together. You have needs that I can fill: money, weapons, people, contacts, political influence. I have all of this."

But Abdullah remained unconvinced. He was a proud man and was not about to have his actions dictated by this *kafirah*. The fact that she was a woman was an added insult. While this infidel might be powerful, Abdullah was not going to turn control of his budding empire over to her. Abdullah al-Harbi was a puppet to no man . . . or woman.

"Ah, I see from your hesitation that you require a demonstration," Ying stated.

Abdullah perceived the threat in her voice and nodded to his two bodyguards. But before his companions could move, the man behind Ying leapt over the tall desk and pounced on the unsuspecting bodyguards.

Abdullah al-Harbi watched in horror as Ying's lone attack dog grabbed one of his bodyguards in a tight headlock while simultaneously delivering a powerful side kick to the other's throat, crushing the burly Arab's windpipe. Without any expression or hint of emotion at all, Ying's killing machine finished the job by smoothly snapping the neck of the bodyguard in the headlock. After the brief *demonstration* had ended, Ying's bodyguard stood atop the two bodies, staring blankly into the distance.

Ying rose from her desk, revealing her full height of almost six feet. "Don't be a fool, Abdullah. I don't want control over your little *jihad*. You go play your games in America and Europe or wherever you want to."

"What is it you *do* want?" Abdullah asked, realizing that he now had a partner, whether he wanted one or not.

"Something bigger. Much bigger."

11

ANGIE SAT ALONE at the end of the dining tent. There were a few refugees still sitting at the opposite end of the long table, even though dinner had been cleared from the buffet thirty minutes ago. After what she had seen that afternoon, Angie had no appetite. She had asked to stay in the medical tent to help, but Gabriela had gently told her that it would be best if she wasn't there when the bodies were brought in. Angie felt helpless but realized that the Peruvian nurse was right. She wasn't ready for that, for the sight of a dozen women and children murdered so violently.

How did they do it? Angie wondered. *The resiliency of the refugees in the face of such fear and savagery was mind boggling,* she thought, watching the refugees finish their dinner.

Angie was beginning to second-guess her decision to come to Africa. Could she even help? Would she be able to make a difference? She hadn't even had the presence of mind to pull out her phone to snap pictures of the brutal murders as they happened.

Jason entered from the other side of the tent. *He looks tired,* Angie thought, *emotionally drained.* Angie waved to catch his attention, and Jason gave her a small smile. He walked to the coffee carafe on the otherwise cleared buffet and poured two cups before coming over to Angie's table and sitting down.

"How are you holding up?" she asked. Jason's eyes were heavy and hair was disheveled. *It must have been an awful sight,* she thought.

"We got the bodies cleaned up as best we could," he said, avoiding answering her question. "I usually write a long report and take pictures to try to document the war crimes."

"What happens then?"

"Usually? Nothing. I give it to Henry, and I know he pushes it up the chain. But no one has ever come to investigate. No questions. No inquiries. At least, not while I've been here."

"How often does that happen?" she asked.

"Fortunately, not often, but even once is too much. I treat a lot of refugees for burns and bullet wounds when they come in. They usually get those injuries when the Janjaweed raid their camps. Obviously, only the survivors make it here. Usually the only dead bodies I see are the ones who die in the camp."

"Do you mind?" Angie asked, pulling out a small tape recorder. She was determined not to miss another opportunity to document the crimes occurring in this forgotten part of Africa.

"No, it's okay," Jason said, rubbing his hand through his hair. "You might as well report what's going on here. You're the only one now."

"What do you mean?" she asked.

"The Kiwis are packing up. They're leaving in the morning."

"Why?"

"I guess what happened this afternoon was a little too close for their liking. They're not the only ones. A number of volunteers and even camp employees are leaving. Even Carey's talking about it. I can't say as I blame them."

"Wow. It's that bad?" Angie probed.

"You saw it yourself. It *is* that bad. Too much dying going on around here. People are scared, and rightfully so."

"You said some refugees die here in the camp? How?"

"Mostly from infectious diseases. Dysentery. A lot of the refugees get sick traveling. Many of them die on the long walk to get here. Some from the elements, some from dehydration or starvation. Some from poisoning."

"Who would poison them?"

"The Janjaweed. They poison the wells in the desert between the villages in Darfur and the refugee camps. They know the routes the refugees use. They take the bodies of villagers they kill and stuff them down the wells. It doesn't take long for the water to become contaminated with many types of bacteria, most of them deadly without treatment."

"What monsters," Angie said.

"Yes, they are."

Yasser entered the tent and walked up to Jason. "Doctor, the ward's full. We have no more beds."

"Well, let's set up the cots in our tent again, Yasser."

From the look on Yasser's face, Angie could tell he was not happy with this solution. But he nodded and turned away to follow the American doctor's instructions.

"His English is good," Angie said.

"I'm lucky to have him. If he leaves, I'll be hurtin'."

"Is he leaving too?" she asked.

"Not yet," Jason answered. "At least, not that I'm aware of. Yasser's from Darfur. He's Arab, but I don't think he wants to go back to Sudan. But he doesn't talk about it much and I don't ask."

Henry Chesterfield entered the tent and joined them. "So, it appears we'll be losing a few of our staff."

"I heard," Jason replied, putting down his cup. "How was your trip to N'Djamena?"

"I'm afraid other than collecting Angie, not very productive. Most of the governments in the region are having their own issues, and getting resources to support our little operation here is becoming more difficult."

"Surely the fact that the Janjaweed crossed into Sudan and murdered refugees on Chad soil will get officials in N'Djamena to act. At least they can send more security," Angie said.

"Technically, they were murdered across the border in Sudan. Besides, I hate to say it, Angie, but the lives of twelve refugees from Darfur are not high up on the list of pressing issues for the government of Chad. They're busy fighting their own insurgency causing havoc across Chad. Don't get me wrong. Chad has been a good friend to us and the refugees. We wouldn't be here if it were not for them. In fact, neither would you. But not too long ago, the Chad rebels pushed their way all the way into the capital in N'Djamena. This government has its hands full at the moment."

"We're running low on medical supplies and medications again," Jason said.

"I know, Jason, I know," Henry said, waving his hand. "I'll address it in Geneva when I go next week. In the meantime, I've called on both the Red Cross and the Red Crescent to step up their assistance. Dr. Serrena Binachi from the World Health Organization is in Wau in South Sudan. There's a big international conference on human rights violations in Africa going on there this week. I'll give her a call today and see if she can get any of her contacts to send us more medicine. She might be able to get something up here in a day or so."

"I hope the refugees make it that long," answered Jason.

"There's just so much going on right now, it's the best we can do. After this attack, I'm not even sure we'll be able to keep our doors open if all our volunteers and employees leave because they feel it's unsafe," replied Henry, rubbing his stubbled chin.

Angie could tell the media coordinator for the UNHCR and de facto UN liaison for the camp was stressed.

"What about your company, Jason?" Angie asked.

"It's not really a company. Medicine International is an NGO—a nongovernmental organization that's funded by donors. I could let them know we could use more security, but they're pretty strapped for money as it is."

"It's worth a try, isn't it?" she asked.

"I'll give them a call, but don't hold your breath."

"Thanks, Jason," Henry said. "I spoke with the UNAMRID commander here. They can't provide any more security than what we have now. In fact, he's being pressured to do more to protect the villagers across the border in Darfur. We may even lose some of the troops we have stationed at the camp."

"If they leave, Henry, the Janjaweed will roll in here and kill every last man, woman, and child in the camp," Jason replied.

"Yes, they will," Henry answered somberly. He took off his glasses and laid them on the table. "I'll do what I can. The commander told me that he has a medical team coming out this afternoon. They'll be here for a day before they push out to one of the camps in Darfur. They're willing to help out while they're here."

"That'll be great," replied Jason. "Yasser just told me the ward's full. We can use all the help we can get."

"You look tired, Jason. Why don't you get some rest?" Henry said.

"I will. It's just been a long day."

"I'm afraid it's about to get longer. The commander also informed me that another village was attacked just across the border. They're on their way out to take a look and bring back the survivors."

"More?" replied Angie. "Does it ever end?"

"It's nonstop, I'm afraid," the UNHCR media coordinator replied, picking up his glasses and rising. He took a deep breath and sighed. "You'd better get some rest. It's going to be a long night."

The two Americans watched as Henry walked out of the tent. Angie noticed that he no longer had the spring in his step that she had first noticed at the airport. The events of the day had been hard on everyone at the camp, probably, she realized, hardest on Henry, who she sensed felt responsible for the workers and refugees. He was the only UNHCR official at the camp and, as such, had access to UN resources. Resources that, apparently, were not going to increase any time soon.

"There's so much suffering here," she said. "Why is it so hard to get help?"

"I'm not a politician. I'm just a city boy from Chicago, trying to do my part."

"How long have you been out here?" she asked.

"I guess it's been about a month now. A friend of mine is with the UN and asked me if I'd come out here to help with the refugees, so I signed up with Medicine International. I had no idea what I was getting into, really. Can anyone truly express the extent of the anguish that goes on here?"

"I don't know, but I'm going to certainly try to do so in my writing. I've already spoken to a number of the refugees. Their stories are powerful," Angie replied, thinking about how she'd use them in her story. "Yasser translated for me. He's been a big help, but the refugees don't seem to like him much."

"Since he's Arab, the refugees don't trust him all that much. They hadn't had the best experiences with the Arab Janjaweed," Jason answered.

"It's so complicated out here. So many tribes and politics," Angie said, staring down into her coffee. "You mentioned to Henry that the women and children will be slaughtered if the UN forces leave. I noticed that there aren't many male refugees."

"Most of the men were killed defending their families during the raids. The Janjaweed kidnaps the boys and forces them to fight in their army," he answered. "Some of the teenage girls are sold as slaves, shipped off to who knows where."

Both Americans were silent for a moment, contemplating the horror that surrounded them. Then Angie decided to change the subject. "So, you're from Chicago?"

"Yeah. Not a very interesting story, I'm afraid. Left home when I was eighteen to go to college at Northwestern, then off to medical school and residency at the Mayo Clinic."

"Wow. The Mayo Clinic. Impressive. Were you in private practice before you came out here?" she asked, trying to fill in the gaps.

"Unfortunately, I only completed my internship year, not the entire three-year family medicine residency as I had hoped. That kind of hampers me a bit, since I don't have the in-depth training to fully treat these refugees as much as they need. I'm still learning on the job, really, much more than I'd like. As much as I might be helping some people, I wonder how much pathology I'm still missing."

"From what little I've seen so far, and from what everyone's saying, you're making a big difference," Angie answered.

"I'm not so sure," he replied honestly. "How about you? What brought you out to this desert?"

Angie suspected Jason was changing the conversation on purpose, but let it pass. "Like you, I wanted to make a difference. I want to expose to the world what's really going on here in Africa. I'm not saving lives like you are, but, in my own way, with my own limited skills, I think I can help."

"Don't sell yourself short. Your work could save many more lives than anything I can do over here," he said. "It's the world's complacency that allows the Janjaweed and Sudanese government to get away with murder. Literally. Your words can change that. The power of the pen, and all that."

"That's why I'm here," she answered.

"But for either of us to make a difference, we have to survive. Unless we get some more security out here, that may be easier said than done," Jason replied.

12

AFTER THEIR CONVERSATION, Angie returned to her tent and pulled out her laptop. It had been a long, exhausting first day. She began by documenting the stories she had heard from the refugees. As vividly as possible, she retraced Taja's journey into the desert to find wood and detailed the agony of her family as they found her mangled body. She described the lesions on Ajou's skin in detail and tried to bring life to the agony of his suffering.

Angie kept writing. Page after page, the powerful stories came alive. After hours of pounding away at her keyboard, she finished by reliving the ghastly scene of the massacre outside the village. Closing her eyes, Angie wrote every detail she could remember, from the chilling sounds of the refugees' screams to the acrid carbon smells of the AK-47 smoke as it drifted slowly into the camp. Finally, she added dozens of pictures she'd snapped of crying babies, children with the thousand-yard stare, and women toiling in front of small white tents that had become their new homes.

After hours of word-smithing and rewriting paragraph after paragraph, Angie was mostly satisfied with her first draft. But there was still something missing. Something she'd have to speak about with Henry. In the meantime, however, Angie allowed herself some sleep.

It seemed she had just fallen off into a deep sleep when she heard it. A soothing voice calling in the distance. The rhythm was slow, calming, almost trancelike as it penetrated her slumber. Still partially asleep, Angie tried to place the lyrical sounds. Finally, the cobwebs in her mind cleared and she forced herself to sit up in bed and listen as the words drifted by her.

"*Allah huwa akhbar. Yella lil salah, hiya lil salah. La Allah illallah.*"

Then she realized what it was. The call to prayer. Muslims pray five times a day. The first call was at dawn. She looked outside the tent, and in the eastern desert, she could see the very faintest first rays of sunlight barely peeking up over the desert.

"Dawn," she said aloud in the empty tent. Looking at her watch, she realized it was now 5:48 AM. Roughly five hours' sleep. Not much, but it would have to do. She threw on a pair of tan cargo pants and a loose-fitting, white, button-down shirt and headed off to the women's showers. Cold but refreshing, the water washed away the last remnants of her sleepiness. She would need all of her focus to convince Henry to act on her plan.

The camp seemed empty this morning, she thought as she walked the lonely sandy trails between the rows of white tents. It was early—breakfast didn't open for another hour—but the camp had been more lively yesterday. Maybe after the attack, the refugees were staying closer to their makeshift homes. The tents didn't provide any additional security, certainly not from a Janjaweed bullet, but there was something to say about "ignorance is bliss." In their tents, perhaps a refugee family could have some semblance of normalcy.

Angie walked into the reception tent. It was empty. The small plastic flower and frame containing the picture of Carey with her husband, the few items that Carey told her she brought with her to remind her of home, were gone. As was Carey. Another victim of the violence.

There was one place that Angie knew would be crowded. She made her way back to the medical tent, where wounded and sick refugees filled every bed. The unmistakable stench of death hung in the air. She had read about the odor many times, but had never thought to become familiar with it herself. The pungent combination of rotting flesh mixed with charred skin filled her nostrils and made her nauseous.

Noticing Jason and Abdullah at the far end of the tent sitting beside an old man, she walked over to them.

"Ask him who was leading the raid," she overheard the doctor say.

"What do you mean?" Abdullah asked.

"What did the Janjaweed commander look like? Did he have a patch covering one eye?" Jason asked.

"Good morning," Angie said, interrupting the conversation.

"Hey, Angie," Jason said, glancing at her then returning his focus on the patient's left foot.

When Angie saw what the doctor was doing, she had to turn away and fight back the urge to vomit. "Is that what I think it is?"

"It is," Gabriela said as she walked over carrying a small basin and a bottle of saline. "We use maggots to clean wounds."

"His foot's gangrenous," Jason said, continuing to apply fly larvae to the wound using tweezers. "The maggots feed off the dead tissue."

"But why?" Angie asked, forcing herself to look.

"Dead tissue is a source of infection. Quite frankly, the maggots will do a better job of debriding it than I could with a scalpel. And they'll leave any living tissue alone. While they're cleaning up the wound, they also leave behind some secretions that help kill bacteria."

"But they're *maggots*," she said, scrunching up her nose.

Jason laughed. "Yes, they are. And I'm thankful for them. Gabriela, can you get me the bandages that arrived last week, please?"

His nurse left to get the supplies. "I first heard about the use of maggots in modern medicine in medical school. But last week, a Swedish doctor who has been doing humanitarian missions in Africa for years came out to help us with his team. They left a few days before you arrived. He left me with some of the medicinal maggots and some special gauzes they used."

"So, young Dr. Russo here is impressing you with his state-of-the-art medicine, I see," Henry said, coming up behind them.

"It's just gross," Angie replied.

"I don't disagree," answered Jason. "Many doctors and patients in the States cringe at the thought of maggot therapy. But, I tell you, it works, especially out here in the field where I have so few resources. It helps prevent a lot of infections."

"Glad to hear it," Henry said. "So, Angie, how is the reporting coming along?"

"Good, I've got a notebook full of stories from the refugees and a lot of pictures," she replied, her eyes still glued to the small wound on the old man's foot filled with wriggling larvae.

Henry noted the hesitancy in her voice and added, "Is that not enough?"

"Well, I want this story to rock the world. It needs to enthrall the readers and capture their attention. Then I want them to feel the suffering that's going on in Darfur. For that, I need to be thorough. The stories I have from the refugees are great. They really paint a good picture of what they've been through."

"But?" Henry replied.

"Well, there's really no safe haven for the refugees. I mean, their villages are destroyed and they lose their loved ones and everything they own and come across the border to this camp

EVIL WINDS: TRADECRAFT PHASE TWO

where they're also attacked. I have that later part of the story, but not the beginning: what their lives were like at home, in the villages."

"Yasser, can you give us a few minutes, please?" Jason asked. Yasser rose and exited the medical tent. After ensuring the translator was out of earshot, Jason continued, "You can't mean what I think you mean."

Henry stared at her in disbelief. "You want to go into *Sudan*?"

"Henry, they're living in fear, every day waiting for the Janjaweed to come and rape and massacre them, kidnap their sons to be child soldiers. *Hearing* their stories is important, but *seeing* it is crucial to understanding how they got here. I need to know what their lives are like *before* the Janjaweed take it all away from them. That'll complete the picture for my readers. Only then will they fully comprehend the story of those living in fear every day. Watching, waiting."

"But all these refugees *were* there," Jason interjected, not liking where this was going. "Surely they can tell you what they went through before they were refugees."

"You don't understand. I need to tell their *whole* story in order to get anyone to believe them and want to help. I need pictures of the kids playing in the villages *before* they were refugees or taken away to some battlefield. I need to show how they live in fear every day, fear that the Janjaweed will come take away everything they have. Then I can add the stories and pictures of their life in the refugee camp *after* their world was shattered by the militia. That, I think, will stir the American people. To see how they lived and loved, only to have their lives torn apart and have to settle in refugee camps in a foreign country. I need to see it for myself to do the story justice. Do you understand?" she asked.

"I understand the Sudanese desert is a dangerous place," Henry replied. "It's no place to wander around without armed guards. Not only do we not have any armed guards we could spare to send with you, we don't even have Sudan's permission to enter their territory. There's just no way, Angie."

"Jason, do you remember the little boy you treated for typhus?" she asked.

"Ajou. Sure. Why?"

"When I spoke with his grandmother yesterday, she told me about a village just over the border that hasn't been attacked. It's not far from here, only about thirty miles or so across the desert. Ajou and his family stayed there for a few days after their own village was destroyed. I could just pop over there in an SUV and be back in a couple of hours."

"I won't have it, Angie," Henry interjected. "There's just no way. It's not safe. And we have no permission to go into Sudan. Before you got here, we specifically asked that you be allowed to see the camps in Sudan and the government adamantly refused. No journalists, particularly from America. If you were caught by the Sudanese government, you'd go to jail for a long time. And their jails aren't very nice, let me tell you. And if you got caught by the Arab militias, I don't even want to think about that. Haven't you heard anything the refugees have said to you? The Janjaweed are cold-blooded killers. They rape and kill their own people. What do you think they would do to an attractive young American woman?" he asked, trying desperately to convince her of the dangers.

"I can't help them if I can't tell their full story," Angie said, not budging.

Henry looked over at Jason, his eyes pleading for help. When he found none, he closed the subject himself. "I'm sorry, Angie, it's just completely out of the question. Now, if you'll excuse me."

Just then Gabriela returned and started applying the special bandage to the wound on the old man's foot. Jason stood up from his stool and watched Henry storm out of the tent.

"Jason, I've got to see this village," Angie pleaded.

"Angie, you heard Henry. He's right. You don't know how ruthless the Janjaweed are." Jason led her outside into the bright sun. "I've seen the results of their torture. And those are just from the few that made it out alive. It's just not worth it."

"It *is* worth it. The story has to be complete if it has any chance of helping the world see the truth of what's going on here. I'm going, Jason. I don't know how. I'll walk there if I have to. This story needs to be written."

"Okay, but at what cost?"

"Ask them," Angie replied, nodding back toward the medical tent.

"I guess there's no way I can talk you out of this?"

"No, my mind's made up. Jason, you make a difference every day here. Let me do my job and make a difference as well. But to do it, I have to go into Sudan," Angie replied.

Jason shook his head. Finally he said, "Yasser knows his way around the border. Let me talk to him, see what he thinks about how safe it is."

A bright smile came across Angie's face. She reached out and put a hand on his forearm. "Thank you, Jason. You don't know how much it means to me. My story, if written right, may be the catalyst to stop the madness."

"I still don't like it. But, if it's safe, maybe we can take a quick ride out to the village for an hour or so. There're no fences or border crossings in the open desert between here and Darfur."

"No, I don't want you to get you into trouble. I'll go alone," she replied. "I don't work for the UN or any NGO, Jason. All they can do to me is send me back home. Once I get my story, that'll be just fine. But you, this is your job. You could get into trouble."

"This is nonnegotiable, Angie," he said firmly. "I won't help you if I don't go with you. I'm not letting you go out there by yourself."

For a moment she was angry, wondering if Jason was being condescending because she was a woman. But, after reflecting on the stories she recorded from the victims in the camp, she realized that Jason was right. The Janjaweed were bloodthirsty killers. Besides, she would feel better if he were there with her.

"Okay," she relented.

"Let's go see Yasser," he said.

They reentered the medical tent. Gabriela had finished dressing the wound and was sterilizing some medical instruments with an iodine solution. Yasser was seated alone at the back of the tent, translating some medical records for Jason.

"Yasser, can we speak with you for a moment?" asked Jason.

"Sure, doc. What can I do for you?" he asked.

After looking around to make sure no one was listening, Jason said, "Yasser, there's a small village, about thirty miles or so from here, across the border into Sudan. Do you know it?"

"Zarundi is there. It's really no more than a collection of huts, actually. About fifteen of them, or so. The last I had heard, the Janjaweed have not yet destroyed it."

"Why?"

"The tribal leader has been paying them off. They're a poor people, but they give most of their harvest to the Janjaweed in order to keep them out," Yasser answered.

"But there's been so little rain over the past few months. Many of the people I've interviewed have told me most of their crops failed this year. Surely it must have affected Zarundi as well," replied Angie.

"Probably. If so, I'm sure they're worried. If they have nothing to give the Janjaweed when they come, they'll be destroyed like their neighboring villages," Yasser added with a nod.

"Jason, we've got to go," Angie cried. "If I can tell their story, maybe we can help them *before* the Janjaweed come. Before it's too late."

"Why do you ask?"

"Yasser, I need you to take us to Zarundi."

"Doctor, it is not safe at all. Why do you want to go?"

"To help," Jason said, looking over at Angie.

"It's not wise," Yasser replied. "The Janjaweed are very active in that area. The men that attacked us yesterday are probably still roaming along the border. It is only a matter of time before they run out of food and go to Zarundi for resupply. If they don't find any, they will surely destroy the village. And everyone in it."

"Angie, the drought has made the Janjaweed desperate," Jason said. "They have nothing to lose. Their lands to the north are becoming more arid every day, driving them deeper and deeper south into the non-Arab villages in Darfur. This elevates our risk. And the danger. Is there any way I can talk you out of this?"

"I have to go," Angie replied.

"Okay," said Jason. "Henry said the UNAMRID medical team will be here this afternoon. We can leave after they arrive and the next wave of refugees are taken care of. Once the UNAMRID team gets here Henry will be tied up getting them settled and won't miss us. We'll still have several hours of daylight if we leave right at dinner time. Yasser, can you get a vehicle ready? Fill it up with fuel and put some extra food, water, and gas cans in the back. Can you meet us back here at five?"

"As you wish, but I'm warning you, it is not safe," Yasser said firmly.

"Please," Jason added.

"All right. I'll do as you ask," he replied, shaking his head as he walked off.

"Thank you, Jason."

"Listen, we go across the border, talk to the villagers in Zarundi for one hour max, then get right back here before it gets dark. Deal?"

"Okay," she said. Something had come over Jason. She certainly didn't know him well, but she was a reporter. Part of her job was to notice things and read people. In an instant, he had changed to become more serious and commanding, solemn even. Maybe he was just worried and being overly cautious.

▼ ▼ ▼

Jason didn't like it at all. Angie had lived a quiet life in California. Her upper-middle-class roots afforded her a security that shielded her from the dangers of the world in which she lived. He, however, had grown up in the slums of Chicago. He was accustomed to fear and danger, life and death. His survival had depended on his ability to accurately weigh the pros and cons of each calculated risk he took. It had kept him alive thus far. In his mind, he summed up the risks of this trip and didn't like the numbers he came up with.

13

"DIG FASTER!" the man holding the AK-47 screamed at the boys in the quarry.

Matak looked to his left and right as he swung the heavy pickax. The soft sand had given way hours ago, and the group of young teenagers were making slow progress in the hard bedrock. He had no idea what the men with the rifles were looking for in this barren desert.

He had long since lost track of how long he had been held captive. The boys were fed only once each day: stale bread and whatever they could pick off the bones left over from the guards' meals. It was difficult for him to concentrate as he swung the pickax at the rocks at his feet.

The big man with the scar and the one eye had returned an hour or so after they had started working this morning. Even the guards became more on edge when the man returned, Matak noticed. They beat the boys harder and made them dig faster when their leader stood over them, as he did now.

"Maseeh ad-Dajaal," Obie muttered.

"What did you say?" Matak asked his emaciated cousin beside him. Obie had been severely beaten after the escape attempt. Now his eyes were glossing over and he was sometimes incoherent. Dehydration and starvation were starting to take their toll on young Obie.

"*Maseeh ad-Dajaal*," Obie repeated, but this time he was looking up at the edge of the quarry. Matak glanced up and saw the one-eyed Janjaweed commander looming over them. He was holding a bag and stared right at Matak, causing the boy to cringe. The Janjaweed grinned and dumped the bag into the quarry. Pieces of cooked meat fell at Matak's feet.

Matak looked down. He felt hands all over him and was pushed out of the way as the other starving teenagers grabbed at the food. Then the fists started flying. Fights broke out between the boys, who were screaming and cursing at each other. At first, Matak huddled into the wall of the quarry, trying to stay out of their way. Starvation caused their primal instincts to take over, provoking them to fight each other for scraps of food to survive.

He looked to his left and saw that Obie just stood there as the other boys rolled on the ground, punching each other. Obie was still staring at the Janjaweed commander standing above them.

Matak knew that Obie wouldn't make it much longer without food so he dropped to his knees and started fighting the other boys for pieces of chicken. For every piece he was able to get his hands on and shove into his mouth, he took another and thrust it into his pocket.

A small, bony fist came out of nowhere and landed on Matak's cheek. The reverberation of the impact made his head hurt. The small boy who delivered the punch lunged at Matak, trying to grab a chicken leg from his hand. Matak wrestled with the boy, rolling on the hard ground of the quarry, delivering his own punches with his free hand to protect his prize. Matak's attacker, sensing defeat, scampered away to attack someone smaller.

Out of breath, Matak sat on the ground, panting. He still held the chicken in his hand but couldn't eat it. He felt a gaze upon him and looked up. Two big hands grabbed him and pulled him out of the quarry.

"What were you going to do with these?" one of the Janjaweed soldiers asked as they went through his pockets and pulled out the meat.

Without thinking, Matak looked back into the quarry at Obie, still staring aimlessly into space.

The man punched Matak in the stomach and he fell to the ground, gasping for air.

"No," the man shouted. "There is no charity here. If he doesn't fight for his own food, he starves. You don't save food for him."

The Janjaweed soldier kicked Matak in the face with the sole of his military boot. Matak rolled over and fell back down into the quarry where chaos reigned. That was what the Janjaweed soldiers wanted.

The one-eyed commander stared down into the quarry, laughing. Obie was right. He truly was an *ad-Dajaal*. The Antichrist.

14

ABDULLAH SAT IN THE APARTMENT overlooking the millennium-old Bab al-Yemen. Smoke from a burning building rose from inside the walled Old City of Yemen's capital, very close to the famed gate. Ever since he could remember, the fifty-one-year-old freedom fighter had been a soldier of Islam. Recruited in the late 1980s during the early days of al-Qaeda, Abdullah had been a faithful jihadist for the cause.

"What perplexes you, my *khalifah*?" Faisal said, bringing chai to his friend.

"Faisal, why are you still so formal with me? You and I are like brothers," Abdullah replied, taking the hot tea.

"Because you have been chosen to unite and lead our *ummah*," replied Faisal, sitting down in the chair beside Abdullah.

"We've come a long way in the short year since we broke away from al-Qaeda," said Abdullah, sipping his tea as he watched the plumes of smoke dissipate around the tall, ornate buildings characteristic of Yemeni Islamic architecture.

"It was time. Ad-Dawlah al-Islāmiyah and al-Qaeda are failing," Faisal replied. "As you've preached many times, war and violence is not the principal method to achieve our *ummat al-Islamiya.*"

One Islamic community that spanned the globe, transcending cultures, languages, and nationalism. That had been Abdullah al-Harbi's dream ever since he picked up his first AK-47 as a teenager in this ancient city on the southern tip of the Arabian Peninsula. The *ummah* was Abdullah's vision of a new world order where Sharia law ruled over a single and united Islamic government that spanned the globe.

"But so many have tried to achieve what we are striving for, Faisal. One nation spread across the globe, without borders, all united under the banner of Islam. The *ummah*. Previous caliphates have tried as well. Numerous *khalifahs* throughout our rich history have been successful at spreading Islam and even united its peoples from time to time. But there has not been a true *khalifah* in a long time. No one to unite the faithful in these modern times. Perhaps the caliphate of the past cannot exist today," concluded Abdullah. "Look at them. Shi'a *Houthis*, Sunni al-Qaeda, Arab government troops and resistance fighters, all battling each other right in front of our eyes." The rare tear formed in Abdullah's eyes as he watched the fires in the once-picturesque Old City of Sana'a. Declared a World Heritage site by the United Nations, yet another Yemeni civil war threatened the ancient buildings with their stained-glass windows. "How can we defeat the infidels abroad and unite our people if we can't even keep from fighting ourselves here at home?"

"Abdullah," Faisal replied sternly, "don't despair. Your vision is righteous. The strategy to achieve a united *ummah* is solid. One nation of the faithful. It will come, under your leadership. You *are* the *Khalifah*. Your plan will succeed and Muslims from across the world will unite. You can achieve where the others have failed. Have faith, my brother."

Abdullah looked over to his second-in-command as a thought came to him. "You're right. Maybe we can use the division within our own community to our advantage. But first, we have to deal with Shao Ying. She's motivated not by faith but by power and greed, just like her father. She wants to influence us, control our actions, as she does with the other mujahideen," he said. "In order for my plan to work, we have to remove ourselves from under her patronage. All she's interested in is chaos and destruction. She doesn't want the *ummah*, as we envision it, to succeed. She's poison, Faisal, and would oppose my plan."

"That won't be easy. From what you tell me, she's a very powerful woman that's used to getting what she wants."

"Perhaps there's a way. Until then, however, we must act the part. Ying wants us to wage war like our brothers in ad-Dawlah al-Islāmiyah and al-Qaeda. We will not disappoint. It's time for us to break out onto the world stage, and we will start in the Sahel."

"Using Hussein of the Janjaweed?" Faisal asked, trying to understand his *khalifah*'s master plan. "But he killed Faris in Toulon. Can you trust him?"

"He is barbaric, but he's also faithful. He wants to be our emir in Africa, and, with our help, he and his Janjaweed army will wage war across the continent. It will be like the great Islamic purification of North Africa during the *Mahdiyya* a century ago. The world will learn the power of the United Islamic Caliphate and they will fear us. Then our brothers and sisters will flock to our cause. That will keep Ying happy while we work behind the scenes elsewhere and enact our plan to create a pan-Islamic world in a way that even she cannot stop."

15

"YOU WERE NOT THERE," Hussein snapped after being summoned to the provincial capital in Shamal, Darfur. "I would have been arrested. You may be the governor of this *wilaya*, Tawfik, but remember that you were once one of my Janjaweed lieutenants."

"I have responsibilities now that you cannot imagine," Tawfik Dahabi replied to the fighter sitting across the desk in his modest governor's office. "You have no idea of my responsibilities, Hussein. More than half of villages in the entire Darfur fall under my control. My police are under constant attack by Sudan Liberation Movement rebels. On top of that, I have to clean up the mess that you and your Janjaweed raiders leave across the province. I was told you killed four men in France, including one of al-Harbi's emirs."

"I take no chances," Hussein replied dismissively. "One of the men pulled out a gun. Obviously, they were waiting for me. I don't know how many of the men I killed were with the authorities. And, frankly, I don't care. They are dead, I am still alive."

"But there are those who do care. If you want to support al-Harbi and his ideological fundamentalist crusade, fine, but remember who pays the bills around here. And remember that I control this province. Khartoum has given me complete authority to run things as I see fit. If word gets out that someone from Sudan was involved in the killings in Toulon, it would bring unwanted attention on our activities. We already have enough international eyes spying on us. We don't need Interpol or the Hague on our backs as well."

"You sit here in El-Fashir in your nice governor's office that your cousin in Khartoum helped secure for you and lecture me?" hissed Hussein, leaning forward in his chair. "You turned your back on your Janjaweed brothers, Tawfik. You gave up fighting for the cause a long time ago. You have your small army of smugglers, marauders, and criminals and are allowed to run this province as you see fit because you are a puppet to both Khartoum and your foreign master. I believe you care more about your bank accounts and making the foreigners happy than you do for the quarter of a million Sudanese under your charge."

"Watch your tongue, Hussein," Tawfik warned. "You are no longer my commander. El-Fashir is becoming a major business and trading center in Darfur, and I am charged with keeping the peace. I will not risk all that our government has worked for because of your crusade to help al-Harbi form his *ummah*. Yes, I know about that."

"You were once a fine soldier, Tawfik. One of my best Janjaweed leaders. But you've become a bureaucrat. You've been corrupted by the foreigner's money, just like so many in Khartoum. I still fight for something meaningful. What I do out there I do to preserve our people, our way of life. I don't do it for money. You mock al-Harbi and call him an idealist. At least he fights for all Arabs and for Islam—something you and your masters know nothing about. I'm tired of serving infidels."

"Those *infidels* passed you information that saved your life in Toulon. Be careful who you betray. You don't see the big picture like I do. That's why I became, as you say, a bureaucrat. The world is a giant chess game with only a handful of people moving the pieces. Choose your side, Hussein, but choose wisely."

Hussein sat back in his chair and contemplated his former subordinate. Tawfik had been one of his best fighters, a brave and masterful tactician on the battlefield. But he was always ambitious. When Tawfik's cousin became the deputy minister of the interior in Khartoum, Hussein's former lieutenant seized the opportunity and used his connections to become a local governor in Darfur. Ever since, Tawfik had been Hussein's liaison with the government in Khartoum, directing his raids and providing him weapons, money, and support.

The Janjaweed commander knew his aggressive actions in Toulon would anger both his current benefactor in Sudan as well as the *khalifah* in Yemen. It was a bold move, but he had to prove his ruthlessness to both men. Soon Hussein would have to make his peace with al-Harbi for killing his emir in Toulon and convince the *khalifah* that his highly mobile, powerful Janjaweed army had a place in executing the grand plan to expand the Islamic Caliphate into North Africa.

"One hundred and fifty years ago, my great-great-uncle, Mohammad Ahmad bin Abdullah, the great *Mahdi* himself, brought the great British Empire to its knees in this very desert. As the leader of the *Mahdiyya,* he was the savior of the people of Sudan. I, Hussein bin Mohammed, a humble servant of Islam, will carry on the work he started. The infidels and non-Arabs must be purged from our lands. You are either with me, or against me. So," Hussein said, standing up to his full height and towering over the desk, "it is you, *my friend,* who should choose more wisely."

16

"LAST CHANCE. Any possibility of me talking you out of this?" Jason asked Angie as they stood in the medical tent. The Toyota Land Cruiser was waiting outside with Yasser in the driver's seat.

"No. But thanks for coming with me."

"It's dangerous. But there's one thing I need from you, and it's not negotiable."

"Everything's negotiable," she joked.

But Jason remained stone-faced.

"Okay, what's the condition?" she asked.

"You listen to me. Whatever I say, you do. Exactly. When I say it's time to leave, we leave. Is that a deal?"

"Fair enough," Angie replied, as she jumped into the passenger seat.

Jason didn't like it. He closed her door and walked over to the driver's side.

"I'll drive, Yasser. Thanks for getting everything ready for us. I appreciate you coming with us. You know this area much better than I do, and we'll need an interpreter."

"No problem," Yasser answered casually as he climbed into the backseat.

I wonder why he's so calm. Maybe I am being too paranoid. After all, it's only thirty miles away or so. We won't be gone long.

Through the window, Jason could see his medical bag sitting in the backseat, bulging with items he hoped he wouldn't need. Having it, however, gave him comfort. He climbed into the driver's seat and put the truck into first gear.

The scenery across the austere landscape was as breathtaking as it was barren. Although sunset was still several hours away, a reddish hue tinged the sand as the sun sank toward the horizon. Small trees or thorny shrub dotted the landscape. The rock formations, hills, and small mountain ranges that jutted out of the desert in the distance were eerily majestic. Angie took pictures as they drove. Over his feigned protest, she even took one of Jason driving.

"Just keep that one out of your story," Jason said of the picture.

"Why?" she said playfully. "Don't you want me to remember you?"

Jason looked over at her in the passenger seat. Her red hair was blowing in the wind. Jason decided he did, in fact, want her to remember him. And more. His gaze was fixed on her radiant smile. He was about to speak when the SUV jarred to a complete stop.

"What happened?" Angie asked, sticking her head out of the window.

Jason shoved the gear shift into low, but the wheels kept spinning. He tried reverse, but was only rewarded with more sand flying up around the rocking vehicle.

"Sand. We must have hit a patch of loose sand." He cursed himself quietly for taking his eyes off the road. He would have seen it, had he not been so focused on Angie.

Jason put the manual shift into neutral and climbed out. Angie and Yasser followed.

"Damn," he said, looking at the back wheels. They were both covered in sand to the axle.

"What do we do now?" Angie asked.

"We dig the tires out," Jason replied. "Yasser, grab the ladders for me."

Yasser nodded and climbed onto the back bumper to reach the roof rack. He removed two four-foot-long metal ladders and tossed them down onto the soft sand. After he got down, Jason opened the back of the SUV and took out a shovel.

"What are the ladders for?" asked Angie.

Jason started digging around the back tires. "We need traction. They'll sit on top of the deep sand and give the tires something to grab on to."

As if on cue, Yasser placed the metal ladder in front of the back tires as Jason dug around them. He stopped for a moment to look up at the sky. *This is going to take some time,* he thought, wiping the sweat forming on his brow. They were losing daylight quickly. The last thing he wanted was to be stuck in the middle of Janjaweed-controlled desert when the sun went down.

17

SHOTS ECHOED throughout the quarry filled with young boys fumbling with rifles.

"Exhale slowly as you pull the trigger, boy," barked the scarred, one-eyed man whom Obie had dubbed *ad-Dajaal*. The Janjaweed leader had lined up his captives in the quarry in which they'd been working since sunrise. After a surprisingly hearty lunch, the Janjaweed gathered all the boys up and handed them rifles but no bullets. Then the Janjaweed lined the boys up and taught them how to operate the deadly tools of *ad-Dajaal's* trade.

Matak struggled with the heavy rifle, trying to keep it steady as he once again pulled the trigger as *ad-Dajaal* instructed. Once again, the rifle's hammer released against an empty chamber. Once again, *ad-Dajaal* was dissatisfied with his performance.

"You won't hit anything if you shake the rifle like that," he screamed, striking Matak on the back of the head with an open hand.

"This is how you kill your enemies," the big man continued, lifting his own rifle to his one good eye and firing off three bullets in quick succession. The line of would-be soldiers watched with a mix of awe and fear as three cans at the far end of the quarry flew into the air.

"You'll learn how to be a fighter or you will die right here in this quarry." *Ad-Dajaal* pulled an empty magazine out of one of the pockets of his tan camouflaged military vest and placed one bullet into the magazine. "Now," he said to Matak. "Fire that weapon like I taught you to."

Matak stared at the magazine. He took it from the hand of his new master and placed it in the empty magazine slot of his rifle. He mustered all of his strength to pull back the heavy charging handle like *ad-Dajaal* had showed him and released the bolt, sending the single round into the chamber.

Many thoughts raced through Matak's mind as he lifted the rifle to his shoulder once more. This would be the first time he had ever fired a live bullet from a rifle. He thought about his family. His mother, brutally murdered by the Janjaweed led by the scarred Antichrist standing beside him. His sister Fatima—he didn't know where she was or what horrible things these evil men were doing to her. Or if she was even alive.

As instructed, Matak closed one eye and looked through the rifle sights with the other eye. He tried to concentrate on his shoulder and arm muscles to steady the rifle. One shot, that's all he had. Would it be enough?

His mind raced at the choices before him. Was he fast enough? Would he be able to turn fast enough and shoot the devil standing next to him? Could he kill a man, even one as evil as *ad-Dajaal*?

He smelled the putrid breath of the Janjaweed commander standing beside him. Surely he would be mowed down by all the surrounding soldiers as soon as he pulled the trigger. But if he had a clear shot and could kill *ad-Dajaal*, would it be worth it? Would it make a difference to his people in the long run?

Matak began to pull on the trigger. It was hard and cold. He took another breath and pulled on his index finger with all his might. Slowly the trigger moved. As he applied even pressure to the trigger, just as *ad-Dajaal* had instructed, he thought about his choices. A quick swing of the rifle and it would be pointed at *ad-Dajaal's* head. One shot and his nightmare would be over.

The trigger pulled back farther. Soon it would be back far enough to release the hammer, allowing it to strike the firing pin. After the firing pin hit the bullet in the chamber, the deadly round would explode out of the barrel. All Matak had to do was to turn quickly enough to swing the end of the barrel at the Antichrist before the big man could stop him. But could he do it? Could Matak kill a man in cold blood? Even this monster of a man?

Matak made his decision just as the weapon was about to fire. He closed his aiming eye, said a quick prayer to himself, and pulled the trigger the rest of the way.

Crack! The sound of the weapon startled him as the can at the far end of the quarry jumped up into the air. Matak finished exhaling and lowered the empty weapon to his side.

"Good," *ad-Dajaal* said. "You have killed your first enemy."

Matak stared at the rocks at his feet, disappointed that he hadn't turned the weapon on his true enemy.

The Janjaweed commander leaned in close and whispered, "I know what is in your mind and in your heart. Your hatred and anger will make you a strong soldier. Know that I will be watching you, boy."

Matak turned to look squarely into the evil man's eye and realized that the fear he had of *ad-Dajaal* was now gone. It truly had been, as *ad-Dajaal* said, replaced by hatred.

▼ ▼ ▼

The Janjaweed leader's phone rang, interrupting the staring contest he was having with this young boy. Perhaps one day he would make a fine Janjaweed soldier, once Hussein and his men broke his spirit. The one-eyed man walked away, pulling his phone out of his war vest. As much as he had come to detest the foreigners and their unholy influence in his beloved Sudan, he was glad that they had brought in cell towers and state-of-the-art satellite communications. Although he was certain they were listening to his every word, at least he had phone coverage to coordinate his strikes against the Fur.

"'Alo," he said.

"You know who this is?" the man asked in Yemeni Arabic.

Right away Hussein recognized the voice of his *khalifah*, Sheikh Abdullah al-Harbi. "Yes, I know." He had been awaiting this call ever since he killed al-Harbi's emir in Toulon. He was about to find out if his bold move had had the intended effect on the *khalifah*.

"I need to know that I can trust you. That you will act in my name," al-Harbi said.

Hussein accepted the rebuke for his actions in Toulon but knew his moment had arrived.

"I will work tirelessly to spread the faith under your guidance," Hussein said. "At all costs."

"Good. It's time, my new emir in the Sudan, for us to make our mark on the world. Prove to me that I can trust you as my new prince in Africa. Show me what you can do against the infidels."

That was all Hussein needed. He realized that now he had a new home. A place of honor that would secure his position in Africa and the world. Like his ancestor, the great *Mahdi* himself who had waged war against the British invaders a century ago. Finally, Hussein bin Mohammed, newly minted and faithful soldier of al-Harbi's global *ummah*, would do what his government had failed to do. Khartoum and their foreign allies were too political. They held back on purging his country of non-Arabs. He and his Janjaweed army would complete this task—and more—in the name of the *khalifah*.

"I understand, *Khalifah*. It will be done."

Hussein put the phone back into his pocket and looked around. The foreigners had ruined his beautiful desert. First, he would take care of the African villagers. The time for the expulsion of all infidels from his beloved Sudan would come soon enough.

In a loud, booming voice, he called out to his Janjaweed soldiers: *"Yella, ya shabab!"* It was time to prepare to leave. He reflected on a different call he had received a few hours ago—one that provided him with some very interesting news. Perhaps he could offer his new master the exact present he needed to usher the Islamic Caliphate into a new era and create a united North Africa for Arab Muslims. He did not believe in coincidences. Allah had indeed blessed him today, a day that would go down in history as the first conquest of Hussein bin Mohammed al-Fadi, Janjaweed commander and faithful emir of the United Islamic Caliphate in Africa.

18

"TRY IT AGAIN!" Jason shouted. The SUV rocked forward as Angie pressed on the gas. Yasser and Jason stood at the back of the vehicle, shoulders against the rear door, pushing as the Land Cruiser inched forward.

"Keep pushing, Yasser," said Jason. The tires moved slowly toward the ladder's metal rungs and finally met their target. The SUV lunged forward as the treads of the two rear tires grabbed onto the rungs. Yasser and Jason almost fell into the sand when the vehicle shot away from them.

Angie drove about ten feet away from the sand pit onto rockier ground and stopped, looking out the back window. The two men were pulling the ladders out of thick sand. As Jason bent down, Angie caught a glimpse of a silver object in his bag. At first, she thought it was a piece of medical equipment, but then she saw a trigger. Angie knew their trip was going to be dangerous, but why would an American doctor have a pistol in a refugee camp?

The driver's side door opened, startling Angie.

"Good job," Jason said. "You California girls know how to drive in the sand. Must be all those beaches out there."

"Huh?" she said.

"What's wrong?" he asked.

"Oh, nothing," replied Angie. She was still trying to process what she had seen.

"We'd better get going. We lost a lot of daylight," Jason said, looking up at the sky again.

Angie got out of the SUV and returned to the passenger seat. Yasser and Jason finished securing the ladders and shovel, and soon the three were back on their journey to Zarundi.

▼ ▼ ▼

A half hour or so later, Jason began to slow the vehicle in anticipation of their arrival. "The village should be right over that small ridgeline," he said. Angie remained quiet, still wondering why Jason owned a pistol. Bahai certainly was a dangerous place, as she had witnessed firsthand in just her first day at the camp. But Jason was a doctor, not a soldier. Why would he own a gun? Maybe he felt he needed to protect himself or his patients, she mused.

"Are you all right?" asked Jason. Angie looked over at him. Although she had spent quite a bit of time at Bahai with him, she realized that she barely knew the man.

"Yeah, I'm good," Angie replied, forcing a small smile.

Certainly, after all of the violence Jason must have seen along the border with Sudan since arriving at Bahai, she could see why Jason would want to arm himself. But she wasn't a gun person. Angie abhorred violence. She knew that her motives for coming to Africa were not entirely selfless. She was chasing the award-winning story, one that would prove her journalistic skills to the world and free her from her father's shadow. But the refugees' stories had touched her, and she wanted to help them. Guns and violence had started this war, and she felt they would do little to end it.

After another half hour of driving in silence, Angie peered up at the sky. The sun looked closer to the desert horizon. She knew their time in the village would be limited. She pushed her worries about Jason and his gun out of her mind and focused on what to ask the Zarundi villagers.

"Remember," Jason said, "we leave when I say. One hour. I want to be out of the village by twilight so we can make it home without headlights. I don't want to attract any Janjaweed that may be roaming around. Lights in the desert can be seen for miles."

Jason seemed more familiar with the dangers of the desert than most doctors, Angie thought.

"Okay, one hour," Angie allowed. After all, he was probably right.

"It takes the Janjaweed far less time than that to raze a village," Jason told her. "I brought my medical bag and some supplies. I'll see some patients while you conduct your interviews. But we stay together at all times, agreed?"

"All right," she agreed.

"That's Zarundi." Yasser pointed to the cluster of huts forming in the distance.

Back in Bahai, Angie had protested when Jason suggested they inform Henry of their travel plans. Angie, fearing that Henry would try to stop them, begged Jason to keep their trip a secret. They hoped to be back before anyone would notice, especially since Henry would be with the commander of the UN troops at a dinner with the local mayor all evening. She was now second-guessing her decision. The village appeared eerily quiet.

▼ ▼ ▼

Jason felt relieved to be nearing the village, but he stayed alert. As they entered the village of a dozen round mud and straw huts with thatched roofs, no children played outside. No women walked by with baskets on their heads, as Jason had seen so often at Bahai. Where were the men? Who was here to protect the village?

Before stopping, Jason made sure to turn the SUV around.

"What are you doing? Why are we leaving?" Angie asked.

"We're not. I just want to be facing the way we came if we have to get out of here in a hurry."

Jason put the SUV in park and turned off the engine. He left the keys in the ignition, although he knew there would be nowhere for them to run. If the Janjaweed were hiding nearby, they would be on horseback and maybe with some small pickups outfitted with high-powered *Dushka* machine guns. Jason knew the SUV couldn't outrun the horses and would be attacked. If the three were on foot in the village, they would be captured, but they might have a chance as opposed to being mowed down in the desert as they attempted to flee.

He grabbed his bag between the front seats and got out, followed by Angie.

"What is the matter?" asked Yasser from the backseat.

Jason didn't answer. He continued to scan the area, trying to figure out what was wrong.

"There're no people," Angie said. "Where are they?"

Jason looked back at Yasser. He was still in the backseat, but, surprisingly, he didn't look nervous at all.

"It's quiet," Angie whispered.

Jason said nothing, focusing on the narrow sandy road between the huts in front of them. At least the village hadn't been destroyed. That made him think that the Janjaweed had not yet come. But the stillness concerned him. What dangers awaited them?

"It's okay," Yasser said, exiting the SUV. "I don't see any signs that the Janjaweed have been here. The huts aren't burned down."

"No bodies in the street," Angie said. "The survivors back at Bahai all mentioned the Janjaweed left bodies strewn in the streets after the raids."

The three walked down the dusty trail into the village center. Jason thought about taking his gun out of his bag but decided against it. He didn't want to alarm Angie prematurely, and he wasn't even sure if it was necessary... yet. Besides, he could pull it out in seconds. He had practiced many times.

They continued on, cautiously surveying the village. Jason saw no movement other than a few chickens pecking between the huts. He heard, but could not see, a goat nearby. Those were both good signs.

"What's going on?" Angie asked. "Are we too late?"

"No," Jason replied. "I don't think so. These huts wouldn't be standing if the Janjaweed had been here. The animals would all be dead or taken. No chickens. No goats."

"Where are all the people, then?" she asked.

Jason just shook his head. He didn't know, but he was going to find out.

"Stay here," Jason told her. He walked to one of the larger mud structures and peered through the open slats of the thatched door. A shadow darted across the hut, and Jason froze, then glanced back at Angie and Yasser twenty yards behind him. He saw the fear and concern on Angie's face, but Yasser looked nonchalant. *That's odd. Why doesn't Yasser fear the Janjaweed?*

Then there was a muffled sound from the hut. Jason decided not to pull his weapon. If the Janjaweed were there, he would already be dead. They had no reason to hide from him. Besides, his pistol would do little against AK-47s. Jason took a deep breath and threw open the door. Much to his surprise, he saw a group of fifty or so women, children, and older people holding each other tightly in a corner of the hut. Jason's heart broke at the look of terror on their faces.

"It's okay," he said gently. "Yasser, come over here."

Yasser and Angie ran over to Jason's side.

"Tell them there's nothing to be afraid of. We are not here to harm them."

Yasser translated Jason's message.

A look of relief came over the villagers, but they remained cautious. Finally, a frail, elderly man approached Jason and spoke as Yasser interpreted.

"We heard your truck approaching from the west. We thought the Evil Winds were coming for us," the old man said, trembling.

"Evil Winds?" Angie asked. "What's that? What do they mean?"

"That's what the non-Arab Sudanese call the Janjaweed. The refugees in Bahai talk about what it's like when the Janjaweed entered their villages. They come like 'Evil Winds' out of the desert, leaving a path of destruction and death in their wake," Jason explained. "Just like the devastating sandstorms that are common in this area."

"Yasser, tell them we're from the United Nations camp across the border. We came to check on them, to see how they're doing," said Angie.

As Yasser translated, Angie took some photos. The sight was heart wrenching. Terrified, starving children hid behind their mothers. Flies were everywhere, feeding on the emaciated villagers.

"I'm Jason. This is my friend Angie. We're from America. We want to talk to you about your life here."

"What life?" the old man snapped. "We live in fear of the Janjaweed. They take everything we have. And now, when they find we have nothing they can take from us, they will take our lives."

"Why?" asked Angie.

"Why?" he repeated. "Can you tell me why evil exists? Explain to me what evil is. Why do men butcher each other? Power, riches, land? I don't know why. I just know it happens all around us every day and no one does anything. No one stops them. We have nothing left but each other. We have no trucks, no electricity. Whenever we hear horses or trucks in the distance, we hide, fearing the return of the Evil Winds. They *are* coming."

Angie looked at Jason with anguish in her eyes after Yasser translated this last part. "We *have* to help them, Jason," she said.

"We don't have much time. Why don't you start talking to the women, get the stories you need, so we can go. While you're doing that, I'll examine the kids. I brought some medicine as well as some extra food and water. We'll leave it with them when we go. That's the best we can do for them for now. Like you said: Tell their story. If you can get people in the UN or America to listen to you, that'll be better for them than anything else we can do for them today. Only do it fast," Jason said, looking up at the darkening sky.

"Everyone fears the Janjaweed," Angie said softly. "Even you."

Jason just looked at her for a moment. "Hurry," he said, turning toward the SUV to get his medical bag out of the vehicle. "We need to be out of here by nightfall."

19

ALMOST TWO HOURS had passed since Jason, Angie, and Yasser arrived at Zarundi. Angie strolled through the village, taking dozens of pictures and speaking with the villagers about their lives and experiences in Darfur. Meanwhile, Jason examined patients and distributed vitamins in a large hut in the center of the community. The children were in much worse shape than he expected. The IVs he started on many to rehydrate them had to be run slowly due to the patients' fragile condition, delaying the trio's departure.

It took the villagers some time to warm up to the American visitors, but, once they realized Angie and Jason were not a threat, they returned to their daily activities. After interviewing several of the villagers, Angie returned with Yasser to the center hut as Jason was finishing up with the last few patients. She watched from the door as he gave some tablets to a young girl who couldn't have been more than twelve years old.

"She has malaria," Jason said, not looking up. "She's probably had it for months. Most of the malaria in this region is caused by *Plasmodium falciparum*—a deadly type. I assume she's one of the few infected with *Plasmodium vivax*, which is much less common but also less lethal. No way to tell out here, though, without any lab equipment. She still has strength, although I don't know how. I saw her carrying water down the street an hour ago. She's one tough kid," Jason continued, rubbing the girl's head and eliciting a smile. "She'll get better with these medications, though, as long as she takes them."

Angie went over to the girl, who wore a white floral shirt and old ripped jeans, her hair short but braided. "What's your name?" Angie asked as Yasser translated.

"My name is Halima," the girl said in English.

"You speak English," Angie replied, surprised.

"A little. My mother was teacher here."

"Where is your mother now?" Angie asked.

Halima's face darkened. "The Evil Winds took her when she was visiting my aunt in a nearby village."

"What about your father?" asked Angie.

"Gone" was the reply.

Angie took a piece of hard candy from her jacket.

"Can she have this?" she asked Jason.

"Sure," he said.

Halima took the candy without any expression as she continued her story. "I wasn't feeling good the day my mother took my brother Matak and sister Fatima to visit our aunt."

"Probably cyclic fevers from the malaria," Jason said, putting his hand on Halima's forehead. "Here, take this pill." After watching Halima take the first dose of the anti-malaria medication, Jason had the girl put the rest of the medicine he had given her into her pocket.

"I stayed here. But my family never came back," she finished.

Angie put a hand on the young girl's arm.

"Halima, can you help me?" Jason asked. Angie recognized that he was changing the subject, trying to get Halima's mind off the loss of her family. "Can you be my helper?"

Halima nodded, but her face remained expressionless as she waited for her instructions. "Do you see those two boys over there?" Jason said, pointing. "They're going to take the same medicine you are. Can you bring these two bottles over to them? I already told them how to take it, they just need the medicine. Can you do that for me, please?"

Halima took the two bottles that Jason pulled out of his bag and walked to the other end of the hut.

"I've filled my notebook with stories, many just like Halima's. Their stories are so sad, so terrible," Angie said sorrowfully. "They're suffering so much here, Jason. Do you know that a week ago a small plane flew over this village and dropped hand grenades out the window?"

"I know. I just treated two kids with shrapnel in their legs from the explosion. Apparently, it blew up one of the huts they used as a school."

"That's inhuman. I can't believe people can act that way toward one another."

"You'd be surprised," Jason replied sadly.

A noise outside drew them out of the hut to see villagers scurrying from hut to hut in a frenzy.

"What are they saying?" Angie asked, watching a woman run in between the huts screaming in terror.

"Evil Winds are coming, Evil Winds!" Halima translated, looking terrified.

Angie glanced off into the horizon and saw a cloud of dust. It looked like a sandstorm was headed their direction. She felt Jason tense up beside her.

"We have to leave. Now!" he said.

Then she saw them. Emerging from the sandy cloud, dozens of men on horseback and camelback stampeded at the village. In their hands were the unmistakable silhouettes of AK-47s.

Halima rushed out of the hut and sped past the two Americans down the dusty road, now crowded with villagers.

"Halima! Hide!" Angie shouted. "Jason, we have to do something!"

"Get into the SUV, fast!" Jason yelled.

"But the people!" protested Angie.

"There's nothing we can do for them. We can't fight off an army. We can help them more alive than dead. Now *move!*" Jason looked around for Yasser but didn't see him. He pulled Angie by the arm and they ran to their SUV and jumped in. Jason slung his pack off his shoulder and it landed next to Angie.

"We need to put as much distance as we can between us and the Janjaweed," he said as he frantically tried the engine.

"Hurry!" shouted Angie.

Jason tried the key again, but the engine wouldn't turn over.

Just then the Janjaweed descended upon the village from the east like a hungry swarm of locusts. Angie listened in horror as AK-47 machine gun fire tore through the hut she'd been in just minutes ago. She watched as the women she had just interviewed were gunned down as they ran for cover.

Finally, the old Toyota cranked over and the engine came to life. As Angie watched, she saw Halima running down the street, heading for their SUV. Two fierce-looking Janjaweed militiamen on black horses barreled after her.

"*No!*" Angie screamed, leaping out of the SUV just as Jason put it into gear and lunged forward.

"Stop! We have to leave *now!*" Jason cried, slamming on the brakes and shifting back to neutral. He grabbed his pack and ran after Angie. "Angie, wait!"

But she just kept running for Halima. She reached the girl and held her close to her chest just as the horsemen swept by them. One of the men jumped off his horse and grabbed Angie while the other turned around and raised his rife.

Crack! Crack! rang in Angie's ears as two bullets ripped through the horseman's chest, causing him to drop his rifle to the sand. The next thing she knew, Jason was stuffing a pistol under his belt as he leapt on top of the man who held her across the waist. She pulled free and dropped to the ground next to Halima. They held each other as they watched Jason grapple with her assailant.

▼ ▼ ▼

The Arab was taller than Jason and easily had twenty pounds on him. He threw Jason off, and the doctor went tumbling to the ground. Jason reached behind his back for his pistol, but it had fallen out. He regretted not shooting the man after he killed the horseman, but he'd been afraid of hitting Angie.

Jason stood up to face his attacker. He was no stranger to street fighting. Jason waited until the man lunged at him then nimbly ducked, swung behind the Janjaweed, and wrapped his arms around the man's neck and squeezed, clamping the man's carotid arteries with his forearm. Within seconds, the man dropped to his knees. But then, to Jason's surprise, the man rolled forward, flipping Jason over him onto the hard-packed sand. The air rushed out of Jason's lungs, and he struggled to breathe. Knowing this was a fight to the death, Jason forced himself up before his adversary could pounce on him.

The fighters stood face to face in the middle of the path between two huts. The Janjaweed soldier pulled a long, curved blade from under his shirt. It was half sword, half knife, and he waved it wildly, taunting Jason to attack. And attack he did, executing a quick roundhouse kick, connecting to the left side of the man's face. The big man fell to his knees, spitting blood. Jason crouched in front of the dazed fighter and finished him off with two quick strikes to the neck. Then Jason stepped over the Janjaweed fighter and pulled Angie to her feet. She embraced him tightly, but finally, he pulled away.

"We have to go," he said, panting heavily.

"Halima!" Angie called, turning back to the village. AK-47 machine gun fire erupted all around them, sending sand into the air and both Americans to the ground to take cover. When they looked up, they were surrounded by dozens of Janjaweed militiamen, all pointing their weapons at them. The men were lighter skinned than the villagers and much taller. The fighters were stocky, obviously well fed, and not emaciated like the Darfurians. Most of the men wore some article of military clothing, probably bought off the street in Khartoum, Jason assumed. The green camouflage trousers did little to hide them in the desert, but it added to their vicious aura.

Jason saw Halima being held by a group off to the side. A huge Arab, apparently the Janjaweed leader, approached them. And Yasser accompanied him.

"Yasser, you son of a bitch," Jason muttered under his breath.

"Who are you?" the one-eyed leader demanded in broken English.

Angie answered defiantly, "We're Americans working with the UN. Why are you doing this?" She got to her feet. *Surely the sight of the horrifically scarred man staring her down unnerved her*, thought Jason. But she stood her ground.

The Janjaweed leader laughed hard and loud, and his men joined in. Including Yasser. Two fighters came up behind the Americans. The smaller of the two, with white hair and a long beard, stood behind Angie, holding her arms. A younger, heavier one wrapped his husky arms around Jason's chest, holding him tight.

"You Americans, always sticking your noses into matters that do not concern you. But who are you, really?" the tall Arab asked Jason.

"I already told you, we came here to help the villagers," Angie exclaimed.

"Is that so?" the leader replied in a deep, bellowing voice. "Tell me, what do you want from these Fur?" he asked Jason.

Jason said nothing. Hussein took a few steps closer and hit Jason in the stomach with the butt of his rifle, sending the doctor to his knees in pain.

"Stop it!" Angie shouted, struggling to get free. "We don't know what you're talking about!"

"You may not, woman, but this spy does. He knows exactly what I am talking about," the Janjaweed commander replied. "What are you looking for?"

Jason remained silent, prompting his impatient inquisitor to knee him in the face. Blood spurted from Jason's nose as he hit the ground.

"Stop!" cried Angie again.

The commander jumped in front of Angie, inches away from her face. "Yasser tells me your friend has been asking about me over the past few days," he hissed. "All of the refugees he treats in your camp across the border, he asks the same thing: 'Have you seen a large Janjaweed with a scar across his right eye?'" he snapped, pointing to his glossed-over eye. "Now, why do you think he asks that question?"

"I don't know anything about you except that you are a murderer!" she hissed back.

"This is a feisty one, eh, Yasser? She will make a fine present for Abdullah. Yes, I believe that you do not know," the Janjaweed commander replied, standing to his full height in front of her.

"Yasser tells me you just arrived a few days ago. But your friend is different. He and his employers think I am a criminal. You see, woman, we take land that is rightfully ours. Is that not right, Yasser?"

"Yes, Hussein. You're right," Yasser said with a laugh.

Jason looked up at Yasser, a man he had been working with for weeks. A man he had trusted.

Hussein noticed and added, "Don't be offended by your interpreter, *Doctor*. After all, he must remain loyal to his tribe. Yasser says you specifically asked about me and the lost men from the Fur villages. How do you know about me? Who sent you? Why are you here?"

Jason's silence angered Hussein.

"Take him to the hut! We'll see how strong you are, spy," he barked, picking up Jason's pistol from the sand.

The Janjaweed crowd howled in excitement as the men dragged Jason away amid fresh protests from Angie.

▼ ▼ ▼

"Leave her alone!" Angie shouted when she saw a scrawny young Janjaweed soldier pick up Halima. He was probably not much older than the girl herself, Angie noticed.

"Don't worry, you're going too," the one-eyed man answered, eliciting more laughter from the Janjaweed horde.

Angie and Halima were brought to a nearby hut and were thrown inside. Angie tried to open the door, but it was latched from the outside. A guard stood on the other side of the thatched door. Halima sat on the ground, listening to the screams of the villagers in the distance.

Angie kept peering outside through the spaces between the slats that made up the wooden door. She caught a glimpse of the old man they had spoken to when they had arrived. They locked eyes for a moment. Although his were sad, they were not fearful. The Janjaweed forced the survivors to lie down in the middle of the dirt street in front of the hut, then covered them with wood and straw they had pulled off some of the huts. To Angie's horror, they threw a lit torch on top of the wood. The dry wood and thatch went up in flames. She turned her eyes away, unable to watch. It only took a few minutes for the screams to stop. Angie was at least thankful that their suffering was short-lived.

She looked down at Halima and saw tears in her eyes. She didn't have to witness the Janjaweed barbarism to know what had happened to her family and neighbors.

Angie wondered what had become of Jason. Where did they take him? Why did the Janjaweed commander call Jason a spy?

"It'll be all right, honey," Angie said as she sat down beside Halima and put an arm around her. "We'll find a way to get out of this."

Soon Henry would realize they had gone. But would he figure out they had gone to Zarundi? She regretted not letting Jason speak to him before they left.

The two waited in silence, wondering what their fate would be. A half hour passed before a Janjaweed fighter opened their door. To Angie's horror, she saw it was the same man who tried to attack Halima on the road. He smiled at her, blood still staining his teeth where Jason had kicked him. The man turned, dragged a body into the hut, and threw it on the ground. Angie, horrified, realized it was Jason. He was covered in blood and wasn't moving. She ran over to him and checked his pulse. It was still strong. She looked up and saw Hussein standing in the doorway.

"You think about my questions, spy," barked Hussein. Then he pointed to Angie. "Tell me who sent you and why you are here or she will go through what you have just experienced.

Only much worse," he said with an evil grin. "Woman, convince the spy to give me answers or neither you nor the girl will see the sunrise tomorrow."

He left the hut.

"Jason, what happened?" Angie asked as he struggled to sit up. "Why are they doing this?" She wiped the blood from his face. "What's he talking about?"

"I'm not a spy," he said, spitting out some blood from his mouth. "But I do work with the CIA."

Angie couldn't believe her ears. "CIA? But how?" she gasped, leaning away from him. "But you said you're with an NGO. You're a doctor."

"Because I'm a doctor, I was placed in Bahai by the CIA to gain access to the refugees. Henry…no one from the UN or Medicine International knows about it."

"Access to the refugees?" she asked in disgust. "For what?"

"Intelligence. They wanted a clear picture of what was going on across the border in Sudan. The stories from the refugees are firsthand accounts of Janjaweed atrocities. From their attacks, my CIA handler was able to track the Janjaweed's movement by putting together a timeline of their locations and mapping out their positions. Not long ago, I received a request from someone at the CIA to find out anything I could about a tall Janjaweed leader with a scar across his right eye. Supposedly this commander, in addition to being a war criminal for what he does here in Darfur, is also joining up with some new terrorist organization. The CIA wants to know more about them. They want to know if the Sudanese government supports the terrorists. If so, they can take it to the UN for more severe action against Sudan. Maybe the US would even consider unilateral action."

"All this time, you pretended like you cared. But you were just using all those poor refugees, just to grill them for information?"

"I do care, that's why I'm here. I want this stopped, just like you do."

"No, you're not like me," she said.

"We don't have time for this. We've got to get out of here. They'll kill you."

"Why? They don't want me. *You're* the spy," she hissed.

"I told you, I'm not a spy. I am a doctor and I work for Medicine International. Yes, I have given information to the CIA, but I did it to help the refugees," Jason explained. "You think they care that we're Americans? The only reason we're still alive is because the one-eyed Janjaweed leader, the man they call Hussein, wants to know who sent me and how much they know about him. I'm sure he's afraid if the CIA knows too much, he'll be targeted for a drone attack. Otherwise, we'd be dead, just like all the villagers out there. We have to find a way out." Jason looked around the hut, illuminated only by the amber light of the burning huts and pyres outside emanating through the slats on the locked door.

"Will he be a target?" she asked.

"I don't know. I don't make policy at the CIA. I just help them with information. Now let's focus on getting out of here before they take you and Halima away and torture you like they did me," he said.

Jason had been beaten and had tried to save both her and Halima when the Janjaweed first arrived. Angie didn't know him well, but she did feel he was genuine in his desire to help the people of Darfur.

"How can we get out?" she asked quietly.

Halima stood up. "I know a way."

20

"THIS IS ONE OF THE HUTS we use for hiding our grain," said Halima. "We keep some underground, hidden from the Evil Winds, so they don't take all of our food." She pointed to a rug in the far corner of the hut.

Angie walked over to the rug and pushed it aside. After moving some sand with her hands, she felt wooden planks underneath. She lifted one of the planks as Jason and Halima came to her side. There was a large hole below. If they crowded in together, all three just might be able to fit into the shallow hiding place.

"It's worth a try," Angie said.

"Better than the alternative," Jason replied.

"But what about the Janjaweed? There's a guard outside. They know there's no way out of here."

"Wait a minute," he said, going over to the other side of the small hut and reaching into the corner where the thatched roof met with the mud wall.

"What are you thinking?" asked Angie.

"I'm going to make an opening in the roof," he said, pushing the straw to the side. The bright moonlight shone through the new opening. "When they come in and don't see us, maybe they'll think we snuck out through here. Go ahead and get down in the hole. I'll be right there."

Halima jumped into the hole. After removing a few more of the planks, Angie jumped down into the hiding place and crouched down beside Halima. It was tight, but by sitting with their knees balled up into their chests, they were able to make room for Jason.

Angie watched as Jason pulled a chair over to where he was working and made a larger opening in the thatched roof. Suddenly he stopped; there were voices outside the door.

"Hurry, Jason," Angie called softly.

"Almost there. I want to make sure the opening's not too big that the Janjaweed walking by outside would notice, but big enough to convince them that we escaped."

Then Jason climbed down from the chair and sprinkled some roof straw and sticks onto the floor before finding his place next to Halima. She helped him replace the boards on top of the hole.

"Halima, your hands are smaller than ours. Can you reach through the boards and pull the rug over the wood so it's covered?" Jason asked. Although Angie couldn't see anything, she felt Halima stirring beside her. After a moment, her movement stopped.

"Okay," Halima said.

"Good girl," Jason replied, just as the sounds of a door swinging open came from above.

Although they couldn't see him, they could clearly make out Hussein's booming voice.

▼ ▼ ▼

"Where are they?" Hussein asked a bewildered guard as he walked around the small, empty hut.

"They didn't leave through the front door," the guard reported shrilly, clearly petrified of the consequences he faced for allowing the prisoners to escape.

"This is impossible!" Hussein yelled, more to himself than the guard. There was nothing in the hut but some chairs, a small table, and a few thick rugs used as bedding on the floor. *How could they have escaped?* he wondered, walking purposefully around the small hut.

▼ ▼ ▼

Angie held her breath when she heard a slight *crack* as sand fell on her head and into her eyes. Hussein must have stepped on the carpet-covered boards directly above where they were hiding. She prayed the heavy Janjaweed commander didn't notice that he wasn't standing on solid ground but hard wood that echoed over a hole underneath.

▼ ▼ ▼

Hussein stopped and looked around. Then he slowly turned his eyes down to the carpet under his feet, pulled his pistol out of its holster, and crouched down. He reached out to a corner of the carpet. As his fingers touched the threads, the guard shouted out.

"Look, there," the guard exclaimed, pointing to a hole in the roof.

Hussein leapt to his feet and ran over to the corner of the hut. He glanced down at the floor and saw the sticks that came from the thatched roof. The moonlight hit his face as he turned it up to the opening in the roof.

"Outside, hurry! They've escaped through the roof," he screamed, pushing past the guard and exiting the hut. "Find them!"

▼ ▼ ▼

For the next hour, no one entered the hut. Outside, they heard voices and vehicles moving. Every once in a while, Angie could make out Hussein's voice. She knew the entire Janjaweed horde must have been searching for them.

The three lay quietly in the dark hole. Angie smelled the unmistakable scent of burning wood and fuel. There was another smell, though. One more foreign to her sense of smell.

"Is that...?" she whispered to Jason, not wanting to know the answer.

"Yeah. Burning bodies," Jason said.

Angie fought back the urge to vomit. An intense fear washed over her. *What if they burn down the village while they were still hidden in the hut? Death would be slow*, she thought, shivering. She only hoped they would succumb to asphyxiation before the flames reached their underground tomb.

"Jason," she whispered, her voice trembling.

"Shh," he cautioned. "Let's just wait quietly until they've gone."

"How long will that be?" she asked.

"I don't know," he said. "I just don't know."

The minutes ticked by as they waited in their shallow hiding spot. To Angie's surprise, Halima had fallen asleep. Angie closed her eyes and rested her head on the hard dirt wall. She remained quiet, both because she didn't want to give away her position but also because she was still shocked at Jason's revelation about working with the CIA.

The refugees and his patients at Bahai had trusted him, and he had used them. She opened her eyes and turned toward

Jason. Although he was only a foot away on the other side of Halima, she couldn't see him in the darkness. Maybe he wasn't much different from her, she realized. After all, she had come to Africa to write an award-winning story. She wanted to break into the world of journalism on her own, without riding her father's coattails. But her trip here had become so much more after hearing the stories from the refugees. Maybe Jason's compassion had become just as real and not just a cover story for the CIA.

Finally, Jason broke the silence. "I think they're gone. I thought I heard them bring the horses up a few minutes ago. I don't hear them anymore."

Angie strained to hear any sounds of life outside their cramped subterranean hiding place. "Why would they leave in the middle of the night?"

"That's when they do most of their traveling. It's the best way to avoid being tracked and keep ahead of anyone looking for them. Wait here, let me check. Don't leave the hole," he whispered.

She could hear Jason begin to move. As he lifted the first plank over the hole, a few rays of moonlight entered, allowing Angie to see Jason pull back the rest of the carpet. Jason climbed out of the hole and covered it back up again, once again blinding Angie.

Concentrating on any sound she could make out, she listened to the creak that she surmised was the door of the hut opening. Then, nothing but silence. Five, ten, fifteen minutes passed. Nothing. She heard Halima's heavy breathing next to her. They were in total darkness. What had happened to Jason?

Angie made her decision. No longer able to sit idly by, she reached up, felt the planks with her fingertips, moved them to the side, and pushed away the carpet. As she stirred, she felt her joints and muscles aching at the sudden movement.

"Where are you going?" Halima asked her, awakened by Angie's movement.

"I'm going to find Jason."

Angie peered into the hut, thankful for the illumination from the moonlight. The hut was empty. She helped Halima up out of their hiding place, then climbed out herself.

Walking through the hut, Angie bumped into a chair. Halima, apparently more accustomed to the dim light than Angie, stepped in front, grabbed Angie's hand, and led Angie to the door. As Angie opened it, the scent of charred flesh made her gasp. Smoldering ashes in front of the hut were all that remained of the villagers, many of whom she had interviewed just hours earlier.

She and Halima slowly walked out into the village. Angie peered deep into the darkness, trying to see something. Anything. Then, out of the corner of her eye, she saw movement. It was a quick flash, moving low to the ground. Was it Jason? Or were the Janjaweed still there, looking for them? She put her hand out to Halima, motioning her to stop. Fearing the worst, she started walking backward, tracing their steps back to the hut.

Maybe we should have stayed hidden.

Before she reached the door, however, she felt a strong hand clasp her right shoulder. She screamed into the night as she spun around to face her assailant. Recognizing Jason, she let out a sigh of relief.

"It's only me," he said. "It's okay, they've all gone."

"You scared the hell out of me!" she hissed. "They're *not* gone. I just saw someone over there, crawling on the ground."

Jason smiled. "It's all right. It's a small dog. I've already been over there. I've walked the entire village. There's no one here. No one left," he said, looking back at the pile of ashes.

Halima stared at the ashes as well. The tear forming in her eye told Angie that she knew exactly what had happened there.

Jason put an arm around Halima's shoulders and knelt down beside her. "We'll take care of you now."

Angie reached down and held Halima tight, but the girl's eyes never left the smoldering ashes. Angie understood that the small Fur girl had grown accustomed to death and pain. For years the Janjaweed had terrorized these villages. Her mother, brother, and sister had already been taken from her. Now the rest of her village was gone. Her father was out there in the wilderness. Somewhere. Maybe. At this moment, there was no one she could turn to.

"What do we do now?" Angie asked.

"We can't stay here," Jason announced.

"I doubt the Janjaweed left us any way out."

"No. I didn't see any vehicles. The SUV's gone," he added.

"What about food and water? Did you see any? There must be a well. Halima, where did you get water?"

"No good," Halima answered, shaking her head.

"She means it's probably poisoned. The Janjaweed usually dump a few dead bodies into any wells before they leave a village. Just to kill any survivors or returning Fur."

Angie couldn't believe people could be so brutal.

"*Waha,*" Halima said, pointing southwest from the village. "Near."

"*Waha?* What's that?" Angie asked.

"Water in the *Sahra,*" Halima replied. "Not far from here."

"She must mean an oasis. There are some closer to the border," Jason explained. "I saw them on the map when I was planning our drive out here. We need to move. It's not safe here."

"But what if the Janjaweed are out there? Surely they're looking for us."

"They'll head west for Bahai, if they are looking for us," Jason answered. "The oasis, if I remember correctly, is southwest of here. Much closer than the refugee camp. We really have no choice. We'd never make it back to Bahai without water."

"What about Halima?" she asked quietly as the girl stood staring at the remains of her neighbors and family.

"I'm sure she's made the trip to the oasis many times to get water for her family. We'll take her with us. She's not safe here and, quite frankly, I don't think we'd make it without her. We don't know the way to the oasis or, for that matter, Bahai. She also speaks the language. We'd better go. It's a long walk," he said, leading them out of the village and into the darkness of the desert.

Angie, a tear in her eye, took Halima's hand. The young African girl patted Angie's hand. "It's all right."

But it wasn't. Angie knew, after this ordeal, nothing would ever be all right with her again.

21

TAWFIK DAHABI stood on the hot tarmac surrounded by stacks of shipping containers. It had taken several days for him to get the merchandise trucked across Sudan to his country's largest port on the Red Sea. He himself had flown out from El-Fashir after his meeting with Hussein yesterday so he would be ready to meet the buyers this morning. It had certainly been a busy week.

The governor stood leaning against the Mercedes-Benz sedan he had rented last evening when he landed at the Port Sudan New International Airport. After a restful night at the only five-star hotel in the bustling port city, Tawfik rose early to meet the driver as he arrived at the port. Although he didn't like taking what would amount to two days away from his operations in Shamal Darfur, Tawfik acknowledged a night away did make him more relaxed.

The constant threat of armed conflict in his province from Sudanese Liberation Movement rebels, orders from his bosses in Khartoum and the foreigners, combined with the stress of dealing with his former Janjaweed commander's transgressions were beginning to take its toll on the young governor. Normally Tawfik wouldn't have taken the time to personally ensure this transaction went off without a hitch. But the buyers were new and offering top dollar.

After paying off the driver an hour ago, Tawfik had been waiting patiently for the Russians. At the appointed time, a large SUV pulled up to the shipping container. Four heavily tattooed, well-dressed men got out of the vehicle and approached Tawfik.

"Sergey, welcome to Sudan," Tawfik said to the man in the black button-down shirt.

The Russian's sharp facial features and pale skin contrasted with the Sudanese governor's own uniquely Arab complexion.

"Let's get this over with. I want to be out of this hellhole as soon as possible."

Tawfik smiled. These arrogant Russians. So tough with their shaved heads, tattoos, and muscles. They aren't real men. They wouldn't last a day in his desert.

"First, the money," Tawfik replied with an exaggerated, contemptuous bow of his head.

The head of the Russian mafia squad nodded over his shoulder. One of the men standing by the SUV reached in and pulled out a suitcase, brought it over, and placed it on the SUV's hood. Two snaps and it was open, revealing stacks of hundred-dollar bills.

"Half, as promised. You'll get the rest when the merchandise is safely delivered. Now open it," the Russian commanded.

Tawfik walked over to the shipping container and opened it. Inside, a dozen Fur girls huddled together in the back corner, terrified as they shaded their eyes against the bright light.

"They've been fed and have water. They are being well taken care of," Tawfik said.

"They look sickly. Will they make the trip? They're worth nothing to me dead," was the terse reply.

"The men on the cargo ship have been well paid. They will ensure your merchandise eat and drink. They'll even let them get some exercise on their voyage across the sea. Don't worry, your investment is safe."

"I'll be back in a month. For your sake, they had better arrive safely. I'm not wasting my time coming down to your stinking country for dead meat. Next time, I want two dozen. And fatten them up a little. You can keep the scrawny ones for yourselves," the Russian said with a smile. Then he closed the suitcase and dropped it onto the tarmac in front of the SUV before getting back into the vehicle.

Tawfik watched his new business partners drive away.

Twice the order. It will be a good year, indeed, Tawfik thought.

Now, if he could only keep his rogue Janjaweed commander focused enough to keep the supply rolling in. It had taken Tawfik months to convince Hussein to not slaughter every living creature in the African villages he razed. The governor had allowed the Janjaweed to kill the adults, but the boys made good slaves while the girls made good profits.

Tawfik closed the container and waved to a man sitting high in a large crane. The man pulled a lever and the shipping container lifted off the ground. Outside the container, even on the relatively busy shipping yard tarmac, the faint, muffled cries of the girls could be heard. But Tawfik was too busy thinking about how he was going to spend his cut of the profits to hear the sound.

▼ ▼ ▼

Inside the dark container, Mobassa's daughter Fatima held the hand of her friend. Nadifa had just arrived and told Fatima what had become of her village of Zarunda. Tears streamed down their faces. Though they could not see anything, they knew they were surrounded by all the other imprisoned girls from the destroyed villages throughout Darfur. Fatima wondered if it would have been better if they'd been killed along with their families and neighbors back in Darfur.

22

"MY BROTHER MATAK and I would make this trip to get water. It became more dangerous once the Evil Winds started coming to our village," Halima told them as they walked beneath the blistering morning sun of the Sahara. "The families would take turns sending people out to *waha*. Matak insisted on coming with me. To protect me."

"What about the well in your village?" asked Angie.

"During the dry season, there would be no water, and people from our village would have to make this dangerous trip or we'd die from thirst."

"How much farther until we reach the oasis, Halima?" asked Jason.

"Not far," she replied.

Angie wondered what "not far" meant to a twelve-year-old Fur child who had survived more physical hardships than most Americans had even seen on television. Angie's calves and thighs were burning from muscle cramps from walking on the mixture of dry packed earth with the occasional sand traps. She licked her chapped, dry lips as they continued walking through the open desert. The heat was intense. She wanted to roll up the legs of her cargo pants but knew she'd burn horribly in the intense, direct sun. And, she thought wearily, it was only morning.

"How are you holding up?" Jason asked.

"We're fine," replied Angie.

"It's already close to a hundred degrees out here. We have to keep on the lookout for signs of dehydration and heat injury. As long as we're sweating, that's good. If your body's heat-response mechanism shuts down—if you stop sweating—that's a sign of heat stroke. Under the best of conditions, the human body can survive without water for two or three days. In this heat, we don't have nearly that much time."

"We're fine," Angie repeated.

▼ ▼ ▼

Jason felt the tension between himself and Angie and decided to address the metaphoric elephant in the room as they trudged along beneath the blazing sun. He slowed his pace, falling about five feet behind Halima, so he could converse with Angie out of earshot of the young girl.

"I was recruited last year," Jason began softly.

Angie looked at him, shielding her eyes from the reflection off the sand. Halima kept walking.

"I had just finished med school," he said. "I was at the top of the class, so I guess it got the government's attention. My roommate at college went into the CIA. He first approached me at my med school graduation, but I turned him down.

"But several months later, halfway through my family medicine internship year, my mother was hit in a drive-by shooting in Auburn, one of the bad areas of Chicago. She was a social worker, going to check out a report of child abuse in a particularly rough neighborhood. She had a police escort. The police officer was a hero. He took a bullet to the head trying to shield my mom and died instantly. The second round hit her in the back as she was trying to find cover. She's paralyzed from the waist down and can't work anymore."

"I'm so sorry, Jason," Angie said.

"Dad had a workplace injury years ago. He worked in a factory and damaged the nerves in his right arm when a machine went haywire and crushed it. He's been disabled ever since."

"Is the state taking care of your mom?" Angie asked.

"No," he said angrily. "Mom was a temp. That's why she was sent to Auburn. None of the full-time employees, even those who lived in that area, wanted to go to that street. Too dangerous. So, they sent the temp. There aren't any benefits for part-time employees. She gets some government assistance for being disabled, but not much. Besides, my parents are old-fashioned. They don't believe in being on the dole. But with his injuries, Dad can't work on the line at the factory anymore, and that's all he knows. He did the same job since he was seventeen years old."

"So, you take care of them?"

"Yeah. That was a hard pill for them to swallow. They're proud, independent people. Mom refused initially, knowing I had hundreds of thousands of dollars in loans from undergraduate and medical school. Residents barely make enough money to take care of themselves, let alone full-time care for their disabled parents. But the money from the CIA goes a long way. They help me with my loans and give me a good stipend. I don't spend much money in Chad, so most of it goes to my parents."

"Surely there's another way. Once you go back and finish residency, you could make decent money."

"That's two more years on a lowly resident's pay. My parents need to eat now. Rent, taxes, and medical bills are due *now*. I hire aides to come into the home to help them. They can't wait.

I can do this for a few more years, continue to take care of them while still putting some money in the bank to keep paying the bills when I go back to finish my residency later. But I'll be honest with you, it wasn't just the money..."

"What do you mean?"

"After I took over paying my parents' bills, I called my friend back. He told me what the CIA wanted me to do. I went to Langley and was briefed on the atrocities being committed here in Darfur. When I heard that, I wanted to help. They told me I could do good work here in Africa. Through contacts they had, the CIA could place me with Medicine International to work as a doctor at Bahai. No one, they said, would question it. And they were right. It made perfect sense. Just an American doctor doing humanitarian work at one of the refugee camps. They made the arrangements and I showed up at Bahai. My CIA handler would ask me for my patient rosters and reports on what type of injuries the refugees were presenting with. Every once in a while, they'd give me specific questions to ask the refuges. Like trying to get information on the Janjaweed. After a recent attack in France, they wanted to know more about their one-eyed leader."

"Hussein?" Angie asked.

"Yep. It didn't seem like I was doing any harm. The more I got to know the villagers, the more I wanted to stay and use all my skills, limited as they may be, to ease their suffering. I needed to do something. You know, my mom was trying to help battered victims. Those murderers in Chicago gunned her down in broad daylight, with a police officer standing right by her side. They didn't care. Just like the Janjaweed. They're thugs. Bullies who indiscriminately use brute force to take advantage of defenseless neighbors with no punishment. In some ways, I did this for my mom and everyone else who suffers at the hands of bullies and criminals. Do you understand?"

"Maybe. But there were so many other ways you could make a difference."

"You saw it with your own eyes. I *was* making a difference at Bahai. And the CIA isn't as bad as what the media makes them out to be. I may not necessarily agree with everything they're doing across the globe, but good people work there. Contrary to popular belief, Langley is not the Death Star, full of storm troopers trying to conquer the world. There are people who care, people trying to make a difference in the world. They pay me to make a difference in the lives of the refugees, and I do. They also pay me to get information on the bad guys who commit these atrocities. I do that as well. That part I'd do for free. And, you know what, I'd do it all over again if it would put terrorists like Hussein and his lackey Yasser in a shallow grave."

"How did Yasser work for you and the CIA if he had ties with the Janjaweed? Don't they vet their employees?" asked Angie.

"Yasser wasn't with the agency. He was an interpreter my NGO contracted locally. We had no idea he was with the Janjaweed. To my knowledge, he wasn't on the CIA's payroll."

"How did he know you gave information to the CIA?"

"I guess he just figured it out. I needed him to translate for me. He probably put it together from all the pointed questions I was asking the refugees and, at times, him as well," Jason said. "Like I said, Angie, I'm not a spy. Not in the way you think, anyway. Back at Langley, I got a crash course on what the CIA does. An overview, at best. I learned about tradecraft, which describes the tools and tricks spies use to gather intelligence, but I didn't get any advanced training on it. That's for case officers and operatives. I'm just a hired hand doing the best I can digging up information from the refugees. Besides, Yasser gave me no reason to be suspicious of him. Maybe he went through my things. Maybe he overheard phone conversations I had with my CIA handler and contacts. I thought I was being careful, but apparently not. I don't know all the tricks of the trade like the real spies do. I guess I got sloppy."

"Maybe, but I do believe you were helping the refugees," Angie allowed. "Certainly from your work as a doctor. And anything you may have told the CIA to help put away the one-eyed Janjaweed leader would no doubt be a blessing to this entire region."

"I'm not sure anyone is really helping the Fur. I put on Band-Aids and may save a few lives here and there. Maybe I make a small difference, but I'm not winning the war. You see, Angie, what I've realized since being at Bahai is that no one really cares about Africa. Not the UN, not the US, not even the CIA. Bandits and extremists are supported by Khartoum and some unscrupulous governments that back the corrupt officials there. The Janjaweed are encouraged to operate freely throughout Sudan. All of these groups, in my opinion, are just as responsible for massacring Halima's village as the Janjaweed."

"Well, then, we both have to continue our work. You with your stethoscope and me with my notebook," Angie said with a smile and reached down to grab his hand.

Jason smiled back at her. "But first we have to find some water and get out of this inferno."

Angie looked out at the bleak, deserted horizon, shielding her eyes from the strong glare. There were no signs of life. Energy drained from her body with each passing step. She began to recognize that, regardless of Jason's reassurances, they would probably not make it back to Bahai. Her head was beginning to pound and she felt lightheaded. No matter how much willpower she had, she knew she wouldn't last much longer walking in this heat without water. She prayed the oasis would appear on the horizon soon.

23

ANGIE REALIZED she had stopped perspiring almost an hour ago. She didn't know how far she could continue in this intense heat as the signs of dehydration became more evident. They stopped once to rest, but they found their muscles tightened up and made it more painful to start walking again. Angie stopped talking to conserve her energy. So did Jason. Even Halima was showing signs of fatigue.

Lightheadedness was beginning to overtake her as she trudged through the sand, her feet getting heavier and heavier. Her dry, parched lips were cracked, but the painful burning sensation had ceased hours ago. The growling in her stomach, however, continued. Her legs ached from the lactic acid release from her starving, aching muscles.

Angie felt her skin. It was hot and dry. From the warning Jason gave them about the signs of heat exhaustion, she knew she was rapidly succumbing to the elements. She scanned the horizon, searching for any signs of water. None. No trees, no shrubs, no life. Nothing. She began to wonder if Halima was lost. After all, she was just a child. How could she possibly know how to navigate this empty desert? But then, off to the left, there was a break on the horizon. Was she hallucinating?

"Look," Angie said, pointing.

Halima broke out into a run.

"The oasis!" Jason cried. He and Angie exchanged a smile and trotted off behind Halima. They were so tired, though, they couldn't continue the pace, and soon the two adults resumed a slow walk. The pain in her legs was so intense, Angie wasn't even sure if she would make it to the watering hole.

After five more minutes, the shape of palm trees were beginning to form. Angie wondered if it was only a mirage but was reassured by the fact that Halima and Jason noticed it as well. As they approached, shrubs and bushes took shape under the bright desert sky. In the middle of the oasis, the sun reflected off the glimmering water.

"I can't believe—" started Angie. Suddenly she fell headlong to the ground. She put her hands into the scalding sand to push herself to a seated position and looked back to see what she had tripped over.

Staring at her, half buried in the sand, was a boy, not much older than Halima, his face frozen in a grimace.

"Jason!" she cried out. "Look!"

Jason hadn't noticed the half-buried corpse until Angie pointed it out. He rushed over and inspected the body.

Only some fingers, bare feet, and the top of the boy's head and face were visible. His hands were outstretched, reaching for the life-saving water in the distance. *He must have seen it,* thought Angie, *but didn't have enough energy to go on.* It looked as if he was struggling, crawling for the oasis, but eventually he succumbed to the extreme heat and unforgiving elements of the Sahara.

Jason examined the boy's open eyes and the decay on his skin. "I don't think he died that long ago," he concluded. "Maybe a day or two. Any longer than that and the sun would have begun to mummify his body."

Angie gasped at the smell. It was horrible. A putrid odor, similar to the smell of spoiled meat but different. Fortunately, Halima had not yet noticed. She was almost at the oasis when she looked back to check on her companions.

"Go ahead, Halima. We're okay," Angie called, waving her arms. "We'll be right there."

Halima stared curiously at Jason and Angie for a moment, then turned and started toward to the water.

"You think he was lost?" asked Angie.

"I don't know. I doubt it. From the look of his skin, hair, and what little clothing I can see, he appears to be Darfurian, not Arab. Maybe in his mid-teens. He would know this desert like the back of his hand. Like Halima. No, I think he knew where he was going. He was probably headed to the oasis just like we were."

"He must have come a long way for his body to have given out like this. We've been traveling all morning, covering miles of desert, and we made it," she said. "Why didn't he?"

"He might have been malnourished to start with," Jason replied. "Maybe even wounded. Looks like these are sutures on his head." He looked at the boy's hands and pointed out marks around both wrists. "Someone held him captive. His hands have been bound recently. These aren't scars. They're fresh abrasions from some sort of leather, or maybe even metal binding or shackles."

Angie looked at the boy's feet to see if they also showed signs of bondage. "Was he a child soldier?" she asked.

"I'm not sure. He was probably abducted by the Janjaweed and escaped or deserted. Maybe he was from a tribe near here and was trying to get back to his village." Jason scooped the sand around the body to search the boy's pockets for anything that might help them out of their own desperate situation.

"Jason, look at his feet. What are these strange bumps?"

The doctor looked closely at the boy's feet. "They're cracked and swollen, not uncommon with decaying bodies left in the heat of the desert. But the soles of both feet—dark, fissured, spotted with wartlike nodules...

"I'm not sure. I've seen pictures similar to this in medical school. I recall it had something to do with some rare toxin or exposure, but I can't remember which one exactly. It might have something to do with why the boy couldn't make it to the oasis. He may have been poisoned and too weak to go on."

Angie watched Jason sit back in the sand, obviously reliving his medical school days in his mind, searching for that one slide or textbook picture that held the clue to the teenager's mysterious death.

Standing up, he said, "I don't know. It might mean something. Let me think about it. In the meantime, let's go get some water. Maybe if my brain's hydrated, it'll work better."

"Don't tell Halima about him. He might have been from her village," Angie added.

"Good idea. How are you feeling?" he asked as they walked to the oasis. "Can you make it?"

"The sight of a dead boy is unsettling. But, honestly, right now I'm thinking more about the water."

"Well," Jason said, "we've been heading southwest for about ten miles. We should be fairly close to the border by now. It won't be long before we're back in Bahai."

"I hope so."

Halima was waiting for them at the bank of the small oasis. The water was not as clear as the Saharan oases that Angie remembered portrayed in Hollywood movies, but Angie didn't care. She knelt down beside Halima, who was running water over her face, and cupped both hands. The water was warm, but Angie had never tasted anything as refreshing.

"How do we know this well isn't poisoned?" asked Angie.

"We don't. But he was headed in this direction," Jason said, nodding back at the corpse. "And Arab Bedouin travel this way all the time. Besides, we don't have much choice. We won't last much longer without water.

"Slowly. Don't drink too fast," Jason warned, kneeling beside her.

Poisoned water, or death by dehydration, or at the hands of the Janjaweed. Angie didn't care anymore. A week ago, she'd been enjoying coffee in the Mission District in San Francisco. Today, she was drinking dirty water in the middle of the Sahara with bloodthirsty bandits on her tail. *What would tomorrow bring?* she wondered, looking at her reflection in the water.

24

NGIE HEARD IT FIRST—an engine in the distance. She stood up to look over the bushes and shrubs.

"I hear it," Jason said, also rising to get a better view.

Halima nervously watched the two Americans and scanned the horizon as well.

Although the land to the north of the oasis was flat, there were some small hills to the east. The hills could be hiding the sound of the approaching engines; they could be closer than they seemed, Angie realized.

"Jason, shouldn't we hide, just in case?"

He covered his eyes to block out the glare.

"Yeah, you may be right. It might..." he started, but was cut off by the sight of a four-wheel drive *Dushka* truck that appeared about a hundred yards over the crest of a small hill in front of them.

"Get down!" he yelled. The three of them dived behind the bushes.

"Here. Behind these shrubs," Angie called as she scrambled on hands and knees to the far side of the small oasis.

Within minutes, the *Dushka* pulled up to the oasis and stopped. With the engine still running, a man in green fatigues stepped out from the passenger's seat. Another man armed with an AK-47 jumped out of the truck's back bed and stood by the first soldier.

Angie peered through the branches as the three soldiers walked to the edge of the oasis.

"Border guards," whispered Jason.

"Friend or foe?" Angie asked.

"Good question," replied Jason, raising an eyebrow.

Angie knew their best option was to stay hidden. If these men were, as Jason suggested, border guards, then they were probably very close to Bahai. They were, after all, in Sudan illegally, and she doubted the border guards would be very understanding of their plight.

Jason, Angie, and Halima quietly waited, hidden by the few bushes that dotted the oasis. Angie's heart stopped when one of the soldiers looked her way. Although she believed she was well hidden, it seemed as if the man were staring right at her. He took a step forward, obviously straining to hear anything out of the ordinary. Then, slowly, he backed away and motioned for the other guard to return to the truck.

As Angie was letting out a sigh of relief, Jason began kicking his feet violently. Wincing in pain, he rolled up his pants leg.

"What is it?" she asked. But then she saw it: two puncture wounds on his calf. She looked around and saw a two-foot long snake crawling toward the desert. The reptile had had a pear-shape head and a tan body with brown and white markings. It resembled the rattlesnakes Angie had seen in the California desert, only it had no rattles.

Her attention returned to Jason. He started to sit up but rolled back to his side, moaning. Angie looked at the pickup starting to pull away from the oasis and made a choice.

"Hey!" she shouted, getting to her feet and waving her arms. "Over here!"

Jason stopped struggling long enough to focus on Angie. "What are you doing?" he hissed.

"I saw the head and eyes on that snake. I spent enough time in the desert to know a venomous one. Henry told me that even the most common snakes in the Sahara were not just venomous but deadly. Walking to the border would make the venom circulate faster. You know that, Jason. We'd never make it. You'd die in the desert well before we make it back to Bahai."

Angie noticed the tail lights flash abruptly on the *Dushka* truck. The men had heard her calls. The three occupants of the truck dismounted, weapons at the ready.

"You stand a much better chance of remaining alive with them. At least there's a chance you'll get medical treatment if we give ourselves up. You'll certainly die out here without antivenin, so we really don't have much of a choice."

"I think I'd gladly take excruciatingly painful death by venomous snake over an eternity in a Sudanese prison," Jason answered.

As the men ran toward her, Angie wasn't so sure she had made the right decision.

25

THE SOLDIERS TIED THE TWO Americans' hands behind their backs and threw them into the bed of the pickup truck near the machine gun tripod mounts. The driver of the truck brought Halima into the cab with him, leaving the other two guards to watch over their prisoners in the back. Angie kept her eye on Jason. He was sweating profusely but from his moans, she could tell that at least he was alive.

After fifteen minutes of bumpy desert driving, they reached a hard-surface road. From there, the truck sped west along the paved highway. The driver was going fast, and she hoped the man was doing so in order to get Jason to a hospital. As the hours ticked by, however, her hopes faded. Jason's moans had ceased, and he hadn't opened his eyes despite her calling his name. The two guards standing over them laughed and said something in Arabic.

Eventually Angie could glimpse concrete houses dotting the landscape. *We must be approaching civilization,* Angie thought. Maybe they were taking Jason to a hospital. After all, if they wanted them dead, three bullets in the middle of the desert would have done the trick and surely would have saved the uniformed men a lot of trouble.

The truck made a quick turn, sending her rolling. When they screeched to a stop in a cloud of dust, the men guarding the Americans jumped out and opened the tailgate. One grabbed Angie's ankles and pulled her out of the truck. The other guard caught her before she could hit her head on the hard ground. The driver exited, dragging Halima with him while the other two guards started to pull Jason out of the bed of the truck.

"He needs a doctor," Angie yelled, lying in the sand. Uniformed men were coming out of the building. *A small police station?* Angie wondered. "Halima," she called after the girl was thrown next to her, "tell them he was bitten by a snake and needs medical attention."

Halima translated, causing a few of the men from the building to walk over to look at Jason. One man, with shoulder boards on his shirt that Angie hoped meant he was in charge, briefly examined Jason. He had a quick conversation with the driver that she couldn't hear. Not that she would have understood the Arabic even if she had been able to hear the words.

The driver slammed the tailgate of the pickup shut and returned to his seat behind the wheel. He revved the engine before peeling out of the sandy parking lot.

"Are they taking him to a hospital?" Angie asked Halima.

"I couldn't hear. But they were talking about him," replied the girl, now sitting up.

Angie watched the pickup pull back onto the road and speed off. She was jarred back to reality when two men grabbed her under her arms and dragged her into the building. Another man picked up Halima and threw her over his shoulder as the girl kicked and screamed in Arabic.

Inside the building was cool but barren. The concrete walls were dirty and cracked. The guards continued to drag Angie across the floor to a back room, where she was thrown into a cell. The guards closed the iron door behind them, locking her in the room alone.

It was dark. The only light came from a small opening in the door and a barred window high up on the concrete wall. Angie's hands were still tied behind her back, but she was able to roll onto her stomach and then up on her knees. She struggled to stand and then walked around the small room, furnished only with a cot.

"Hey!" she yelled through a six-inch window in the door. "I'm an American. I need to speak with someone from the American embassy!"

But all she could see through the opening was the other side of the empty hall. She listened for moment. There was no sound.

"Halima?" she asked, hoping the girl was in an adjacent cell. "Are you there?"

But there was no answer. She was alone. Deciding to save her energy and strength, Angie sat down on the cot. A moment later, she jumped up as she heard footsteps approaching. When the metal door was unlocked, she tried to run out, but a guard pushed her back. She fell onto the cot as another man dropped a metal tray onto the floor, making a loud clanking sound. The man who had pushed her pulled a large knife from a sheath on his belt, put his hand on her shoulder, and forced her to lie on her side. Angie closed her eyes tightly and braced for the worst, knowing screams would not help her. She felt the cold steel on her arm, but let out a sigh of relief when the guard used the knife to cut the rope binding her hands, then released her.

Angie sat up and watched the men leave the cell, slamming the heavy door behind him.

She looked at the rope burns on her wrist. They weren't bleeding, but the skin was rubbed raw. Despite all that had happened to her—the pain, fear and concern over Jason—her primal, survival instincts took over. She was starving and fell to the ground and began devouring the food. Although they had drunk plenty of water at the oasis, she hadn't eaten for close to twenty-four hours.

The bread was moldy and most of the water had spilled out of the tin cup when the guard dropped the tray onto the floor. Angie lifted the tray and poured what water had spilled onto it back into the cup. There wasn't much bread, but at least her stomach had stopped growling.

Angie looked around her cell again. The window was much too small for her to fit through. Besides, it was barred. There was no way out other than the steel door in front of her. She knew what was going to happened when she pushed on the door, but tried it anyway. It didn't budge. She was trapped.

26

ANGIE AWOKE TO THE SOUND of the heavy door swinging open on its creaky hinges. She jumped up from the cot and rubbed her eyes, not knowing how long she had been asleep. Glancing up at the window, however, she realized that the sun was now shining brightly; the last time she had looked, it had been dusk.

A guard entered the small cell but this time, rather than carrying a metal tray of food, he had a wooden chair. He placed it in the middle of the room, facing the cot. He then turned without a saying a word and made his way to the corner of the cell where he stood guard.

A man of medium stature with a greasy black comb-over across his tanned, leathery forehead walked in and sat. At first, he said nothing. Angie could feel his eyes roam over her body and could see the lust in his eyes. The sight of him terrified her.

Finally, he grinned at her with a scraggly, unshaven face. He spoke to her in broken English. "I am Tawfik Dahabi, governor here in in Shamal Darfur. You are in El-Fashir. Capital city. You understand?"

"Yes. I understand. Where are my friends? What did you do with the other American and the girl?"

"Yes, yes. Friends are fine. No worry. You, though, not so fine. No passport. That is big crime in Sudan," he told her, shaking his head. A few strands of his long, thin hair fell into his eyes, and he pushed them back with his hand as he continued to speak. "Now, tell me why you are in Sudan."

"We're with the UN. We came to help and were captured by the Janjaweed. They're the criminals. They destroyed Zarundi and murdered the inhabitants. I saw it with my own eyes. That's what you should be investigating."

"Yes, but any proof?"

"We saw it, all three of us," she continued, then realized perhaps she had said too much. She had learned in her research that many Sudanese officials were allied with the Janjaweed; if this man realized they were the only witnesses to an act of genocide, she may have just signed their death warrants. "The American I came with. Is he in the hospital? How's his leg?"

"You worry about you, not him," he said, pointing at her. "If you will not tell me exactly what you were looking for in Darfur and why you are here, I will have to send you to Khartoum for more official questioning. Believe me, you will not like that."

Angie believed his threat. But there was nothing else she could say. Technically, she was there because of the UN and did enter into Sudan to learn more about the plight of the people of Darfur. "I've already told you everything. I told you the truth. We came to see what life was like in a village in Darfur. To understand how the people live."

"Why? I am governor. We take care of our people. We help our people. But there is no one to help you," he said, and stood up. One last terrifying smile came across his face before he turned and left. The guard, however, remained, watching over her and the open cell door.

A knot rose in her stomach, making Angie feel nauseous. But it wasn't from a lack of food. Would she spend the rest of her life here? She had heard of people "disappearing" in Darfur. Would she be one of those statistics? No one at the camp knew where they were going. Jason was gone. So was Halima. She was all alone. She looked down and noticed her hands were shaking. Something was about to happen. She had the feeling it wasn't going to be good.

A moment later, a man in his late twenties walked in. His blond hair gave him away as a Westerner. Or maybe a Russian. Either way, he wasn't from Sudan.

"Miss Bryant," he said with a slight East Coast accent. "How are you?"

Angie smiled broadly and gave the man a hug. He was American. "Thank God you're here. Are you from the embassy?"

"Yes, I came from the U.S. embassy. My name's Steve Connors. I got here as soon as I could. Unfortunately, Khartoum is quite a distance from here. I had to fly."

"How long have I been locked up here?"

"Well, I got the call from the Ministry of Foreign Affairs yesterday evening. They said they found you in the desert near the border yesterday morning. They got you here in the late afternoon. It's morning now."

"I came with another American. Dr. Jason Russo. He got bitten by a venomous snake. I don't know where they took him."

"He's in a hospital not far from here," Steve said.

"And a girl from one of the villages near the border. Her name's Halima," Angie informed him. "Her village, Zarundi, was just destroyed."

"I know. Let's get out of here. We'll talk more on the road."

"On the road? But we can't leave them."

"We won't." He smiled. "Come on before the governor changes his mind."

▼ ▼ ▼

Tawfik waited patiently in the dark hall as the man from the U.S. Embassy led the woman out of the cell.

"There's a girl. From Zarundi," the American said in fluent Arabic. "Where is she?"

"That wasn't part of the bargain. You have what you paid for. Go before I change my terms," replied Tawfik. *These Americans are so arrogant and demanding.*

"You were well paid, Governor. The girl is of no significance to you. This woman is a reporter. She'll stop at nothing until you release the girl. And neither will I," the American diplomat replied with a not-so-veiled threat.

Tawfik normally wound not bow down to anyone making demands in his province, but he did have his orders. Boss told him to get rid of the Americans quickly and quietly, but in a way as to not cause an international incident. The sooner they were out of North Darfur, the sooner Boss's operations would continue unnoticed, or so Tawfik had been told. The foreigners were already annoyed that Hussein and his Janjaweed army had taken their raids too far and now the Americans were involved.

"Fine. You may take the girl," Tawfik said, nodding to a guard who went to a cell at the end of the hall. "But that will cost more. Double the price of the Americans." *I might as well profit from this concession,* he thought.

"You're a bastard, *Governor,*" the American answered, shaking his head. "I don't have that much cash on me. You've already taken everything I brought as your bribe."

Tawfik smiled. He liked this American. He was young and bold, not afraid to speak his mind. And he was willing to barter for what he wanted. "No worries, my friend. You can send someone with the payment. I trust you. You may take the girl."

"I'll send a courier from Khartoum by the end of the week with your money."

Tawfik smiled and nodded, pleased with the outcome. The three had landed in his lap yesterday, and today he had just made two years' worth of salary bargaining for their release. That was, of course, his government salary. His profits from his dealings with the Janjaweed and the foreigners were much more.

Both his own government in Khartoum and the foreigners would be well pleased with him for defusing the situation Hussein had caused without causing an international incident. Perhaps their appreciation would translate into a nice little bonus. *Yes, it has been a good day indeed.*

"Give this note to the guard at the hospital and he will release your friend," Tawfik said, scribbling on a piece of paper he took from the guard's desk.

▼ ▼ ▼

A few minutes later, another guard returned with Halima, who ran into Angie's arms and gave her a big hug. Tawfik and the guard led the women and the American diplomat into the police station's main reception area.

"Are you all right?" Angie asked Halima.

She nodded vigorously.

"Let's go," Steve said.

"What about Jason?"

"He's in the hospital, not far from here. But I don't know why."

"How is he?" asked Angie.

"I don't know," Steve answered.

"He was bitten by a venomous snake," Angie replied. "The guards took him away when we first arrived."

"Damn. He probably needed intensive care. The snakes around here can put you into shock right away. These hospitals aren't like back home. We'd better get there quick," Steve said.

"You Americans think you have the best of everything. Our hospitals are very good," Tawfik said, standing at the door. "Best equipment from China."

"He'd better be okay, *Governor*," Steve warned.

"Yes, yes, he is fine," Tawfik answered dismissively. "But next time you come to Sudan illegally with no passport, you may not be so fine," he said to Angie.

Angie put her arm around Halima. "Let's get out of here."

27

"YOU ARE A FOOL, HUSSEIN," Tawfik hissed into the phone. "This time, you've gone too far. I warned you. Now the American government is involved. You should not have gone after them in the village."

"Remember, Governor," Hussein replied calmly, "it was you who authorized the destruction of Zarundi."

Hussein routinely checked with Tawfik before razing any villages. In fact, usually Tawfik told him what villages to raid when the foreigners needed more workers for their operations. Hussein had been careful to call Tawfik to get his "permission" to attack Zarundi after he'd gotten the idea from Abdullah al-Harbi.

"I didn't know there would be Americans there," Tawfik snapped. "Had I known that, I never would have agreed to your request to raid Zarundi. You should have left them alone. The Americans would have returned to Chad peacefully and quietly, witnessing nothing."

"And continued their search for me," Hussein stated.

"That's not my concern. Toulon was another of your many mistakes of late. Your reputation as a ruthless butcher is quickly growing, my old *commander*. But, don't worry, I have cleaned up your mess once again. The American embassy sent a diplomat from Khartoum to collect them. As part of the bargain to secure their release, he assured me that they will be on the next plane back to America."

"And you believe this diplomat? Is he not a government lackey? Like you?" Hussein asked.

"Enough!" Tawfik barked, annoyed at the jibe. "You're not seeing the big picture. You know how powerful our foreign friends are." Hussein and his Janjaweed army had been useful to them—once. But he was now going rogue. Tawfik decided to try one last time to reel him in before it was too late. "You are being seduced by the terrorist Abdullah al-Harbi and his crusade to form an international *ummah*. That has been tried by al-Qaeda, ad-Dawlah al-Islāmiyah, and every other group of jihadists in the world today. What makes you think al-Harbi will succeed where others have failed? There is no future with him, Hussein. But there is future with the foreigners. That is where the true power in this world lies. Can't you see that? And you have angered them."

"Tawfik, with the help of al-Harbi, I will save our people. Not the bureaucrats in Khartoum and certainly not your foreign friends. The United Islamic Caliphate, with al-Harbi at the helm, is growing. I will carry their banner in the Sudan at the head of my Janjaweed army. You will soon see who holds the true power. Our people are faithful. The *khalifah* will sway them much more than Boss's money."

Tawfik sat back in his chair, convinced that Hussein was completely lost to al-Harbi's foolish jihad. "Boss wants to see you. Because of your brash actions, he needs more security for his operations. And they want a Sudanese face to it."

"We are not night watchmen, Tawfik. My men are proud nomads. They follow orders from me alone and do not babysit foreigners who are afraid of two Americans and a little girl."

"You have your orders, Hussein. I suggest you follow them."

Tawfik hung up the phone. Hussein would soon learn a valuable lesson. Tawfik knew that there are those in the world that you don't provoke. There is always a bigger fish. He had learned long ago that there were masters who offered sticks and others who offered carrots. Boss wielded both. Tawfik wondered which one Boss would use to put Hussein back in his place before the unstable Janjaweed commander wreaked more havoc.

28

DRIVING THROUGH the shantytown of El-Fashir, Angie was still amazed by the poverty she witnessed. Street after dirt street in this city of over a quarter of a million people was lined with mud-walled homes and emaciated inhabitants. Henry had briefed her about the UN camps on both sides of the border. Many international relief efforts were funneled through El-Fashir; she had expected the town to appear wealthier. But with officials like the governor in charge, she was certain any money that flowed into the region went to corrupt officials, crime lords, and the Janjaweed.

▼ ▼ ▼

"The hospital is a few blocks away. It's not a pretty sight," Steve told her.

"Have you been here before?"

"Once. Last week. I was helping a colleague at the French embassy. They had an aid worker out here who had appendicitis. I arranged for a US military MEDEVAC flight to land at the airport here and take the patient to France. I came out here to help translate and coordinate the transfer." In truth, his "colleague" worked for the Direction Générale de la Sécurité Extérieure, the French equivalent of the CIA. But Angie didn't need to know that.

"Did the Sudanese government contact you at the embassy? Is that how you knew where we were?"

Steve wasn't going tip his hand just yet. She didn't need to know that this same DGSE colleague at the French embassy had alerted him only this morning that his countrymen were in El-Fashir. It was Jason's name that concerned him most and prompted his expedited trip to El-Fashir. Were it just Angie, he would have let the UN and U.S. State Department officials negotiate her release. They probably could have done it more efficiently and certainly less expensively. But it would have taken far too long and may have exposed Jason's cover. "Not sure. I was just told you guys were here and to come get you out of prison and on a plane out of Sudan."

"You had to pay to have us released?"

"A way of life here in Africa, I'm afraid. Call it a finder's fee," he said with a smile. "Here we are. General Hospital, Sudanese-style."

The small, dilapidated hospital was nestled between a demolished building and an animal market on a busy street in downtown El-Fashir. Angie could tell at one point there had been white and red paint on the hospital building, but that had long since peeled away. The concrete was in poor shape, and there was no glass in any of the windows. Dozens of people were sitting or lying in the small courtyard of the hospital, and there was a line to get in.

"Let's go. Don't touch anything. If you think our hospitals back home are a breeding ground of infection, imagine what dangerous bacteria reside here. Let's get in and out quickly," Steve told her.

EVIL WINDS: TRADECRAFT PHASE TWO

The two Americans, with Halima in tow, left Steve's rented SUV in front of the hospital and made their way to the busy entrance. Steve followed the Arabic signs hanging from the ceiling directing him to the inpatient wards. The hospital looked more like a rundown motel than a hospital, with rooms opening up into outside walkways and open courtyards. The main inpatient ward consisted of several large rooms with iron beds crowded together on either side. Over twenty patients were crowded into the first room they entered.

While Steve spoke to the charge nurse, Angie scanned the room, searching for any signs of Jason. What she saw horrified her. Old men and women lay on blood- and vomit-covered sheets. Their wounds, open and exposed, attracted flies and other insects.

"There!" Halima called out, pointing to a bed in the far corner as she tugged on Angie's sleeve.

Jason sat on the edge of the bed, arguing with a doctor as he buttoned his shirt.

"I'm fine. I'll keep an eye on the leg," he said in English. The doctor obviously didn't understand a word Jason was saying.

"Steve," Angie called from across the crowded ward, pointing to the corner then hurrying over to Jason.

"Jason, how are you?" Angie asked as the doctor walked away, shaking his head in frustration. She was so happy to see him alive that she couldn't resist hugging his neck. He was perspiring. "You're burning up."

Up close, he looked pale.

"I'm all right," he said, smiling at her and grasping her hand. "I keep telling these doctors that I'm better and that I'm a doctor, but I can't get them to understand me. I think they want me to stay here longer. How did you get out of the police station? Did they hurt you?"

"No. Mr. Connors from the embassy came for us," she said, nodding over her shoulder as Steve approached. "He got us out. We're fine."

"Steve?" Jason asked as the CIA agent reached the bedside.

"Hey, buddy. How are you?"

"You two know each other?" Angie asked.

"It's a long story. One best told in the car when we're on the road," Steve said. "The doctor says you were probably bit by what they call *rashasha*. I think he means the carpet viper. It's the most common venomous snake in the area. Also, one of the most deadly. You're lucky to be alive. Fortunately, because it's so common, they stock plenty of antivenin here. But the doctor says you still need to rest. They want to follow your labs, make sure you don't have any complications from the bite."

"Well, that's kind of him. Tell him thanks, but no thanks. I'm fine. I feel better. Let's get out of this house of horrors."

Jason rose without finishing buttoning up his shirt and, with Angie and Steve's help, walked off the ward with a slight limp to his gait. The Sudanese doctor and two nurses followed them to the outside breezeway, protesting Jason's departure. Steve told them in Arabic not to worry, and the four walked out of the hospital compound.

Halima stayed close to Jason, keeping her arm tightly around his waist. Jason smiled at her.

"Thanks, Halima," he said, and gave her a hug when they got to the SUV.

After the group got into the SUV, Steve pulled out onto the dirt road, careful to avoid the crowd of sick and injured patients walking across the street toward the hospital entrance.

"Steve, they told me you were shot in Toulon last week. I thought you were dead," Jason said.

"What?" Angie asked. "Don't tell me you're with the CIA as well? Is any American in this country *not* part of an intelligence organization?"

Steve gave Jason a look, annoyed that a reporter knew his true identity. "So, I guess your cover's blown?"

"Yep," Jason said. "Angie, meet Steve Connor. CIA operative and, until recently—after he was shot and presumed dead—my handler."

"A fine introduction, Jason," Steve replied. "A little more information than I'd like out on the street, but I guess it's a little late now."

"The Janjaweed knew who I was," Jason continued. "Yasser was one of them. He turned us in to Hussein."

"The Janjaweed commander? You saw him?" Steve asked.

"We all did. He and his marauders razed Halima's village," answered Angie, putting her arm around the young girl's shoulders.

"Your interpreter worked with the Janjaweed and knew you were passing us intel?" Steve asked, flabbergasted that Hussein was so organized.

"'Fraid so. I guess I wasn't as careful as I should've been. What happened to you back in Toulon?"

Steve paused for a moment, wondering how much he should divulge in front of Angie and Halima. Angie obviously picked up on it right away.

"Listen, we're all in this together now, so you might as well fill us in on what we're dealing with," she replied.

Smart girl, Steve thought. He still needed their help to find Hussein. Besides, having a reporter on his side might come in handy. It seemed enough to spook the governor into letting Halima free, even with the additional bribe. "Okay. Not long ago I was given the name of the top UIC emir in Europe."

"What's an emir and who's the UIC?" asked Angie, clearly not well versed in the most current events of international terrorism.

"*Emir* is the Arabic word for prince. But some terrorists use it as a title for a regional commander or lieutenant. The UIC is a new terrorist organization. Its leader, Abdullah al-Harbi, used to be high up in al-Qaeda but decided to go solo not long ago. He created his own offshoot radical Islamic group he called the United Islamic Caliphate. I was given the name of one of al-Harbi's top men in France on a recent trip to the Persian Gulf." Though Steve was giving out a lot of information, he wasn't about to divulge that his contact in the Emirates was actually a member of the Iranian intelligence service.

"French intelligence was trying to uncover who was stealing weapons from French military bases. Weapons found in Mali were being used against French soldiers fighting there. We teamed up with the DCRI, or French intelligence, on this one, especially since I had a lead that ended up being a break in the case. The name I was given was the leader of a particularly nasty gang in Toulon, but he was also one of al-Harbi's top men in Europe. His emir."

"So, this new terrorist group is recruiting gang leaders and thugs into their organization?" Jason asked.

"Seems like it. Al-Harbi's creating a ready-made army by swaying established criminals and warlords to join the UIC," replied Steve.

"Like Hussein and his Janjaweed army," Angie added.

"Bingo," Steve said. "So the DCGI tapped some phones, traced some emails, and we raided an apartment full of weapons. Some of the weapons had been earmarked for Hussein. But at the drop, he received a phone call that tipped him off that we were there. That's when I was shot."

"I thought you were dead," Jason repeated.

"I took a round to the shoulder, then one to the back. Sent me into the French Riviera, actually. That's how I was able to get away. I hid under the edge of the promenade while Hussein was looking for me. Luckily the DCGI had given me a bulletproof vest right before the raid. It saved my life. And fortunately, the shoulder wound was soft tissue only, no bony involvement. I recovered for a few days, then went to Khartoum to find Hussein. Since then I've been using all of my resources to find him and al-Harbi."

"How did you know to look for Hussein in Sudan?" Angie asked.

"Well, he spoke Sudanese Arabic and wanted weapons for five hundred horsemen in the Sahel. That gave away his nationality and profession. That description could only fit the Janjaweed. Besides, they have the reputation of being as brutal as Hussein was in Toulon. A number of people died that day, including a good DCGI agent," Steve said.

"Hussein's a monster," Angie replied. "What he did in Zarundi was unimaginable."

"Are you sure this man is the same guy from Toulon?" Steve asked Jason.

"Your people didn't tell me you were all right, but they did give me the description of the man who shot you. Six and a half feet tall, big, and burly. Clean shaven and bald, which is not very common with the Janjaweed. Thick eyebrows and a long scar across the right side of his face, all the way down his cheek. Forks out a little near the corner of his mouth. His right eye's still intact but glossed over. The cornea must have been cut with the initial injury, then eventually scarred over. He probably doesn't have much vision out of it."

"Sounds like him," replied Steve.

"How did you find us here?" Jason asked.

"When I got to Khartoum I tried to contact you at Bahai. I heard that you went AWOL," said Steve. "Henry Chesterfield reported it to the US embassy in N'Djamena. A friend of mine in Khartoum told me that a couple of Americans crossed over into Sudan and were in jail in this hellhole. I took a chance it was you. Where's Hussein now?"

"Don't know. We escaped the Janjaweed but were caught by border guards at an oasis. That's where I got bitten by the snake."

"Do you think that's what happened to the boy?" asked Angie. "Could those marks on his feet have been from the toxins of a venomous snake?"

"What boy?" the CIA agent asked.

"There was a body of a teenager near the oasis," replied Jason. "He hadn't been dead very long. Had a head injury but it seemed like it was repaired. I don't think that's what killed him. He had the strangest lesions on his feet. I've seen them before, but I just can't place it."

"Bite marks?" Steve asked Jason as he drove.

"No, I don't think so. It has something to do with a toxin, I'm sure of it, but not from an animal. I remember seeing pictures of similar lesions when I was in med school, but I just can't recall what they were related to. Sorry. Is it important?"

"I don't know. Maybe," Steve replied. "Every scrap of intelligence is important. It helps me put together a picture, like pieces of a puzzle. Men and boys from villages all across northern Darfur are disappearing. It's not like when the war started years ago. The numbers have increased exponentially over the past several months. I'd sure like to know what's happening to them. Maybe, if that corpse was one of these boys and he escaped, those marks may be the only clue we have as to where they're being taken."

"We could go back there. Halima knows the way," Angie added.

Halima shook her head. "From my village, I know. But I don't know where we are. This is a new place."

"I have a better idea," Steve said, pulling out a cell phone. He looked through his contacts while he was driving and dialed a number back in the States. It was a long shot, but if anyone knew if a toxin was related to the physical signs Jason described, it would be her.

29

IT WAS ONLY 6:45 in the morning in Boston but, like
every other day, Dr. Emma Hess was at her desk hard at
work. She had tried to slow down a few months ago after
an exciting, eye-opening trip overseas, but the work just
kept coming in. She recently published a landmark article in the
New England Journal of Medicine warning about how genetic
research could be misused to create ethnic weapons. She knew
firsthand how evil forces could twist this valuable and poten-
tially life-saving science. Since the publication, her phone had
rung off the hook with offers to join committees, conduct further research, and speak about her position and experiences.

Normally, she wouldn't have interrupted her work to answer
the phone, but the ringing came from her cell, and only a select
few had her personal number.

"Hello," she said, wondering who was on the other line of the
blocked number.

"Emma," Steve said, "it's Steve Connors. I hope I didn't wake
you."

Emma leaned back in her chair. She hadn't heard from Steve
since they'd left Lebanon several months ago. Although, in

truth, she didn't really expect to hear from him often, knowing he was with the CIA.

"No, not at all. I've been up working for hours."

"Man, you have to take it easy, Doc. All work and no play..."

"Look who's talking. I bet you're in some exotic location on a mission right now, aren't you," Emma said with a smile.

"Well, since you asked," replied Steve, "I need a big favor. I have a doctor here with me who saw some very interesting marks on a dead body, but he doesn't know what could cause them. He thinks it may be from a toxin. I know that's right up your alley."

Dr. Emma Hess was a preeminent Harvard physician and researcher with multiple board certifications, toxicology being one of them. This was not the first time she had helped Steve with a case, even though she wasn't on the CIA's payroll.

"Do you want me to talk to him?"

"That'll be great. Thanks, Emma. Here he is."

▼ ▼ ▼

Steve handed Jason the phone but covered the handset. "No names. She's a friend, but doesn't need to know who you are." Steve then pressed the speaker phone. "Okay, Emma. You're on speaker."

"Hello," began Jason. "I came across this body. Male, approximately fifteen years old. Looks like he had been deceased for twenty-four to forty-eight hours. He was out in the hot sun. But he had these lesions on the soles of his feet. They were hyperkeratotic and had thick spotty pigment changes. There were some on the hands, but mainly on the feet."

"Was there leukodermia?" Emma asked, obviously wondering about any blanching or whitish lesions.

"Yeah, actually, about two to four millimeters in size."

"Nodular, verrucous lesions, some dark pigment mixed in? Skin looked gritty, right, with some cracks and fissures throughout?"

"Exactly. What is it?"

"Classic chronic arsenic poisoning," Emma answered. "Rare to see in the U.S. nowadays due to strict OSHA regulations. I assume you're overseas. Don't tell me where, I don't want Steve to have a heart attack," she said.

Steve smiled.

"Yes, we are," Jason answered. "You're right. Now I remember the slides from my tox classes. India, right?"

"Yep. And Bangladesh. Arsenic exposure from well-water sources," Emma replied, referring to well-known but sad cases where millions of people had been exposed to well water contaminated with arsenic. "So, arsenicosis can come from ground-water contamination since many areas have rich inorganic arsenic deposits not too deep in the soil."

"Probably not here," Jason replied. It was unlikely that the tribes that had lived in the region near the oasis for so long were depending on contaminated wells. If the villagers started dying from poisoning, they would have switched water sources long ago. "What else causes arsenicosis?"

"You can get arsenic release from natural ground sources, like the wells I mentioned, pesticide exposure, wood preservers, or burning treated wood. Another ground source is from mining."

"Mining? What kind of mines?" asked Steve.

"Coal, for one. Gold mining also exposes workers to high levels of arsenic."

Jason looked over at Steve, wondering why he was so interested in mining. Dr. Hess was listing a number of other, plausible possibilities.

"Don't forget murder as another etiology," she said.

"Tell me more about harmful exposures from mining," Steve pressed.

"Well," Emma continued, "I'm no expert on the mining industry, but I worked on some coal mining cases in the past. First of all, natural gas is often found when mining for minerals. This gas is, obviously, dangerous and needs to be siphoned off or extracted and stored to prevent any unwanted explosions in the mines. You can certainly have exposures to other toxic gases like methane or carbon monoxide, aka the 'canary in the coal mine.' As for arsenic exposure, cave-ins and inhaled dust and minerals during the actual mining process can cause arsenicosis. Arsenic is a very common element. It's used in the smelting process but is also released naturally in mines. Miners are commonly exposed to arsenic compounds while mining underground."

"How about in gold mines?" asked Steve.

"Yep. That's a common one, actually. Many gold mines have to be shut down because there's just too much exposure to arsenic and the cost of remediation is too great for the mine to be lucrative, even if the end product is gold. By the way, the lesions on the feet your friend described to me fit chronic arsenic contact rather than a one-time exposure. This can certainly occur in miners working for prolonged periods in areas with arsenic release."

"Thanks, Emma. Extremely helpful, as always," said Steve. "We're going to have to put you on the payroll."

"No, thanks. I like the quiet life," she said. "But do stop by next time you're in Boston."

"You bet. Appreciate it. Take care," he said, and hung up the phone.

"What was all that about gold mines?" asked Angie.

"Sudan gets some of its GDP from oil," Steve explained. "But the country is really revving up its natural resource production. The demand in Asia for gold and other precious minerals is huge and foreign companies look to the third world for untapped resources."

"To exploit," added Angie.

"You got it," Steve answered, laying down his personal cell phone and pulling out another. "There're a number of gold mines in Sudan. The largest concentration is in the eastern part of the country, but I remember hearing about a couple of them out here in Darfur when I got my country brief."

"You think that's where that boy was from?" asked Angie.

"If Dr. Emma Hess from Harvard School of Public Health thinks what you saw on his feet could be from arsenic exposure from a gold mine, I wouldn't second-guess her."

"That must be what's happening with the young men from the villages. The Janjaweed are taking them to the mines to work," Jason mused. "Forced, slave labor. That would also explain the scars on his hands and feet from the bindings."

"Yep. To die is more like it. There are no mine safety protocols over here. They're probably being sold to the mine companies to work as slave labor. I'm sure the government would rather Darfur villagers die from all the accidents and toxins than Sudanese Arab workers," added Steve.

"What about child soldiers? I thought that's what was happening to the boys from the villages," asked Angie.

"I'm sure the Janjaweed sell their captives to the highest bidder," Steve replied as he dialed a number on the new phone. "Captives that can be trained as soldiers could be sold to warlords or used in the Janjaweed army while others slave away in the mines. Doesn't matter to men like Hussein."

"Major Rivera," a young woman answered on the other end of the speaker phone.

"Hi, Mercedes. This is Steve Connors."

"Hey, Steve. How's my favorite spook doing?"

"Not bad. You know what I'm going to ask, don't you?"

"What, you need another favor? Not you," she said in jest.

Steve chuckled. "You Air Force intel nerds are just too smart. Listen, Mercedes, do you remember when we were looking for al-Harbi in southern Libya? Do you still have the images your bird took while flying over Darfur?" When Steve first uncovered the existence of the UIC, he was working on a weapons smuggling case on the U.S.–Mexican border. After apprehending a couple of Libyans with ties to al-Harbi, Steve began working with U.S. Africa Command to uncover potential UIC facilities or safe houses in their hometown in southeast Libya, near the border with Sudan.

Major Rivera controlled all the Air Force's drones operating in the region. Working out of a secure air base, she was responsible for tasking the drone missions for USAFRICOM.

"Should. I usually store several months of data here locally. But I'm not sure we captured much over Darfur. I was focusing on Libya."

"I remember we started imaging on the Sudan side of the border just to make sure al-Harbi wasn't on the border somewhere."

"Yeah. I kind of remember that. Hold on, let me pull it up on my monitor," she said. "Okay, pulling it up. I got it. What are you looking for?"

"A mine," replied Steve. "Probably not too big. They wouldn't want to draw attention to it."

"It'll probably have a lot of security around it," Jason added. "Especially if they're trying to keep in forced labor."

"Right. Mercedes, look for a couple of rows of fences, maybe even a guard tower or two."

"That doesn't help me much. Darfur is a big place. This is like looking for a needle in a haystack. Can you give me a starting point at least?" replied Rivera.

"Start on the Sudanese border with Chad," Jason chimed in. "We had to have been close to the border since the Sudanese border guards are the ones that picked us up. We found the body near the oasis where we were captured."

"A body?" Mercedes asked. "Steve, you do lead an interesting life."

"You don't know the half of it," replied Steve. "Start with the lower half of North Darfur, scan down along the border through West Darfur, then pan out to about fifty miles inland. That'll take you into South Darfur." The area Steve described was large, but probably marked the limits of the area the young man could have walked from.

"Still a good chunk of land. Let me see what I can do. Hold on, I'm scanning now."

"Steve, earlier you said that you were surprised they let us out of the jail so easily," Angie mused. "Do you think they were trying to get rid of us? Maybe not draw international attention to this area? If they knew Jason was CIA, I'm sure Yasser told them I'm a reporter. The governor is obviously corrupt. You said you had to bribe him to release us. Maybe he was hiding something in his province—like a mine being run by slaves and child labor?"

"Maybe," Steve replied. The theory was certainly worth investigating. "Mercedes," he said into the phone. "focus near the border but just in North Darfur."

"Okay. That helps. Give me a minute. Scanning..."

After a few minutes, which seemed like hours, the major said, "Okay. This may be something. A good bit west of El-Fashir, but still in North Darfur. It looks like a large crater but with contours. Obviously, a man-made pit. Only a single fence surrounds it, but there are guard towers. A few military trucks, structures, and storage containers."

"That's got to be it," Steve replied.

"It's the only thing that matches your description that close to the border," Major Rivera said.

"You're the best, Mercedes. I owe you one."

"One? Your counting is off, spook."

"You're right. How about a case of Coors next time I'm in town?"

"Actually, I can't get any Diet Dr Pepper in this place."

"You got it. A case of Diet Dr Pepper it is."

"Now you're talking. That's a starter, anyway. When we hang up, I'll text you the coordinates. You be careful out there, Steve. Let me know if you need anything else."

"Will do. Thanks again." Steve hung up and waited for the coordinates. He almost missed the sign for the airport exit and took the next ramp.

"She found it?" asked Angie.

"I think so."

"Let's go, then," Angie persisted.

"Go? Listen, the only place you two are going is back stateside. Doc, your cover is blown, and I'm pretty sure both the UN and your newspaper are going to be very upset with you for getting arrested for illegally crossing into Sudan," Steve told Angie.

"I don't care about that. Our job's not done yet. We still need proof that those kids are being taken to work as slaves in mines."

"You think my brother might be there?" Halima asked.

"Maybe, honey," Angie replied.

"Listen, I'll look into this," promised Steve.

"Angie, let Steve handle it," Jason added.

"No offense, Steve. I know you saved us back there in that prison and I do believe you will do all you can for the Darfurians. But I don't trust the U.S. government. I know if I can get pictures of this into the national media, I can make a difference. We might be able to save these kids—Halima's brother included, if he's there."

"I have strict orders to put you on a plane," Steve said, pulling into the airport parking lot.

"And you have never disobeyed orders before?" Angie asked.
Steve didn't reply.

"You're not trained for this, Angie. It's dangerous. You've
seen firsthand what the Janjaweed can do. You know that the
Sudanese government is their strongest backer. Let Steve deal
with this," Jason pleaded as Steve found a parking space.

"I'll take my chances," Angie said, opening the door and getting out of the car as it rolled to a stop.

Halima followed, seeming every bit as determined as Angie.

"Come on, Angie, you can't be serious," Jason said, going
after the two as they walked away from the car.

"I *am* serious. There's a UN aide office here in El-Fashir.
I know there are also NGOs. I'll find someone to help me.
Someone willing to help them." She stopped and at looked at
Jason determinedly.

Jason stood beside her, looking toward Steve, who was watching through the open driver's-side window.

"No way. You two can't do this," Steve told them again.

"Steve, we *have* to go," Jason stated. "Even if you find something and report it, do you really think the U.S. government can
make a difference? Will they even try? Politics will get in the
way. You know that."

"No, I *don't* know that. I still have faith in the system. I'll
pursue this lead and find out what's going on at that mine," he
said. "I promise."

"Good. So will we," Angie said, turning and walking away
again. This time, Jason joined her and Halima.

"Stop!" Steve shouted, knowing he had just lost this battle.
The three turned around to look at him. Steve was reaching
over and grabbing something from between the two front seats.
Angie held her breath. Was the CIA agent going to pull a gun
on them and force them back into the car? Then Steve got out

and left the door open. He was holding a small black bag. Steve threw Jason the keys.

"Take the SUV," he said. "It has four-wheel drive. You'll need it. There's plenty of water and some food in the back for emergencies." He took out yet another cell phone from his pocket and programmed in a number. "This is my local cell. It's not encrypted, so don't say anything you don't want the Sudanese government to hear." He handed the phone to Angie. "You can also use it to take pictures or even recordings."

Angie leaned over and kissed the CIA agent on the cheek.

"Thank you," she said with a smile.

"I can't go with you. I'm meeting with one of the leaders of the Sudanese Liberation Movement in an hour," Steve said. The SLM was a non-Arab, Darfurian rebel group that had been waging war against the Janjaweed militias and the Sudanese soldiers since early 2000. "I can't miss it. You take your pictures, then get right back here and call me. We have a safe house not far from here. We'll protect you and get you out of Sudan."

"I understand. One more thing," Angie said.

"Oh, like this isn't enough?" replied Steve.

"Can you take Halima with you and keep her safe? Maybe that rebel group can find someone to take care of her."

"No!" Halima shouted. "I'm going with you. Maybe my brother and sister are in the mine."

Angie knelt down beside the girl. "Halima, it's too dangerous for you. If they're there, we'll find them."

"No. I'm going," Halima said, resolutely making her way past Steve and climbing back into the car.

"Actually, these guys with the SLM may be from Darfur, but they don't exactly wear the white hats. They can be just as brutal as the Janjaweed," Steve said. "She might be safer with you. Besides, you might need her to translate."

"I don't think we have many options, Angie," Jason replied, looking at the girl with her crossed arms in the backseat of the SUV. "Besides, we're just going to take a look and take pictures, right?"

"Yep. That's it. Just enough to prove what's going on," Angie said.

"That's what you said when we left Bahai," said Jason. "I hope we have better luck this time around."

"I know I'm just a reporter. I don't have guns and grenades and wouldn't know what to do with them even if I had them. I saw what the Janjaweed can do. I can't fight them. But I certainly can expose them," Angie said, holding up Steve's phone. "After I get what I need, I want to get back to the U.S. and see it pushed out to all the media outlets."

"Okay," Steve replied. "Jason, there's a GPS in the SUV. Put these coordinates in it." Steve pulled out his work cell, opened the text message he'd received from Mercedes, and handed that phone to Jason.

"How many phones do you have?" Jason asked, taking the phone and walking back to the SUV.

"Too many," replied Steve. "I programmed my number in the phone I gave you. Here's a couple hundred U.S. dollars in case you need it." Steve handed Angie almost all the money he had left.

"What about you? How will you get around?"

"I saved enough cash to get another car from the airport and I can get resupplied at our safe house. Don't worry about me. I've been left alone in worse places with far less than this."

"I can't thank you enough, Steve," Jason said, handing back the phone after he'd programmed the potential mine's coordinates into the GPS.

"Just make it back safely. Angie, we're all putting a lot on the line for this. Make it count. That's all I ask."

"I will," she reassured him.

Steve turned and walked toward the airport. As Angie watched him leave, she wondered if she'd ever see the CIA agent again. Thinking about the trip ahead of them, she wondered if she was making the right decision and if she would see *anyone* ever again.

30

"WHAT'S HAPPENING, HUSSEIN? Why are we going back to see the foreigners?" Yasser asked.

"We all have our orders. You follow mine and I, unfortunately, follow those issued by the bureaucrats in Khartoum," Hussein replied as he drove the truck at the head of his Janjaweed army. Two pickup trucks with mounted *Dushka* machine guns followed their commander, surrounded by dozens of fighters on horseback. "For now, at least."

"But I thought we were done with the foreigners. Didn't Abdullah al-Harbi want us to join his jihad?"

"Patience. Today, I will be a good soldier for Tawfik and his foreign puppet masters. They want us to protect their operations. Fine. We will bide our time. As we speak, Sheikh Abdullah is contacting the best fighters and commanders from al-Qaeda, ad-Dawlah al-Islāmiyah, Islamic Brotherhood, Boko Haram, and even our brothers from the Jema'ah Islamiyah and Abu Sayyaf in Asia. He's gathering the faithful who are disgruntled with the failure of these organizations that have been corrupted by power and greed, unable to win costly crusade after crusade against the infidels. But I've spoken with Sheikh Abdullah. He is a great man. A true *khalifah*. He's the one man able to unite all Muslims, regardless of their nationality, race, or origin. Yasser, a second *Fatuhat al-Islamiyya* is about to begin. This new Islamic conquest, led by our *khalifah*, is on the horizon. He will succeed where others have failed. A world united under one Islamic flag, led by a powerful Arab army. Think about its glory, Yasser. Its strength."

"We've lost so much land. So many brothers have died fighting the infidels, decade after decade. Many fear what you speak of is unattainable."

"Ah, but our *khalifah* is a smart man. I have faith that he will succeed in his quest. And we will help him. He will lead the jihad and it will spread like fire across the world," Hussein said. "Our beloved Sudan has opened the doors to foreigners to control our sacred Arab land. Tawfik and his family in Khartoum have been bought by these foreigners and are under their control. Sudan has been divided under their failed, corrupt leadership. Tell me, brother, is there really any difference between these foreign infidels who steal our natural resources and destroy our nation and the Americans we have been fighting for so long? Today, they are a convenient ally and we will play nice with them. But tomorrow, those in Khartoum who strayed from the teachings of Islam along with their foreign allies will feel the sharp sword of our jihad at their necks."

"Allah-hu-akhbar," Yasser murmured.

"Mark my words. A holy war *is* coming to Sudan. Soon I will place my Janjaweed army under the command of our new sheikh, the wise *khalifah*, and we will beat down the gates of Khartoum and all the capitals across North Africa. Soon, brother. Soon."

"Who are all these new faces?" Yasser asked Hussein as they stopped at the thick chain-linked gate.

"These are not my men," Hussein replied, surveying the armed men on the other side of the gate. The hardened faces staring back at him were not welcoming. Hussein continued through the gate, followed by his band of Janjaweed warriors. The *Dushka* trucks pulled up on either side of Hussein to protect their leader as the men on horseback fanned out in the open area just inside the gate. Hussein noticed that the atmosphere at the gold mine seemed different. A number of the guards inside the compound encircled the arriving Janjaweed army, their AK-47s held at the ready.

"Yasser, stay here with the men. Be on alert," Hussein commanded. "Something's not right."

"Yes, Commander," Yasser answered with a slight bow.

Hussein exited the truck and walked to the middle of the circle of fierce-looking men facing off against his Janjaweed.

"What is this?" he demanded.

No one answered. Two men in the circle took a few steps back, opening a path for Hussein to traverse. Hussein knew he was being summoned to Boss's office.

Hussein stepped confidently out of the circle and walked the beaten path in the sand to a small trailer. On the way, he passed the dirt road leading down to the large open crater that took up most of the fenced-in area. There were more Sudanese militia standing around the trailer, each one silent but giving Hussein a harsh stare. He stormed into the trailer through a door that had a sign reading "private" in both his language and that of the foreigners.

Inside, two foreign guards dressed in black military fatigues stood at the entrance to Boss's office. Clean shaven, tall, with dark, razor-sharp crew cuts, the foreigners eyed the contentious Janjaweed commander as he made his way to the office of the gold mine's director. The Janjaweed or other Sudanese militia might suffice for outside security, but protecting what really mattered in the camp—the boss—was a job for highly trained and deadly paramilitary

"What's going on here?" Hussein asked as he brushed past the guards and barged into Boss's office.

Unfazed, Boss leaned back in his swivel chair and stared at Hussein. His fingers were interlocked across his ample waist.

"Who are all those men?" barked Hussein, standing in front of the desk. "You brought me and my army all the way back here, away from our work purifying the villages. For what? You have plenty of protection here with your *new* army."

"I summoned you here because of your recent actions. You have brought a lot of attention to us here in our little corner of this desert. My superiors are concerned that you may be a threat to our operations and interests in Sudan," Boss said in heavily accented English.

"You question me? My loyalty?" Hussein barked.

"Let us examine the facts, Hussein. First, you go to France to join with the jihadist and negotiate for weapons. That ended up a disaster and was splattered on the front page of major European newspapers. Then you capture two Americans, a reporter and a CIA spy of all people."

"I have served you faithfully. I have done what you and your slaves in Khartoum have asked. I have provided security for your operations and have given you my captives for you to profit from and use to labor in your mines. But I also command a great Janjaweed army. We have responsibilities to our people. Regardless of what you may believe, our world does not revolve around your financial needs."

"Ah, but you keep the best men for yourself. You send the weak and diseased boys for our work here at the mine, but you keep the stronger ones for your growing army."

"Do I not supply you with the numbers you request?" hissed Hussein.

"Yes, *Commander*, you are *very* obedient," Boss answered. "Tell me, why did you provoke the American spy and reporter? First, they came across the border to search for you. Then, you foolishly attacked the village they were in. You should have been more careful. If you would have left them alone, they would have returned to Chad and there would be no issues. No calls from the American embassy to our friends in Khartoum. No threat of news exposés that could embarrass us or threaten what we are trying to do here. When you did capture them, you allowed them to escape, which posed additional risks to us. It was Tawfik who cleaned up your mess and arranged for the Americans to be put on a plane out of Sudan. What am I to do with you, Hussein?"

"I am not your dog. I am a Janjaweed commander. I am feared in the desert."

"Yes, I know," Boss allowed with a dismissive wave of his hand. "The savior for your suffering people. Perhaps. But in my camp, you are just another hired gun. Make no mistake, Hussein, you and your 'army' are expendable."

The door opened behind Hussein, and he turned and glanced at the man standing in the doorway, flanked by the two foreign guards. Suddenly Boss' true intentions became clear to the Janjaweed commander.

31

"**G**UNS," SAID THE LEADER of the SLM rebels. "You want to help us? Then give us more guns."

"How many more people have to die, Mobassa?" asked Steve. "I want to help you, yes. But this war between you, the Janjaweed, and the government of Sudan won't give you the peace you seek. Especially if you try to go toe-to-toe with the Sudanese army. It's a professional military organization with modern weapons, despite years of arms embargoes."

"This isn't about winning or even about peace any longer," snapped Mobassa. "We are way past that. This is about survival. Right now, I only seek to protect my people from the Evil Winds. Our villages are getting fewer in number every day as the one-eyed devil and his army their sweep throughout Darfur. Me and my SLM fighters are all that stand in their way."

"Okay, then come with me down to this mine. If my intelligence is correct, it may contain Fur villagers held against their will," said Steve. "Save them."

"There are Fureen held against their will all over Sudan. Child soldiers, sex slaves, prisoners. I can't help them all. But

I can prevent more villagers from suffering the same fate if my men and I stop the Janjaweed," replied Mobassa.

Mobassa's trusted lieutenant Fidail walked up to the two men standing in the middle of a small village south of El-Fashir and handed his commander a rusty old AK-47.

"I have my own intelligence," Mobassa told Steve. "The Janjaweed are on the move, heading south. There are three villages in their path. We're going to protect our tribes, with or without your weapons."

Mobassa turned and walked away with Fidail, leaving Steve standing next to his SUV. Around him, dozens of SLM fighters were climbing into pickup trucks, armed with the same old weapons their leader carried.

"You may be their only hope, Mobassa," Steve called out. "Children from Darfur are dying in the mines. Who'll save them if not you?"

"I cannot save everyone," Mobassa repeated as he continued to walk away.

"Not everyone, Mobassa," Steve said, running up to him. "Just these children. Right now, two American colleagues of mine are going there to take pictures and get the proof I need to get the United States and the world to do more to help in Darfur. We need you and your army, Mobassa. They have a girl with them from a village that was just destroyed. She's looking for her brother. How many other families have been torn apart by the Janjaweed? Maybe they're at the mine. You can help put these families back together."

Mobassa stopped in his tracks. "What village?"

"What?" Steve asked.

"What village is the girl from?" the SLM leader repeated.

"Zarundi," replied Steve.

Mobassa turned around to square off with the American.

"What is the girl's name?" he asked.

32

T HE DRIVE FROM EL-FASHIR to the coordinates Steve gave Jason and Angie only took a couple of hours despite the rough, sandy terrain. They found the mine tucked away in the middle of some high rock formations. It was still in North Darfur, but on the border with the province of South Darfur and not far from its capital city, Nyala.

When they were less than a half mile away from their destination, Jason slowed his SUV to make a quiet approach to the mine. Ahead of them, just to the left of the road was a large outcrop of rocks. Jason pulled the SUV behind the stone formation. "Let me get a bird's-eye view of the mine from the top of that rock before we get any closer," Jason said, turning off the SUV. "Wait here for a few minutes until we know what we're up against, okay?"

Angie opened the passenger door and began to climb out.

"I guess that means you're coming with me?" he asked, realizing once again that Angie was not one to be sidelined. He looked in the backseat and said, "Halima, will you stay here in the car and make sure we're safe?"

Halima nodded dutifully and crossed her arms.

Angie smiled at Halima and was rewarded by one in return. She was an amazing girl. She was so strong, even after living through such harrowing events over these past several days. Angie herself had been pushed to the edge of sanity. She couldn't imagine what this young girl was going through. How was she able to keep it all together?

Jason and Angie climbed the rocky projection with relative ease and found a lookout spot on top. The sun was nearing the horizon to their left and, from their vantage point, they could see the entire valley in front of them, including the gold mine one hundred yards to their front.

"It's not as big as I thought," Angie commented.

"No. But it has a lot of guards," replied Jason. "I see a guard tower on each corner with a fence along the perimeter."

"There are a lot of armed people inside the camp, she said. It looks like they're facing off with each other.

"Yeah. And they have their rifles at the ready. Something's going on."

"How are we going to get in?" asked Angie.

"You're kidding, right? We can't go in there. Look at all the men with rifles. Take your pictures from here, then let's get out of here."

"We have to get closer. The pictures have to show some detail, and the range on camera phones is limited. A flash would give away our position, so we can't wait until nightfall. Besides, I need to show that there are children being forced to work the mines. Right now it's just a bunch of men standing around. All this way, Jason . . . we can't leave empty-handed."

Jason nodded in frustration. He knew Angie was right, but it was just too dangerous to try to get inside the camp.

"What if we just go to those rocks over there?" Angie continued, pointing to a formation closer to the perimeter gate. "I might be able to get some shots from there that might work. It's closer to the mine. Maybe we'll be able to get a picture of some faces that Halima or other survivors at Bahai may recognize. It would give them some hope knowing their family members are still alive."

Jason wasn't convinced. "As dangerous as that sounds, it's still safer than going into the compound," he responded. "Okay. But we have to be very careful. There's fifty yards or so of empty desert between here and those rocks. And remember, if you're close enough to get a picture of the kids working in the mines, that means you're close enough for the guards to see you as well. Those guard towers are there for a reason. And I'm sure the guards have binoculars."

"Let's do this," Angie said.

The two slowly climbed back the way they came. Jason glanced at the SUV and saw Halima still sitting in the backseat, watching them through an open window. They made their way to their first lookout spot at edge of the rock formation.

The no-man's land between their current lookout atop this rock and the outer perimeter fence was a kill zone. The five-foot boulder Angie wanted to get to was halfway in between. If they were spotted before they reached the rock, the tower guards would mow them down. They wouldn't stand a chance.

Jason glanced over at Angie. "You know there are guards with rifles in those towers. Probably put there because they were the best marksmen."

"Yes, I do. You know there are children in chains slaving away in a deadly mine on the other side of those towers."

Jason smiled at her. "Okay, the tower on the left is the closest to the rock we're trying to get to. Fortunately, it seems like all the attention is focused on the standoff inside the compound. When we're sure that the guard in the tower is looking away, we'll make a break for it. Run as fast as you can. Ready?"

She nodded. Jason watched the guard in the tower on the left. She hoped the guards in the other towers would continue looking away, giving them a slight edge to make this dangerous sprint even remotely possible. As soon as the guard looked away...

"Go!" he said, taking her hand as the two sprinted across the open desert.

33

"TAWFIK, YOU DOG! I should have known," snarled Hussein.

"Hello, old *friend*," Tawfik replied with a grin. Hussein's former lieutenant stood before him wearing military fatigues instead of his usual trousers and a button-down shirt. The AK-47 slung over his shoulder and the pistol on his belt confirmed to Hussein that he had walked into a trap. "We have been waiting for you."

"You are no friend of mine," Hussein snapped. He turned back to the foreigner still seated behind the desk. "So, this is what you've been up to? This is why I was summoned here? You're replacing me with him? His men out there are not even Bedu. Not true Janjaweed. They're just common criminals that Tawfik picked up out of the gutters and alleys in El-Fashir."

"And what are you?" Tawfik taunted his rival.

"Do not provoke me, Tawfik. I am purging my homeland of infidels. I am the commander of the Janjaweed army and descendant of the great *Mahdi* himself and will deliver our lands back to our Arab brothers and sisters."

"Maybe you're right, Commander," Boss replied, still sitting calmly behind his desk. "Tawfik does not have a long list of impressive victories like you do, nor is he as feared as you are. But he has vision. Not the delusional kind, where he believes he is the *Mahdi* or whoever you think you are. He is also loyal and he follows orders. He does what he is told, Hussein. I cannot say the same for you. You are not content in making a fortune doing my bidding as you carry out your foolish ethnic cleansing raids against the Fur. We are conducting much more important work here, Hussein, one that your government is very interested in protecting. You have put this project in jeopardy on more than one occasion in pursuit of your foolish crusade."

"*My* government? *My* government would have rolled tanks into Darfur to destroy all villages that weren't Arab. *My* government would not fall slave to you, foreigner. No, Tawfik's kin in Khartoum and others that you have bought are not *my* government, nor do they represent the Arab people of Sudan. But there are those in Sudan who do support my work. Do you not think I have my own friends in Khartoum? Your money cannot buy everyone, *kafir*," replied Hussein, calling Boss an infidel. "There are still true believers in the faith among my Sudanese brothers in the government. They want what I want. We will have a new *Mahdiyya*, a revolution to rid my beloved Sudan from all foreigners, non-Muslims and non-Arabs, once and for all. And these powerful brothers will soon come forth and join me in this holy jihad."

Boss leaned over on his desk. "Who do you think ordered me to bring you here today? Everyone has a price, Hussein. Except for you, apparently. You see, there can be no *Mahdiyya* or jihad without the money and weapons that we provide to your government and to your movement. It would be wise for you to remember that. Your faith in Abdullah al-Harbi is misguided. *We* are the true masters here. Even al-Harbi bows down to us.

Yes, we have met with your precious *khalifah*. Al-Harbi realizes the power we wield in the world. He knows he needs us, just as you need us. But perhaps your feeble mind cannot grasp this reality. And that is dangerous. For both you and me. Your arrogance has caused external eyes to peer into our secret little world hidden here in the desert. That, Commander, is why you have been called here today."

From the corner of Hussein's good eye, he noticed Tawfik moving closer to him. His instincts had kept him alive for decades living in the most inhospitable and dangerous places in Africa. There was only one chance to escape. One chance to live. But would he be fast enough?

Hussein drew his dagger from his belt, spun on his heels, and released the weapon into the air. But before Tawfik even realized he was in danger, one of Boss's guards raised his arm in front of his face. The dagger struck the guard's forearm, shielding Tawfik from certain death.

34

JASON KEPT HIS EYE on the guard in the left tower as he and Angie sprinted across the open desert for the safety of the large boulder between them and the fence. His leg was still throbbing from the snake bite, but the antivenin had prevented the venom from spreading throughout his body. Still, his stamina had taken a hit and he panted as he limped trying to keep up with Angie.

Forty yards. *So far, so good,* Jason said to himself.

Thirty yards. The guard was still looking away from them.

Twenty yards. Jason allowed himself to look ahead to their target.

Ten yards. "Almost there," he muttered aloud through heavy breaths.

Jason noticed that his limp was causing his foot to drag slightly, creating a small dust cloud behind him. He concentrated on his gait and sprinted the short distance remaining to meet Angie at the rock.

"Are you all right?" she asked.

"Yeah," he said, still panting heavily. He peered over the edge of the rock. The guard on the left was looking right at them through binoculars.

"Damn," he said. "I think he saw me."

Angie took a look for herself. The tower guard pulled back the charging handle on his Russian-made PKM machine gun and was aiming it in their direction.

"He's looking right at us," she said.

Jason knew they would be cut to pieces. The boulder they were hiding behind would not last very long against heavy firepower. Soon RPGs would eliminate what little cover they had. He grabbed Angie's hand again. He thought about standing slowly with his hands in the air. Maybe his surrender would be accepted. It was worth a chance. The only chance they had, really. But before he could summon the strength to stand up from behind the rock, he realized it was too late.

Gunfire erupted from within the camp, and both of the Americans cringed. But after a few seconds, they realized the shots weren't coming anywhere near them.

35

HUSSEIN CRASHED through the bay window of Boss's office and landed on the hard, rocky sand. In a moment he was on his feet, grappling with one of Tawfik's soldiers.

"Get him!" Tawfik screamed at his men through the broken window. "Kill the Janjaweed!"

One of Boss's guards appeared beside Tawfik and raised his rifle to take out Hussein while the other guard calmly pulled the dagger out of his bleeding forearm. But Hussein was too quick. The big man proved quite nimble as he ducked to avoid the incoming bullet and rolled underneath Boss's trailer.

Tawfik drew his own pistol and fired indiscriminately into the floor of the trailer, hoping to kill the Bedouin leader. Tawfik was showered in splinters as shots from Hussein's men hit the window frame. He and Boss ducked for cover as the foreign guards returned fire. Hussein's men, still on horseback or behind the mounted *Dushka* machine guns, had heard the commotion and rallied to their commander, firing into the trailer. Hussein rolled out from underneath the trailer and jumped on a horse to lead his men against Tawfik's militia.

The guards in the tower turned their machine guns and fired inside the camp.

There was an explosion under the right tower after one of Hussein's fighters threw a grenade to silence the elevated machine gun nest. The tower fell to the side, crushing the front fence and entrance gate of the gold mine.

▼ ▼ ▼

Angie and Jason watched as horsemen in the camp exchanged fire with the guards on foot.

"What the...?" Jason said, standing to get a better look. "I don't know what's happening."

Beside him, Angie stood up and snapped as many pictures with the smartphone camera as she could. A shout from Jason stopped her. "Halima, *no*! Get back to the car," he shouted, running after her. The girl had a good head start and almost made it to the gate when Jason jumped on top of her, shielding her from stray bullets that flew all around them.

"What are you doing? You need to get back to the car," Jason exclaimed

"No. My brother," she said, struggling to get away from his strong grasp.

Jason looked inside the camp as Angie scrambled up next to them. He saw half a dozen teenage boys hiding behind a bulldozer inside the camp.

"My brother," Halima repeated, pointing to the construction vehicle.

"What is it, Jason?" Angie asked.

"Those boys. They must be some of the Darfurian children taken as slaves. Halima says one of them is her brother."

"Matak," Halima said, nodding wildly. "My brother."

"Let's go, Jason. We have to get them out. Now's our chance while the Janjaweed are preoccupied fighting each other. Hurry." Angie grabbed Halima's hand and helped her up.

Jason shook his head. It was too dangerous being this close to the fighting.

"What are you talking about?" he said. "Remember what you said to Steve. You were right. We can't fight an army. You can save more people with these pictures. If we go in there, we risk losing it all."

"I know what I said. But they're right there. We can do both. The Janjaweed are fighting each other. They won't even see us," Angie exclaimed.

"We can't. There's too many. We'll get hit in the crossfire." Jason knew what Angie's answer would be before she spoke.

"We have to try."

Angie stood and ran to the front gate with Halima.

"Angie, wait," yelled Jason, following them. They crouched low as they climbed over the mangled iron gate, crushed by the fallen guard tower. Reaching the top of the heap of metal, Jason, Angie, and Halima paused behind a wooden panel that had been a tower wall. They surveyed the chaos inside the compound.

To the right, men dressed in a mix of fatigues and street clothes stood around a trailer, firing automatic weapons at a group of men on horseback riding wildly through the camp.

"Angie," Jason said, pointing in the distance. "It's Hussein. He's here."

▼ ▼ ▼

Hussein rallied his men into an effective counterattack against Tawfik's well-armed mercenaries. Although leaderless, the foot soldiers still outnumbered Hussein's more experienced fighters three to one. To add to Hussein's woes, Boss's two guards aligned against the Janaweed, and their deadly accurate rifle fire was decimating his troops.

"*Yella, ya shabab!*" screamed Hussein, encouraging his men to fight on. "*Allah-hu-akhbar!*"

A dozen of Hussein's horse soldiers swinging machetes rode through a line of Tawfik's men, cutting them down.

▼ ▼ ▼

Avoiding the melee, Angie, Jason, and Halima quietly made their way to the bulldozer. They stopped in their tracks as they rounded the vehicle. Six emaciated boys leaned against the vehicle, watching the battle. Halima strode past the two Americans and right to the group of teenagers.

"Halima, what are you doing here?" a boy called out in the Fur dialect as he ran out to meet her. It was her brother, Matak. He and Halima hugged tightly. "Where's Baba? Is he here with you? Have you seen Fatima?"

Halima switched to English for Angie and Jason's benefit. "No. But my friends are here. They will help us."

Matak regarded the Americans suspiciously as the rounds flew all around them, some bouncing off the heavy bulldozer as he spoke.

"Help? How will they help us? They don't even have any weapons."

"We need to get out of here now," Jason said to Halima and Matak.

"No. There are still boys in the mine. We won't leave without them," Matak stated defiantly.

"Didn't you notice the battle going on around us? We can slip out of here now, while they're busy fighting each other," replied Jason.

"No. We go together or not at all." With that, Matak turned and began speaking to the other boys, planning the rescue of their comrades trapped at the entrance to the gold mine.

"This is crazy!" Jason cried out.

"Jason, we've got to do something," pleaded Angie.

"We're all going to die here if we don't get out now."

"They're already dying," Angie replied. "Every day, Darfurians are dying. How is today any different?"

Knowing he had lost another battle and that she was determined to get all the children out, Jason searched the surrounding sand for a weapon. He spotted a couple of Janjaweed corpses on the other side of the bulldozer.

"Matak," Jason called, getting the boy's attention. "Weapons. If we're going to do this, let's at least take some of them with us."

Matak smiled and spoke to the other boys again. Two of them crawled to the other side of the bulldozer and stretched their arms out to retrieve the dead Janjaweeds' rifles. Matak approached Jason and said with a grin, "You're okay, American."

"Yeah. Okay, but crazy for agreeing to this."

"We need to get guns for us," Matak said, pointing to a dead militiaman. Jason shook his head. The corpse was a good twenty yards away, in the middle of the encampment.

"How about we make our stand from here?"

Matak only smiled. "Let's go, American."

"Jason, be careful," Angie said.

The Fur teenager led Jason out into the open.

Halfway to the body, a barrage of gunfire hit the sand around them. Jason looked up and saw two Janjaweed in the distance, running right at them and aiming their weapons in their direction. Matak, reaching the dead militiaman first, rolled in the sand as he scooped up the man's AK-47. Matak was already returning fire on the men shooting at them before Jason reached him. Seeing a pistol sticking from the corpse's belt, Jason grabbed it.

Then, lying in the sand with their elbows propped on the dead man's chest, Jason and Matak returned fire and quickly silenced the two approaching Janjaweed.

"We need to get to the mine. It's safer there and we can rescue the others," Matak said. Over his shoulder he shouted to the other boys in his native tongue. "Pick up more rifles and ammunition along the way. Let's go!"

Matak sprang to his feet and took off for the open pit. Angie and Halima ran to Jason.

"Matak's right. It probably is safer in the mine," he said, getting to his feet.

"My thoughts exactly," answered Angie, keeping her head down.

"That brother of yours is one brave boy," Jason said to Halima.

"Must run in the family," Angie replied, causing Halima to smile.

The three ran after Matak, who had been stopping to pick up rifles off the dead fighters he passed. The pit was at least a football field across, maybe more. It reminded Jason of pictures of strip mining back in the U.S. Concentric rings of sand swirled down 150 feet deep where the current mining was taking place. As they reached the first ring, they looked down and saw four boys younger than Matak huddled behind a rock.

"Is this all of them?" Jason asked.

"Yes. We are all that's left," Matak replied, helping one of the boys to his feet. "Here, Obie. Take this rifle. It's time for us to stand up to *ad-Dajaal* together." Matak placed a rifle in the young boy's hand. As the boy gripped the rifle, life returned to his eyes. He looked at Matak and nodded.

There were now ten teenagers, all armed with rifles. Jason could see the anger in their eyes. Their innocence had been stolen from them, replaced with pain and revenge. But there were dozens of armed, experienced, and cutthroat fighters in the camp.

The boys' quest for vengeance would give them blind courage and make them feel invincible. But that sense of courage would also make them foolhardy, Jason realized. Many would die if they tried to take on Hussein and the others head on.

"Matak, now is not the time for revenge," Jason cautioned. "Your sister is here. We need to get her out of here safely. Angie has pictures of what's going on here."

"The story you boys tell me—and that I will publish—will be your revenge," Angie said. "The world will know what went on here. Trust me, the Janjaweed and the Sudanese government will pay for all they've done to you and your people."

But Matak was not convinced. His angry eyes continued to focus on one big, scarred rider in the middle of the camp, slashing two of Tawfik's mercenaries with a bloodied machete.

"Let it go, Matak," added Jason. "We'll get them. I promise."

Halima, noticing that the Americans were not getting through to her brother, walked over to him and reached for his hand. Matak turned his gaze from the enemy and looked down at his sister.

"Please, brother. I don't want to lose you too." Halima put her arms around his waist and leaned against his chest as she hugged him tightly. "Take me away from here, Matak. Enough have died in this place. Please?" Halima looked up, a tear in her eye as she pleaded with him.

Matak gave her a soft smile. "Okay, Halima. Let's go."

Just as they were preparing to move, a bullet grazed the shoulder of one of the teenagers standing next to Jason. The boy winced in pain but returned fire on the attacking Janjaweed. Jason pulled the boy down out of the incoming fire as the rest of the group took cover on the slopes of the pit.

"They're closing in on us," Angie cried, watching as the Janjaweed descended into the outer rings of the mine.

Suddenly the two Arab armies stopped fighting each other and seemed to unite against the Fur children and the Americans. Hussein himself turned his attention on Matak. He jumped down from his horse and started walking towards the mine, his machete raised high in the air as his men followed closely behind him. The Fur teens returned fire, but they would be no match against the united Arab advance.

"There's too many of them," Angie screamed. "Is there a way out through the mine?"

Matak shook his head. "Only through the gate," he said, pointing to the broken fence behind their attackers. "We have to get through them to get out."

Suddenly, when Hussein was about fifty yards from his target, he stopped abruptly. His band of Janjaweed stopped beside him. Hussein looked around, his eyes scanning the outer perimeter of the camp along the fence line. Without saying a word, he turned around and returned to his horse. His fighters followed his lead and mounted their steeds as well.

Hussein turned back to look at Matak once more before leading his men through the broken gate. Like a flash, they were gone. Out of the camp, disappearing around the rocks behind which Jason parked their car.

"I have no clue," Jason said aloud to everyone, who all had the same question. He noticed Tawfik, who had been standing in the trailer watching the battle through the broken window, was also gone. "But the Janjaweed departure evens the odds a bit, wouldn't you say, Matak?"

Matak smiled as he continued to fire on Tawfik's militiamen who were still slowly advancing on foot.

A boy standing next to Angie took a bullet to the thigh and let out a high-pitched scream, dropping his rifle. Angie had just reached out to him to apply pressure to the wound when another bullet whizzed by her and hit the boy in the head, splattering blood on her shirt. Angie stood frozen in shock.

"Angie!" Jason shouted. But she just stared at her bloodied hands. "Angie!" He reached over and grabbed her arm. "Shake it off."

She broke her stare and looked at Jason. "We're all going to die," she said.

"We need to surrender," Jason said.

"No!" shouted Matak. "We will not give up. We're not going back to the mines. They killed our families. Our villages were destroyed. It ends now."

"We can't win," Jason pleaded with the young boy from Zarundi.

"Then we will die. You two take Halima and go down into the mine. You'll be safe there until this is over."

Looking out at the approaching soldiers, Jason saw a structure that reminded him of something Dr. Hess had said on the phone earlier.

"Angie," Jason said to her, his eyes softening, "no matter what happens, remember: You have to get out of here and tell their story."

"What are you talking about? We're *all* getting out of here."

Jason gave her a sad, small smile and touched her face. "Just promise me you'll make it back home."

"Stop it, Jason. We're both gonna make it, okay? Why are you talking like this?"

"Matak, cover me," Jason shouted as he turned and ran out into the open, straight at the band of Arab fighters.

"Jason!" screamed Angie.

"Fire at them," Matak yelled to the boys who were could still hold a weapon. It wasn't much of a suppressive fire.

A hail of gunfire erupted around Jason as he ran to the cover of a small pickup truck. Beside him on the ground was a dead

Arab fighter with an RPG lying on top of him. Jason didn't know if the man had belonged to Hussein's Janjaweed army or was a guard at the mine, but, either way, it hadn't ended well for the man. Nor would it for Jason, he realized as bullets from all directions ricocheted off the truck's frame and whizzed close to his head.

"Jason, get back here!" yelled Angie. "You'll be killed!"

He knew it was a long shot and prayed Dr. Hess was correct. It was the only chance they had against the well-armed fighters closing in on them.

Taking a deep breath, Jason squatted down and reached out to the body lying near the rear bumper. He withdrew his arm in terror as bullets hit the ground around him. Fortunately, none of the rounds found their mark. Yet.

He knew he was running out of chances. It was now or never. After another deep breath and a small prayer, he reached out a second time. This time, as he stretched his right arm as far as he could around the front bumper, he felt the cool touch of the rocket launcher's metal receiver on his fingertips. He grasped the RPG and pulled it close to his chest, barely hidden behind the truck. Although he had never fired an RPG before, he knew this was the only chance they had of getting out of this camp alive.

Jason hurried to the front side of the truck to get a clearer shot of his target. He lifted the heavy weapon and aimed as carefully as he could. He only had one shot. Fortunately, it was a big target and would be difficult to miss. He would need that advantage. Closing his eyes, he pulled the trigger and was rewarded by a swishing sound. His right shoulder recoiled hard with the force of the projectile leaving the launcher. Jason watched as if in slow motion the projectile sailed at its target.

▼ ▼ ▼

MICHAEL SHUSKO

A few seconds later, a huge explosion and fireball erupted just above and behind the approaching militiamen. The advancing troops had been crouched beside the tank farm when Jason fired the RPG at the largest gas storage tank in the center. The blast was deafening, much louder than Jason expected, and it engulfed anything within a fifty-foot radius.

Angie and the Fur youth ducked for cover in the pit. After the blast wave and fireball passed over them, they cautiously poked their heads out to survey the damage.

"The gas tanks!" Matak shouted, pointing to what was left of the large tanks across from the pit. The explosion from the stored natural gas siphoned from the gold mine incinerated most of the militiamen. The remaining few were rolling around in the sand trying to put out the fire on their clothing while reeling from their agonizing burns and shrapnel wounds.

Matak and the Fur teenagers shouted in joy as they danced around shooting their AK-47s in the air in celebration. Angie released Halima and the two of them looked over the edge of the terrace trying to catch a glimpse of Jason as the smoke cleared. Angie gasped at the horrific site of burning bodies and militiamen writhing in pain coupled with the stench of charred flesh.

"Jason!" she screamed, and ran out of the pit. The pickup that Jason had hidden behind was overturned, its frame twisted in a macabre shape from the force of the blast. There was no sign of the doctor.

"Where are you?" she yelled, looking under the smoldering wreckage. Had he been crushed by the overturned truck? But she could see nothing. No one. If he was pinned under the cab, she couldn't see him.

"Jason!" she shouted again, but there was no answer.

36

"**O**VER HERE!" cried Halima, standing next to a body about twenty feet from the truck.

Angie and Matak ran over to see what the girl had found. She recognized Jason's clothes, but shuddered at his motionless body, splattered with blood.

"Oh, no," she cried as she bent down and gently rolled Jason onto his back.

"Is he...?" asked Halima, hiding behind her brother.

But before Angie could reply, Jason began to moan.

"He's alive!" she screamed. "Jason, can you hear me?"

Jason opened his eyes. "I guess Dr. Hess was right about the natural gas storage tanks," he muttered, trying to get up onto his elbows.

"Are you hurt?" asked Angie.

"Just some scratches and bruises, I think. The truck shielded me from most of the shrapnel, although the blast threw me way over here."

"I thought you..."

"Nope. Can't get rid of me that easily," he said with a smile as Matak helped him to his feet.

"Yes, you're okay, American."

"And you, my friend, are one tough kid. Can we leave now?"

"Not quite," a voice came from behind them.

They turned and saw a small man flanked by two fierce-looking bodyguards. All three were Asian, but the man in the middle, wearing brown cargo pants and a button-down gray safari shirt, was much shorter than his tall, beefy companions. Angie thought he looked to be in his late fifties or early sixties. He wore wire-rimmed glasses and had a thin mustache on his portly, scowling face. The two men who flanked him were stoic, their countenance void of any emotion. Each held a QBZ-95 Chinese assault rifle aimed directly at the Americans.

"You have caused me and my company a great deal of trouble," the Asian man stated.

"And you have kidnapped Fur children and used them as slaves in your mines," Angie hissed.

"I have done nothing. Am I to blame if the Sudanese barbarians enslave their own people?"

"You bastard. Do you know how many people have died in Darfur?"

"Not my business. *This* is my business. This facility that you helped destroy. Now, what am I supposed to do with you?"

The two guards raised their weapons to their cheeks, preparing to fire.

"You know I cannot let you leave here. You had your chance to leave when you were back in El-Fashir. That was your mistake. Now you will pay for it."

"No, it is *you* who will pay," a deep, boisterous voice rang out. All eyes turned toward the sound. Two dozen heavily armed men were climbing over the twisted metal of the fence into the compound littered with bodies. "You will pay for the crimes you have committed against the Fur people."

"*Baba!*" shouted Halima as she and Matak rushed to greet the man. Jason spotted Steve Connors among the approaching men.

"Fur rebels," Jason exclaimed. "Steve said he was meeting with one of the rebel groups from Darfur. He brought them here."

"*Baba?*" Angie replied, watching Halima hug a Sudanese man in his forties, apparently the rebel leader.

▼ ▼ ▼

Boss and his two bodyguards warily eyed the new band of fighters joining the melee. The SLM rebel leader and the American continued to approach them as half the SLM rebel fighters fanned out into the camp to round up what was left of Tawfik's wounded fighters. The other half surrounded the three foreigners. Boss nodded to his guards to lay down their weapons, knowing the rebels would kill them if they resisted. This battle was over, but with the help of his allies in Khartoum, he would ensure the war continued to be waged against the rebels. Someone would pay for his destroyed camp and the loss of revenue from the cessation of this lucrative mining operation.

▼ ▼ ▼

"Looks like we missed the battle," Steve commented, eyeing the destruction around him.

"You still saved the day," Jason said, shaking hands with the CIA operative.

"I didn't think we'd get out of here alive," replied Angie. "I'd say you got here just in time. Is that Halima and Matak's father?"

Both children stood proudly with the leader of the rebels as he ordered his men to retrieve all the weapons in the camp and round up the wounded guards.

"Apparently so. During my meeting with Mobassa, I mentioned this mine to see if he knew anything about it. I wanted to see if I could get him to come down here with me to help you. At first, he refused. But I noticed his interest piqued when I mentioned you were travelling with a little girl. A survivor from Zarundi. I saw hope in his eyes and he immediately ordered his men to mount up and we rushed down here. Now I see why."

The Americans watched the SLM rebel leader with his children.

"Mobassa and his family lived in Zarundi. He was out in the desert searching for his wife and two children, Fatima and Matak, who went missing after a Janjaweed attack on a village named Hileh Tamim," Steve explained. "He found his wife's body in the village, but not the children. So, he and his men went searching for Hussein, hoping that by finding him, he would be able to uncover what had happened to his older children. But the Janjaweed commander slipped right under Mobassa's nose to attack Zarundi. Apparently, Hussein's a hard man to track in the desert. You know the rest of the story, I believe."

"Hussein was here," Angie said, causing Mobassa to turn toward them at the sound of his adversary's name. "He and his Janjaweed army just left. It was strange. He was just about to attack us, then turned and left with his men."

"Hussein is Bedu." Mobassa spoke up, approaching the Americans at the tail end of their conversation. "And is very good at surviving in the desert. He knows the Sahara better than anyone. That's why he's so difficult for us to catch. He can smell our sweat when we approach, hear our trucks from miles away. Surprising him has proven impossible, especially when he's out in the desert."

"You mean he could literally *smell* you coming just now?" Angie asked.

"What you eat comes out of your pores, even more so in the heat of the desert. We eat different food than the Bedu. Different spices. The sounds of our trucks carry in the desert. The dust cloud is visible as we approached. The Bedu have lived in the desert their entire lives. Their senses are very strong. Especially Hussein. He has mastered the art of detecting his prey in the desert. That's why he's so elusive."

"What will happen to them?" Jason asked, nodding at the three foreigners being led away.

"No harm will come to them," Mobassa replied.

"Their government won't want an international incident any more than ours does. After all, that's one of the reasons I was sent to get you out of that prison," replied Steve.

"We'll leave the foreigners alone," Mobassa answered. "We have enough trouble fighting our enemies in Khartoum. The last thing I need is for foreigners to send in their armies against us as well because we harmed their citizens."

"I'm sure the Sudanese army will be here soon enough. No doubt our three friends here contacted them when all the shooting began. And they most definitely won't be on our side," Steve said. "We'd better be going soon. There's not much time."

"Going? To where?" asked Jason. "Surely every Sudanese cop, border guard, and soldier will be looking for us after what happened here."

"I have pictures and stories," Angie added. "The U.S. government and UN may turn a blind eye because of pressure from other countries that still support the government in Sudan, but I will not. This *will* get published. The world will know what's happening here."

"You're right. And because of that, you are now a marked woman in this country," Steve answered.

"*We*'re marked," Jason added.

Angie smiled. She didn't want him in any more danger, but she was glad she would not be alone in her quest.

"We've got to get you two out of Sudan," Steve said. "The borders will be heavily guarded, for sure. I can't risk bringing you to Khartoum. To be honest with you, after the political mess here, I'm not so sure our own embassy would even want to get involved at this point. There'll be a lot of pressure from Sudan to turn you in as criminals."

"Criminals?" Angie asked. "For what crime?"

"You're still in Sudan illegally. No passports," Steve explained. "Whoever runs this mine has deep pockets. And you've just put a substantial dent in their profits. On top of that, you witnessed firsthand the human rights abuses going on here. I bet they also don't want the world to know what they're doing here in the middle of nowhere. If word gets out, they'll spin this to try to keep themselves clean. They'll say you were snooping around taking pictures, maybe even blew the place up. It wouldn't be the first time activists have tried to shut down mines."

"That's crazy!" Angie looked outraged.

"Yes, it is, but I stay alive by worrying about worst-case scenarios and trying to stay one step ahead of the bad guys. Right now, it's best for you two to lay low and slip out of Sudan as fast and quietly as possible," replied the CIA agent.

"I cannot spare any men to take you out," Mobassa said. "I need to send half a dozen men to take these children back to find what's left of their families. We are already losing precious minutes. You say Hussein has just left? I don't want to lose this chance to find him before he disappears in the desert again."

"Wau," Angie said.

"What?" Jason asked as they looked at her, puzzled.

"Henry said there was a human rights conference going on in Wau," she answered, referring to one of the larger cities in neighboring South Sudan. "There'll be a lot of high-ranking UN staff, NGOs, international reporters, and government officials there, right?"

"Probably," Jason replied.

"Well, if the Sudanese army is looking for us at the airports and along the border with Chad, maybe they wouldn't expect us going a different direction to South Sudan. We're near the southern border anyway, aren't we?"

"Not far. Maybe a hundred and fifty kilometers or so," answered Mobassa. "But, as I have told you, the Bedu are masters of the desert. If we do not find Hussein and the remaining Janjaweed, they might still come after you. And he *will* find you. Many more of our villages will be destroyed if we let them slip out of our grasp again. We cannot take the time to get you all the way to the border, with Hussein on the loose threatening our villages. He's close. This is our one chance to stop him for good."

"But the Janjaweed live in the north and most of their raids are in Darfur, in western Sudan. They wouldn't look for us in the south. Nor would the Sudanese authorities. They'd expect us to return west to cross the border back into Chad or go to the nearest airport or the embassy in Khartoum. When I was researching Sudan back home, I read about the revamped train system here. New engines just donated from China. Isn't there a line near here that goes down into South Sudan?" she continued.

"Fidail!" bellowed Mobassa. In a moment, the white-haired man appeared at the side of his SLM leader.

"Does your brother still work for the railroad in Nyala?" Mobassa asked.

The man nodded and replied in the affirmative in the local dialect. Halima translated so the Americans could understand what was going on.

"Fidail's brother lives in Nyala," Mobassa explained after the conversation concluded. "He works for Sudan Railways. He says the train from Babanusa to Wau is not officially operational yet, but the new trains are running. Fidail is a great warrior. He's my second-in-command and I trust him like a brother. He will take you to Nyala. I can spare him and one other man, but just to Nyala. It's not far from here. From there, you can take the train to Babanusa and continue down to Wau in South Sudan. That is the best I can do."

"I am going with them, Baba," said Matak.

"Me too," Halima added, standing proudly next to her older brother.

"You cannot," Mobassa answered, not wanting to risk losing two of his children again.

"Your father's right," Angie said. "It's much too dangerous."

"Baba," protested Matak. "We have no home to go back to now. No village. Nowhere left to go. Our home is with you. But it's too dangerous for us to go with you now. You're going after the Janjaweed. We'll slow you down. You are our only family left, now, Baba. Besides, we can help the Americans. I can tell all who will listen how the Janjaweed imprisoned us and were training us as soldiers for their army. I'll tell them how we were forced to work in the mines and how they took away the girls. I told you, they still have Fatima. We need to find her, Baba. These people in Wau, they may be able to help us find her. Maybe if Halima and I told our stories in person, we could convince someone to help us. Help *all* of us."

"I'll tell them how the Evil Winds destroyed our homes in Zarundi. That they killed everyone. I was there, Baba. I saw it all. We can help," said Halima. "You taught us to be strong. To fight for our people."

"Baba. I need to do this. Let me help find Fatima," Matak said solemnly.

Mobassa stared into the eyes of his children. For the first time, he realized they were not children any longer. Their innocence had been stolen from them. It was replaced with desolation. But there was also something else there. Justice. Determination. Strength. Retribution. At that moment, Mobassa felt two of the strongest emotions he had ever felt in his life: a profound sadness for the loss of their youth coupled with a great pride in his offspring for fighting for what they believed in. For their bravery and dedication to find their sister and fight, as he did, for their cause. He hung his head low as he announced his decision.

"You may go with the Americans. Tell our story to all who will listen. Tell them the plight of the Fur. And find Fatima."

Halima smiled at Angie as Matak bowed at his father's words. Mobassa reached out and hugged his children simultaneously. Angie saw sadness in his eyes.

"Take care of them. I will join you in a few days," Mobassa said, and turned to round up the rest of his men.

"I can't go with you," Steve said to Angie and Jason. "I still have some work to do here. The owners of the mine may try to spin this for the media before you have a chance to tell what really went on here. But the intel I can get on this place and on what the Janjaweed are doing here may convince even Sudan's staunchest international allies to support us in the UN for more international action in Darfur. While Mobassa is mopping up, I want to see what I can squeeze out of this squirrely mine boss."

"But how will we get into South Sudan?" Jason asked. "We have no passports."

"Fidail will get your tickets in Nyala and his brother will ensure you get through security and onto the train without any problems," Mobassa said. "They won't even ask Matak and Halima for a passport. The train won't stop at the border with South Sudan. There's no town there, no train station. They'll wait and check for your passports when you arrive at Wau in South Sudan. You are on your own from there."

"I'll see if I can have the U.S. Embassy in Juba make you a couple of expedited passports," Steve said. "Embassies do that all the time if someone's passport is lost or stolen. I have a contact there. I'll give her a call and see what she can do. If we can make it happen, she'll be waiting for you with them in Wau."

"If not?" Jason asked.

"If not, you'll have to improvise," Steve said.

37

STEVE OPENED THE DOOR of the trailer carrying three ID cards in his hand. Boss stood defiantly behind his desk as his two guards sat quietly along the wall. Three of Mobassa's SLM rebels stood watch over them, rifles pointed at the foreigners.

"So, you run the show here, isn't that right, Feng Wu?" Steve asked, reading the Arabic on Boss's ID.

Feng sat quietly but resolutely at his desk.

"Well, this is a big mess, isn't it, Feng?" Steve asked, grabbing a wooden chair from the corner and sitting in the middle of the room. "I mean, a Chinese company operating a gold mine in Sudan using forced child labor from destroyed villages in the Darfur region." Steve shook his head for effect. "But wait, no, while you may be Chinese, your company is not. At least, not anymore. Shao Mining Corporation lost its license to operate in mainland China, didn't it?"

Feng and his two guards sat stone-faced.

"And your two henchmen—Chinese as well?" Steve asked. "Unlike you, they didn't show up in our database." Steve ran the names he had taken from the Sudanese ID cards the three

211

foreigners carried. It only took a few minutes for his CIA col-leagues in Langley to conduct the extensive search, which included the Interpol database. "It seems you've had some legal trouble back in China, Mr. Feng. Suspected of bribery? Corruption? Extortion? Now we can add child labor and kid-napping to that impressive list. I guess I was wrong. China won't be coming to your aid after all. As a matter of fact, they may be quite appreciative of us turning you over to them."

Feng smiled. "Don't play your amateur mind games with me, American. My company was invited here by the government of Sudan. There is no proof of our involvement in anything illegal here. You and your *friends* have destroyed my camp and are trespassing."

"Really? That's how you see this?" Steve asked. "I'm afraid the international community may see things differently. You won't have many friends left, even in Khartoum, when the word gets out that you enslave children and work them to death in these unsafe conditions. But there may be a way to still salvage your reputation. I mean, you're a businessman, right? You just run the mine for your company. I get that. I'm sure that neither you nor your employer cares about the genocide occurring in Darfur. You just care about profits. The bottom line. Gold."

Feng listened quietly.

"So, let me make it easy for you and your superiors wher-ever they're hiding. At this point, I'm not really focused on your business dealings. Don't get me wrong, I think you're scum for using forced child labor to steal precious minerals and resources from the people of Sudan. Resources that could be used to end suffering here in Africa. But right now, I have another problem. Tell me about Hussein and the Janjaweed. I need to know where to find them. Who controls them? Who gives them their orders?"

Feng laughed. "You Americans. So arrogant yet ignorant of the world at the same time. There is so much going on right under your noses yet you only see what you want to see."

"What do you mean?"

"What I mean doesn't matter because my purpose here is not to enlighten your simple, oblivious mind," retorted Feng.

"That's right. Your purpose here is to rob from the Sudanese people and kill their children," Steve answered, standing from his chair. "But you'll pay for your crimes."

"And who will make me pay? You? Your CIA? The SLM rebels?" Feng asked, sneering at Mobassa's guards. "I don't think so. I'm afraid you and your countrymen are the ones who will pay for your lack of insight. Your enemies around the world continue to grow in number and power, and you don't even see it."

"I know all about the United Islamic Caliphate. That's why I'm after Hussein. And once I prove that you and the government of Sudan support him, now that he and his Janjaweed army have teamed up with the UIC, international pressure will come down hard on your little operation and your backers in Khartoum."

Feng let out a hearty laugh. "Hussein is not with us. You fool. Open your eyes. Look at the bodies scattered around. You think I did that? Don't get me wrong; my two guards here are quite capable of doing such carnage as you see outside. More capable than you realize, I might add. But it wasn't us. Nor was it your two young American colleagues who have been sticking their noses where they don't belong for the past several days and have been allowed to live only due to the benevolence and intervention of my superior. The Janjaweed commander that you seek is no ally of mine or my company. His army is responsible for the death and destruction you see out there."

"If Hussein did this, then why do you protect him?" Steve asked, walking over to Feng.

"Hussein was a tool. But he has outlived his usefulness to us and became, as you say in America, 'too big for his britches.' His arrogance and impertinence have made him a liability. He feels he's a savior to his people. That's why he turned his back on us to join the UIC. We do not protect him. So, you see, spy," continued Feng, sitting back smugly in his chair, "you can spin what you see here any way you want. But we can do the same. When I look outside that broken window, I don't see a company using child labor, as you said. I see a Sudanese-sanctioned joint venture that brings much-needed jobs and revenue to this impoverished nation destroyed by the Janjaweed. A Janjaweed army, I might add, led by a man recently recruited by the UIC. So, you see, *we* are the victims here. My company, the world will see, does not support these terrorists but is a *victim* of the UIC. We are here to help the Sudanese government mine their own resources to benefit their people. That's how I see it. And that is how the world will see it. The world will also see that your two meddling Americans are on the side of the Janjaweed."

"You're crazy. No one will believe that," Steve said.

"No? Look outside that broken window. You'll see cameras all along the fence line. Most face outward, but some also face inside the camp. They're for security, you see. I'm sure there's plenty of footage of your friends breaking into this camp and even of the young doctor shooting an RPG at my gas storage tank. There was much damage from that explosion, I'm afraid, and many of my men were killed in the blast. Sudanese men, just trying to make a living, protecting their jobs. Their only livelihood. Killed by American activists taking their protest of strip mining too far. I'm sure some good video editors can use that footage to create a nice picture for the international media outlets."

"You bastard," Steve exclaimed, looking out the window.

"And don't bother looking for the tapes. That's a live feed that goes via satellite to my company's headquarters far away from here."

The door swung open and Mobassa threw Yasser to the ground. "Look what my men found curled on the floor in the backseat of one of the cars, hiding like a woman."

"I'm just an interpreter," protested Yasser. "I have nothing to do with the Janjaweed."

"Yasser, fancy seeing you here," Steve said to translator he had hired to work with Jason in the refugee camp. "Dr. Russo tells me you and Hussein are best buds. What happened, you were hiding during the firefight here and didn't see him leave with his Janjaweed army?"

"No, that's not what happened," Yasser pleaded.

Realizing that Feng's company would do anything to protect their lucrative interests in Africa, Steve decided to play his final hand. He was losing this battle, but the war was not yet over. "If you're not willing to assist me, Feng, perhaps our friend Yasser knows how to find Hussein. I'm sure he would be kind enough to fill us in on the missing pieces we need to shut this place down and put you and your goons behind bars—in exchange for leniency, of course," Steve said, looking directly at the interpreter still curled at Mobassa's feet.

"You cannot shut us down. You have no authority here," Feng replied. "Nor do you have any idea of what's going on around you, spy. You and your pathetic SLM friends are no match for us. The power we control is far beyond your grasp. You cannot possibly win. Go home and leave Africa to us."

"We'll see about that," Steve replied, wondering how much of what the man said was true. Was there more than meets the eye to this hidden desert camp?

"We've collected all the weapons. Now we have to go. We're running out of daylight and Hussein is getting farther away," Mobassa stated.

One of Mobassa's men entered the room and said something to the rebel leader.

"Come," the SLM leader barked to Steve angrily. "My men will watch over the foreigners. Bring him with us," Mobassa ordered, pointing at Yasser.

"What is it?" Steve asked, but Mobassa was already out the door.

Mobassa walked quickly and purposefully to a small square building not far from Feng's trailer.

"Mobassa?" Steve called again, but the rebel commander kept walking. SLM sentinels stood outside the door. Mobassa ducked his head as he entered the cinder-block building. Steve followed and stopped cold in his tracks at what he saw inside.

"What is this place?" asked Steve. He gazed at the state-of-the-art medical equipment that filled the room. Telemetry units were attached to three gurneys that were in the center of the brightly lit interior. Bright industrial surgical lights hung from the metal room over each gurney. Metal shackles lay across the gurneys, but all were empty. Rolling tables filled with drills and other surgical instruments sat beside each one. The gurney closest to him had a red stain on the plastic at one end. Steve walked over and looked closely at the stain.

"Blood," he said, crouching down and following the flow of fluid as it dripped down into a puddle on the tiled floor. "And it's fresh. What is this place?"

"My men caught these two throwing papers into that furnace," Mobassa said. Beside him, four SLM guards held the arms of two foreign scientists. The men stood motionless in their white coats. Steve approached them. Behind them, the yellow glow of flames shone through a small glass window in a burning furnace.

"What the hell where you doing in here?" asked Steve, wondering what other evidence had been thrown into the fire.

But the scientists only stared off into space, expressionless. If they were afraid, they didn't show it.

"These men are coming with me," Mobassa said. "They'll tell us what they've been doing with our children in this room."

"They're probably Chinese citizens, just like Feng," Steve said. "Like him, I'm sure they're wanted in Beijing for some crime or another."

"The hell with that. They've taken this too far," barked Mobassa, pointing to the furnace.

Steve cringed at the thought of what other horrors the furnace was used for.

"They'll receive their justice here with me," Mobassa continued. "Today."

Before Steve could protest further, the two scientists began to twitch simultaneously. One let out a slight groan as his convulsions grew, and both men fell to the floor in epileptic fits. Steve ran over to one to try to render aid.

"What's happening to them?" Steve wondered. The men continued to convulse, foam emanating from their mouths. He crouched down but could do nothing to stop the life-threatening seizures. After another moment passed, the tonic-clonic jerking of the scientists' limbs ceased. Steve checked the men's heartbeats, but the bluish color on their faces gave Steve the answer that their lack of pulses confirmed. They were both dead.

"But how? Both men having seizures at the exact same time?" Steve asked, confused as he crouched next to the bodies.

Gunfire erupted nearby. One of Mobassa's men entered the room and said something to the rebel leader while pointing out the broken window.

"Our time is up. The Sudanese army is here. We have to leave right now," Mobassa said after looking out the door himself.

Steve just stood over the bodies, still wondering what had happened to the men. He took out his smartphone and snapped pictures of the bodies as well as a panoramic shot of the room, being careful to zoom in to capture images of the equipment and tools. Anything that could provide a clue into what went on in this room. He wished he could take the computers, but Mobassa grabbed him to leave before he had a chance to collect any evidence.

"We may have to leave now, but I'll be back. Whatever went on here, I'll find out!" Steve shouted as they ran out of the make-shift lab.

"People die in Africa every day, my friend," Mobassa replied, leading his American ally back to their horses and vehicles for their hasty escape as the Sudanese army closed in on the camp. "But no one ever comes back."

38

THE SUV RIDE SOUTH through the desolate sands was short. Both Angie and Jason sat quietly contemplating all they had been through recently. Perhaps their struggle would be over when they reached South Sudan. There, they could focus on bringing relief to those left behind in Darfur. As they approached the sprawling outskirts of Nyala, Angie was surprised at the size of the capital of this southern Darfur district. Over half a million inhabitants occupied this former Daju empire stronghold.

What a contrast with the dusty streets of El-Fashir, Angie thought. She marveled at the organized structure of the city as they drove through the center of town en route to the rail station. Although it was unmistakably still part of the Sahara, Nyala was much greener than the surrounding villages. Trees shaded many of the houses in the walled compounds lining the paved main road through the provincial capital. There were also more people walking the dirt side streets than she had seen in other villages. Most were women wearing colorful yet modest abayas, some with floral patterns, but all still wearing head scarves.

They passed a number of small, ornate mosques and even a relatively modern and clean-looking hospital before turning off onto a sandy desert path toward the Nyala rail station. Soon the car stopped and Mobassa's lieutenant Fidail got out of the passenger seat. Angie watched as he approached a small shack that was selling tickets. After a moment, Fidail emerged from the station and waved for his charges to come to the waiting train.

They approached the platform and gazed at the new diesel engine at the head of the long train of passenger cars, loaded with people heading east to the first stop at Babanusa.

"It looks brand new," Angie commented upon gazing at the large blue locomotive.

"Sudan just received a dozen or so new diesel engines to revamp their railroad system. What used to take a day's travel to Babanusa will now take only four or five hours, and about the same down to Wau," Jason explained.

"He says we need to hurry," Halima told her American friends, interpreting Fidail's words as he handed Jason the tickets. "They're about to let the people on the train and we'll need to push our way up front if we want a seat together."

"Follow me," Matak said. The Fur teen was about Jason's height but, despite his light weight of only 120 pounds, he was able to push through the crowd and lead them to the front of the line. Noticing the first car behind the engine was set up as a stable car for animals, they moved their way down the crowded platform to the door of the second car just as the conductor stepped off the train and allowed the passengers to embark. Jason stood on the platform, using his body to shield the door from the mob trying to push their way onto the train as Matak, Halima, and Angie boarded. He quickly followed behind them and the four travelers hurried down the aisle of the passenger car and found two rows of seats facing each other, separated only by a thin table.

"Okay," Angie said to Matak and Halima as they sat down just as the aisle beside them flooded with dozens of passengers vying for seats on the new train. "We need to stay together."

Halima nodded, but Matak only stared through the window. Angie put her hand on his shoulder. "Are you all right? You've been through a lot."

But Matak continued to stare at the people on the platform outside the train.

Inside, the train was crowded. Passengers occupied every seat, some with caged chickens or birds in their laps. The modern interior of the shiny new Chinese train contrasted with the passengers' traditional tribal clothing. Soon the passenger car jolted as the train pulled away from the station.

Angie leaned over close to Jason and asked, "What will happen to them?"

"When we get to Wau, we'll find this refugee meeting you mentioned and get Halima and Matak in front of the UNHCR delegation," Jason said, referring to the UN's main refugee agency.

"I know that. I mean, their childhood has been stolen from them. They'll never be the same."

Jason glanced over to Matak. He noticed something in the boy's expression that Angie did not. It wasn't just a loss of innocence. It was anger. Matak wanted revenge. Retribution for what had happened to him, his family, and his village. Jason could see this because he'd seen the same expression in the mirror after his own mother had been injured by senseless violence.

"Let's keep an eye on them. They've been through hell," he replied.

The train continued its journey east to Babanusa. As they headed out of the crowded provincial capital of Nyala, the greens and blues faded, replaced by the red hue of the sun setting over the desert. The four companions sat in silence for some time.

Finally, Angie looked over at Halima, who was resting her head on Matak's shoulder. "Halima, that was your father back at the mine?"

Halima smiled and nodded.

"He's very brave. He saved all of us," continued Angie.

"Baba is the hero of our people. He and the other men come together to protect the villages from the Evil Winds. But he's gone a lot."

"But now you have your brother back," Angie said.

The smile returned to Halima's small face as she nodded again and hugged her brother's arm. Matak was still deep in thought, staring out of the window. He spoke without turning his eyes away from the darkness that had overtaken the desert.

"But not Fatima."

"Fatima? Who's that?" Jason asked.

"Fatima is my twin sister. I could not protect her from the Janjaweed. They took her from the village after they killed our mother." Matak's hard face looked at the two Americans. "I wasn't brave enough to save her."

"Matak, you are one man, literally against an army. There was nothing you could have done to prevent them taking your sister," replied Angie.

"I should have fought them. Like my father does."

"If you had tried," Jason added, "you would most likely be dead right now instead of on your way to South Sudan to help us provide evidence of the bad things the Janjaweed are doing. There were two of us back in Zarundi, and I had a gun and I couldn't stop them. But you're going to save your people with what you're doing. And no one asked you to come with us. You did it on your own. You are brave, Matak. The bravest young man I know."

"They took her away with the other girls. After they dropped off the boys at the mine, they drove away with Fatima in the back of their truck. I don't know what's happened to her."

Angie looked over at Jason, her anger at the Janjaweed's actions evident in her eyes.

"We're going to get help, Matak," she said. "Help for all of Darfur. Once the UN hears what went on in the mine and in the villages, they'll help. I'll make them. I'll continue writing about this until someone listens. I promise."

Matak looked at the American woman for a moment, then returned his gaze to the window.

Jason reached out to the table and held Angie's hand, squeezing it softly.

"Is the train slowing down?" Angie asked.

The four companions looked at each other.

"We must be arriving at Babanusa," said Jason.

39

TAWFIK PULLED INTO his parking spot in front of the small government building on the dark street in El-Fashir. He turned off the car and took a deep breath. He had barely made it out of the mine alive. Fighting alongside Hussein for all those years had taught him to follow the lead of his old commander. When Hussein sensed danger, it was time to leave. Seeing Hussein and his men flee in the middle of the battle caused Tawfik to suspect that there was a serious threat approaching.

He was fortunate that he was able to slip out to the SUV he had hidden outside the gate so Hussein didn't see it when he arrived at the mine. Boss wanted Tawfik's presence to surprise the Janjaweed commander, so he left his SUV outside the compound.

Tawfik got out of his vehicle and walked the few feet to the door of his building. As the governor, Tawfik's usual attire was a white dishdasha, not the battle fatigues he was currently wearing. He'd decided to stop at his office to change before going home. His wife and three children would be horrified if he arrived home in military fatigues and battle gear. They were happy believing that their husband and father was a civilized governor, not a Janjaweed brigand.

Tawfik entered the building and crossed the short hallway to his office. After unlocking the door, he turned on the light, tossed his AK-47 on the small couch, and walked over to the window. *It's been a long day*, he thought, staring out at the dimly lit courtyard adjacent to the building. That was where he negotiated his first sale of Fur women after taking office as governor not long ago. He had gone through several local trading partners since then, but his lucrative international partner became available only after he had teamed up with his foreign benefactor. The Russians, although hard negotiators and difficult to deal with, were willing to pay more for the captured Fur women than the Somali pirates and Nigerian warlords with whom he had been dealing prior. Tawfik stretched out his arms above his head. This hiccup with Hussein would soon pass and his side deals, now shifting from transcontinental to international, would soon resume, making him a very rich man.

Startled by the noise of a slamming door behind him, Tawfik turned quickly. Standing at the door were two men, the American CIA agent and the only Sudanese man besides Hussein who Tawfik truly feared.

"So, I hear you were at the mine but managed to sneak out before we arrived," Steve Connors said dryly. "Good instincts."

Tawfik glanced at his AK-47 on the couch beside the American spy. Knowing it would be impossible for him to reach his rifle, he inched his hand slowly toward the holster strapped around his leg.

"Go ahead," Mobassa snarled, aiming his AK-47 squarely at the governor's chest.

Tawfik decided against the move, instead raising his arms in submission. Steve walked over to him and pulled the pistol out of the holster. "Wise choice. Now we have some final business to attend to, Governor. You have committed the most heinous crimes against your people. You stole Fur children and put them to work in gold mines. Recruited them into the Janjaweed army. Sold them as slaves. For that, you'll be judged. But that's for another day. A truckload of Fur girls was taken from a village a week ago. The boys we rescued today told us they were taken away just after they arrived at the mine. Where are they?"

"I don't know what you're talking about," Tawfik said, his arms still raised.

"Yeah, I thought that would be your answer. Well, I don't really have time for this, so I'll just wait in the car outside," Steve replied, turning his back and making his way to the door. Steve stepped outside the office then turned around. "I'll just leave you two alone to discuss this," he said. "Just to save you some pain, *Governor*, in case you thought that you could hold out long enough for Mobassa to give up his search for these girls, know that his daughter was on that truck."

Tawfik looked in horror at the pure rage in Mobassa's eyes.

"Mobassa, take your time. We have all night," Steve said before shutting the door behind him.

▼ ▼ ▼

It was late afternoon in Boston when Emma Hess received another call from her friend Steve Connors.

"Yes, Steve, I got the pictures you sent me," she said, sitting down at her office desk. Happy for the break from packing, she cleared boxes off of her desk to get a better view of the computer screen. "I've seen quite a few disturbing images as a physician, but, I must say, the ones you sent me were particularly troublesome."

"Why?" Steve asked. Emma could tell the call was being placed from overseas but had no idea where the CIA operative was currently working. "What are your thoughts about what was being done in the room?"

"Hard to say, exactly, without being there. But, from the close-ups you sent of some of the equipment, I think medical procedures were being conducted. Probably on the brain, since I noticed a craniotomy saw and other neurosurgical tools. There were pediatric instruments as well, so I would guess that at least some of the patients were children. That, along with the images of the metal shackles and chains lying across the operation table, is what makes this scene so troubling to me."

"You think this room could have been used as a torture chamber?" came the reply.

"Possibly," Doctor Emma Hess replied, grimacing at Steve's choice of words. "But, I doubt it."

"Why do you say that?" Steve asked.

"There are surgical procedures that have been conducted illegally throughout the world for the purposes of torture and intimidation, but neurosurgical operations aren't commonly included in this group. In fact, even if the patients were awake, surgery on the brain would not be extraordinarily painful. If they were doing procedures on the brain, as the equipment suggests, I doubt it was to torture anyone."

"But why would they have an entire surgical suite for just procedures on the brain?" asked Steve.

"Most hospitals that have neurosurgery capability would have setups like this. Without the metal chains, of course."

"This wasn't a hospital, Emma," replied Steve.

Emma sat back in her chair and closed her eyes. She guessed that Steve's mention of "torture" meant the room wasn't used for benevolent purposes, but she had held out hope it was part of a hospital somewhere helping people. But now she imagined the horrors occurring in the room.

"Let me guess. Gold mine?"

"Any reason a gold mine would need this capability?" Steve pressed.

"Not that I could think of," replied Emma. "There could certainly be blast injuries from dynamite, if explosives are used in the mine. Maybe some head traumas from falls from rocks. But I can't think of any reason to have just a dedicated neuro suite. Besides, I didn't see any sterilization equipment when you took the panoramic shots of the room. Unless you found other medical or sterilization rooms, either these procedures were done by amateurs who didn't know about sterile techniques—which, based on the presence of the high-tech equipment and sophisticated neurosurgical tools, I highly doubt—or they didn't expect the patients to live after the procedure, so the surgeons didn't care about post-op infections."

"Nope. This was the only medical room that was found, as far as I could tell," Steve answered.

"Then, I would guess the latter is true. So, putting this all together, I would conclude that some sort of neurosurgical procedures were being conducted on children chained to a gurney by individuals that didn't care if they lived or died."

"But for what purpose?" the CIA agent asked.

"Experimentation."

"What kind of experiments?" he continued, thinking aloud.

"That, I cannot deduce from the pictures. Based on the equipment, probably on the brain. I don't know what else to tell you, Steve."

"No, as always, you've been incredibly helpful, Emma. Sorry to keep bothering you with my medical questions, but you get me answers much quicker than if I went through my official channels. Besides, as your new fiancé Lee likes to say—and I wholeheartedly agree—you are one of the smartest people I know," replied Steve.

"Nonsense. Some of the best doctors I know work for the government. I'm sure they'd be just as helpful as I am on these cases."

"Maybe so, but I don't have them on speed-dial," Steve replied with a smile. "And they probably wouldn't answer my two a.m. calls like you do."

"That's probably true." Emma chuckled, then looked more closely at the picture on her computer screen. "Hey, one more thing: There are a couple of computers set up right next to the operating table. I'm no computer expert, but they look fairly new and powerful to me. Any chance you have access to them?"

"No, why?"

"Well, we don't normally use computers during surgery. Not PCs anyway. Even in the high-tech world of neurosurgery, I couldn't even imagine why those two computers would be there. So, I asked a friend of mine at Mass General. He's the head of neurosurgery there, and he agreed. They don't bring desktop computers into the OR and roll them up next to a patient on the table. I just can't figure out what they were for."

"That *is* interesting. Unfortunately, I don't have access to the computers, and my time in the room itself was rather limited. All I have are the pictures," Steve replied.

"That's all I got for you. If I think of anything else, I'll send you an email. Next time you're in Boston, stop by. Lee and I would love to see you."

"Will do. Tell Lee I said hi. I hear you guys are heading to DC?"

"Yep. Lee's being transferred back to the headquarters of Homeland Security and I'll be at Johns Hopkins."

"Well, I'll sleep better now knowing Special Agent Lee Jansen is moving up the DHS ladder. It's about time those bureaucrats at

DHS recognized his hard work and promoted him. Well, thanks again, Emma and I'll see you next time I'm in the Beltway."

▼ ▼ ▼

Steve Connors leaned against his SUV outside the governor's office. Mobassa would surely focus his questioning on finding his daughter, but Steve had asked the him to press Tawfik on the purpose of the surgical room as well. He doubted Tawfik knew many of the details of what went on internally at the mine. After all, a foreign company ran it, and Asian scientists obviously were in charge of the surgical suite—scientists who died simultaneously and mysteriously. He thought about asking Emma about that, but decided against it. For now. Perhaps he'd bring it up with her next time he was back in the States. He had a gut feeling that there was more to this mine and the foreign company that ran it.

40

I T WAS DARK when the train pulled into the small station
at Babanusa. Angie looked around as many of the passengers stood up to gather up their belongings. More than
half of them seemed to be disembarking.

The rail car was dimly lit, but she could see two men enter
from the rear as the passengers exited the car from the front.

"Jason," she said quietly. "Look."

Jason turned his head and saw them. The first man, dressed
in slacks and a white button-up shirt, also wore a conductor's
cap. It was obvious that he was checking passengers' tickets.
But the man behind him wore a dark blue beret and solid blue
uniform.

"Police," Jason murmured.

"Are they looking for us?" asked Angie.

"Don't know and don't want to find out," he replied, starting
to stand. "Let's mix with the other passengers and get off."

"Wait," she said, grabbing his arm. "We're still far from the
border. We don't know anyone in Babanusa. If they're looking
for us at the train station, our pale skin will surely stick out.

231

Besides, even if we get out of the station, what then? We have no transportation. No way of getting out of North Sudan."

Jason sat back down. "Maybe you're right."

"We have to figure out a way to get by this guard. The front exit leads to the station, so we can't go out there. The guard and the conductor are blocking us from getting to the rear door," Angie mused aloud. "Maybe we can go into the car with the animals and hide there?"

"Wait. I have an idea," Jason said. Reaching into his pocket, he produced a wad of Sudanese pounds that Steve had given him. It was quite a sum, by Sudanese standards. He handed their four tickets and some money to Matak. "Give the tickets to the conductor when he asks for them. See if the man sitting behind you will sell you his *'imma*."

Matak nodded as the crowd began to thin out. There wasn't much time left before the conductor and his police escort reached the middle of the car where they were seated. Jason hoped they could enact their plan while there were still enough passengers moving around the car to hide them from the guard's view.

After concluding his transaction with the passenger behind him, Matak handed Jason the long cloth used as a male head covering in Sudan. Jason struggled to wrap the *'imma* around his head, his poor efforts at creating a Sudanese turban eliciting a smile from both Matak and Halima. Matak leaned over and helped him wrap the *'imma* into a correct Sudanese head covering.

"What are you doing?" Angie asked.

"Like you said, we're going to stick out in a crowd. We need to cover up."

Halima, catching on to Jason's plan, turned and asked a nearby woman for her blanket. Unlike Matak, however, Halima was able to conclude the transaction using only her charm and warm smile.

"Lie back against the window and cover yourself with this," Halima said to Angie, handing her the small blanket.

Angie covered her head with the blanket and, turning toward the window, buried her face into the space between the seat and side of car. Halima leaned over and made some adjustments, ensuring Angie's skin and hair was completely covered by the blanket.

"There. Now you look like a Sudani. Except for your face," Matak told Jason when he was finished arranging the 'imma loosely over Jason's head.

"I'll put my head down on the table. Matak, hand the conductor the tickets, tell them we're your parents but we're sleeping and you don't want to wake us."

"Okay," Matak replied, and adjusted the loose-fitting turban over Jason's exposed skin as he put his head on the table, hiding his hands and face under the long 'imma.

▼ ▼ ▼

After Matak and Halima finished disguising their American friends, they leaned back into their seats just as a large woman with three children moved from the aisle beside them, allowing the conductor and guard to reach them.

"Tickets?" the conductor asked in Arabic.

Matak handed him the four tickets.

"Those are your parents?" he replied.

"Yes. They're sleeping," Matak answered. "It's been a long day."

The conductor glanced over to the guard who leaned across the table.

"Please don't wake them. They say that I wear them out with all of my energy!" Halima added, flashing him a bright smile.

Matak looked at the guard's face, wondering what was going to happen. But a smile slowly crossed the man's face. He laughed loudly and the conductor joined in. "I bet you do wear them down, little one. I have a daughter your age and I think I get more rest at work than I do at home."

Halima laughed with the men and even Matak feigned a smile.

"Let your parents sleep in peace," the guard said, and walked away. The conductor tore the tickets in half and handed the stubs back to Matak before turning to follow the guard.

"They're gone," Halima whispered.

"Let's just stay like this until they're off the train and we start moving again," Jason replied.

It took another ten minutes for the crowd to thin enough for the conductor and guard to finish checking tickets and leave the train.

▼ ▼ ▼

Jason felt the car pull out of the station and raised his head.

"What was that conversation you had with those men about?" Angie asked, pulling the blanket away from her face.

"Halima was sweet-talking that guard, like she always does with Baba to get her way," Matak explained.

Once more Halima smiled brightly while tilting her head slightly to the side.

"Well, you're very good at it," Angie said, touching Halima's nose with the tip of her finger.

"You may have just saved our lives, Halima," Jason replied, unwrapping the *'imma*.

"Do you think they were looking for us?" asked Angie.

"Maybe. Although I don't think anyone expected us to be on a train headed south. I'm sure the governor notified all his security forces and border guards to be on the lookout for two Americans. I doubt he would expect Halima and Matak to be with us."

"Well, from what we were told, this was the only stop before Wau," Angie said.

"Yep. I only hope Steve's contact will be there with our passports. Steve sounded optimistic about our chances there without them, but there's a reason our relations with the South have deteriorated. Their human rights record may not be as bad as the North, but believe me, we don't want to end up in one of their prisons because we tried to enter South Sudan illegally."

"I'd rather not end up in any more prisons. One was enough," answered Angie.

"We'll know soon enough," Jason replied as the southbound train pulled out of its last station in North Sudan.

41

THE SOUND OF A CRYING BABY woke Jason up from his short nap. He glanced at his watch. Based on the train schedule, it would be another two hours before they reached Wau. He was about to move and stretch but realized Angie was leaning up against him. He put his arm around her shoulder, enjoying the sound of her soft breathing, her face only inches from his. Soon the baby stopped crying and the only other sound was the rhythmic clickety-clack as the train moved along the old rails, cutting through the darkness.

It had only been about four days since he first met Angie but so much had happened in that time. Danger elicits extreme emotions in people, and a deep bond had formed between the two of them. There was no question that he had fallen for the beautiful journalist, but it was more than that. Even though their relationship was new and initially had been strained by the revelation of his CIA work, they had weathered that storm and emerged stronger. Closer.

But could it last? What would happen when they arrived in Wau? His cover was now blown, and he couldn't return to the refugee camp or even to his work with Medicine International.

Perhaps it was time to go back to complete his residency in family medicine. He had some money saved to help take care of his parents. Maybe it would be enough, and maybe it was time to go home. Hopefully, Angie would return as well. After all, there were many good residency programs near San Francisco.

Angie stirred beside him. She sat up and rubbed her tired eyes. "What time is it?"

"Early morning. We have a couple of hours left, but we're almost there. We've probably already crossed into South Sudan, actually."

Halima was asleep but Matak was awake, still staring out of the window.

"I'm going to see if there's anything to eat or drink on this train," Jason said. "I think we can all use some nourishment."

"I'll stay here," replied Angie.

Jason stood up and walked to the back to make his way through the interconnecting doors to the next car in search of food.

▼ ▼ ▼

"How are you doing, Matak?" Angie asked.

"Fine," he replied.

"We're almost at Wau. Are you ready for this all to end?"

"This won't end until that Janjaweed commander is dead."

"I understand, but his death won't bring back your mother," she said.

"To you, revenge may be a bad thing. But it is a part of our culture," the boy replied.

"But look at what it's doing to you. It's eating you up inside. All that anger and hate. Is that what you want?"

"It's not about what I want anymore. The Janjaweed commander is *ad-Dajal*. He destroys everything he comes in contact with. He has to be stopped."

"*ad-Dajal*? What is that?" Angie asked.

"We believe an evil spirit will come one day. He is the false prophet and will pretend to unite us. But he lies. He's the devil."

"Hussein is just a man. Not a devil or evil spirit, just a very bad man."

"A number of signs will occur before *ad-Dajal* makes his appearance. People will lose their faith. Those who lie and take bribes and sell their own neighbors for profit will be everywhere. Famine and disease will destroy our lands, and they will become barren like the Sahara. All of this is happening in Darfur."

"Those are bad things, yes, but that doesn't mean the Antichrist has come to Earth," she answered.

"It also doesn't mean that he *hasn't* come," Matak replied, once again staring out at the darkness. A moment later, he continued quietly, more to himself than to Angie. "Maybe, like you said, the Janjaweed commander is not *ad-Dajal*. But I know these bad things are happening to my country. In my homeland. Evil is all around our villages. What are we to believe?"

Angie didn't know how to respond. Matak's words were true: There were evil men and evil deeds throughout Sudan. How could she, a relatively well-off woman from the California suburbs, explain to this young boy who had been through so much pain why his land and people had to endure so much hardship, when she herself had no answer?

▼ ▼ ▼

Jason walked through the third train car in search of a dining car. There were fewer people on the train than before they arrived in Babanusa. As Fidail mentioned, this second leg of the trip to Wau had not yet been opened officially. The train had stopped running after South Sudan became its own nation in 2011. Fidail had told them both Sudans wanted to increase commerce between the two countries, and after obtaining the new Chinese trains, they decided to see if reopening this route would have any economic benefit.

The train was still relatively dark as most of the passengers slept through the southbound journey. At the end of the car, Jason passed an open door on the right. He stopped for a moment and stepped through the accordion doorway of the small bathroom. His hair was a mess, he had bags under his eyes, and, overall, he just looked terrible. Jason bent down over the sink and splashed some cool water on his face. As the water dripped off his chin, he pondered their next move once they arrived at Wau. Although they were out of immediate danger, their ordeal was in no way over. He still had to prove the atrocities they witnessed to the UNHCR and the world. They had firsthand witnesses and some photos, sure, but he had learned that the world saw only what it wanted to see. Would their evidence be enough?

Jason lifted his face from the sink and returned his gaze to the mirror. His eyes widened at what he saw staring back at him. But he had no time to react. A strong, leathery hand grabbed the back of his neck and slammed his head forward, shattering the small, dirty mirror.

42

ANGIE HAD NO MORE ANSWERS for Matak, who had remained quiet after their brief conversation. Now that Halima was awake, her brother put his arm around her so she could rest more comfortably. At least the two of them were safe, Angie mused. She had no idea how she was going to help them find their sister Fatima, if the girl was even still alive. She hoped Steve and their father would be able to find out something about them from the men at the mine in North Sudan.

"How much longer?" asked Halima, stretching her arms.

"Not long, honey. We should be in Wau in a few hours. Jason went to see if he can find some food," Angie replied.

But Halima didn't acknowledge Angie's answer. She stared right past the American with a horrified look on her face.

"What is it?" Angie cried.

At the fear in Angie's voice, Matak turned from the window and followed her gaze to the far end of the car, then pointed. "Janjaweed!"

Hussein was barreling down the aisle, headed right at them.

"Hurry! Let's go!" Angie said, grabbing Halima's hand and half-dragging her into the aisle.

"There!" Matak said, nodding to the front door of the train car.

Although Hussein was closing in on them, he was slowed down by two women standing in the aisle deep in conversation. He knocked them aside as he barreled through the car in pursuit of his prey.

Angie tried turning the handle on the sliding door at the front of the car, but it wouldn't budge. Matak put his hand on top of hers and together they were able to depress the handle and slide the door open. The three hurried into the next car, slamming the metal door behind them.

"Animals," Angie said, looking around the stable car.

"You two, go. See if there's a way into the engine. The driver may be able to help," Matak said, pointing to a door on the far end of the car.

Angie, still clutching Halima's hand, continued down the narrow aisle. On either side, caged animals, crates, and wooden gates opening into stalls containing sheep, goats, and mules blocked their escape and left them no place to hide.

Matak stood with his back against the wall next to the door. Waiting.

A moment later, the door was thrown open. Hussein strode into the livestock car and slammed the door shut behind him. He smiled and slowly raised a pistol to fire on his targets.

Matak, still hiding along the wall next to the door, seized the moment. He stepped up on the wooden gate beside him and jumped onto Hussein's back. The big Bedouin clawed his left hand behind his head, grabbing the collar of Matak's shirt. But the boy wrapped both arms around Hussein's neck, squeezing with all his might. Angie watched in horror as Hussein's face turned a deep shade of red and his good eye began to bulge out of his head. The Janjaweed commander dropped to one knee, blindly clawing at the arms that were choking him to death. As Hussein struggled for air, the pistol slipped from his hand and hit the floor.

Angie moved to pick up the pistol, but before she could reach it, Hussein leaned forward and kicked the weapon behind him. The Janjaweed commander then lunged backward. Matak crashed against the closed door to the stable car, cracking the window as he became sandwiched between Hussein and the door. Matak let go of Hussein and collapsed onto the floor.

"Matak!" Halima screamed.

Hussein leaned against the door, rubbing his neck with both hands. He finally caught his breath as the color returned to his face. He began staggering down the narrow aisle. But as he regained his full strength, his gait steadied and he closed the gap between himself and Angie and Halima. Angie turned toward the door at the end of the car. Like the door in the passenger car, the lever to open this door also wouldn't budge. Unfortunately, unlike Matak, Halima wasn't strong enough to help Angie lift the heavy handle. Angie looked over her shoulder as Hussein approached. She frantically tugged on the handle, but it was stuck.

"He's getting closer!" Halima cried out.

"You thought you could get away from me, Hussein bin Mohammed al-Fadi, commander of the Janjaweed army?" he snapped in a hoarse voice.

Angie realized that it would only be a few seconds before he was upon them. She leaned back, pulling on the handle with all of her might while looking around searching for anything she could use as a weapon.

"You Americans never learn. You come where you are not wanted. Stick your nose where it doesn't belong, as you say," Hussein continued.

He noticed Angie's eyes darting around behind him.

"No, your American spy is not coming to save you. Not this time. I have already dealt with him."

Hussein reached out and grabbed Angie's long red hair in a strong grip. She shrieked, wincing as he pulled clumps of her hair out. She reached up and grabbed Hussein's hand, hoping to relieve the pressure on her head.

The man smiled.

Halima began kicking the large man in the legs, but Hussein swatted at her with his free hand, knocking her down. He pulled Angie close to his face. "You are not so brave now, are you, woman?" His intense, wild eyes were only inches from Angie's, and his fetid breath filled her nostrils, making her gag.

A wave of hatred and disgust overtook her, replacing her fear. She spat in the Janjaweed's face.

Hussein raised his hand up higher, pulling Angie's hair and forcing her to stand on her toes. The Janjaweed commander wiped his face in her hair and smiled even more broadly. "Feisty," he replied, withdrawing the longest knife Angie had ever seen from a sheath on his belt. "Good, I like that. You will die well."

Angie stared wide-eyed at shiny blade as Hussein waved it slowly in front of her face. "The only question left for me is who to carve up first. You, or the little girl?"

"Face me," hissed a voice from behind the Janjaweed commander.

Hussein snapped his head around to see who was challenging him.

Standing in the middle of the aisle, Matak stood defiantly facing *ad-Dajal.*

"It's time for this to end," the Fur teenage boy said.

43

"MATAK, NO!" Angie screamed. "Run!"

"No more running," Matak replied.

"So, you are a soldier, after all," Hussein said, letting go of Angie. He turned to face off with the much smaller adversary. "Let's see if you can fight like a soldier."

"I am no soldier," answered Matak.

"You *are* a soldier. Like me," Hussein continued, slowly inching his way toward his foe. "You and I are more alike than you think. We both fight for the survival of our people. I will make you a deal, young Matak. Join with me and I will let your sister live."

Matak glanced at Halima, still lying unconscious from Hussein's blow. He noticed blood on her forehead.

Angie bent down to check Halima's pulse.

"I need men like you in my army. Brave men. Strong men. I have a new enemy, Matak. I now fight the *Kufar*," Hussein said, referring to the infidels, or those who do not follow Islam. "Foreigners and nonbelievers who are ruining our country. Defiling our religion. You are Muslim, so you are my brother. Let's fight them together."

While Matak was still looking down at his sister, Hussein closed within striking distance.

"Matak, look out!" Angie cried.

As Hussein lunged toward the boy, Matak raised his right hand and pointed Hussein's pistol at the Janjaweed commander.

Realizing the barrel of the cocked weapon was aimed directly at his face, Hussein froze and stared at Matak.

"Exhale slowly as you pull the trigger," Matak said, curling his index finger around the cold steel trigger. "Isn't that what you told me?"

Hussein remained motionless.

"Don't shake or you won't hit anything. Isn't that how you taught us to fire a gun?" the boy continued, bringing up his left hand to steady his grip on the weapon.

Knowing he only had one chance left to live, Hussein cried out in a loud voice and lunged forward. "*Allah-hu-akhbar!*" he shouted, wielding the knife in a high striking position as he sprang.

Crack! The sound of the pistol echoed loudly through the stable car.

▼ ▼ ▼

"No!" screamed Angie as Hussein and Matak fell to the ground. She jumped up and ran to the middle of the aisle where Hussein lay on top of Matak. Neither was moving. Finally, with a grunt, Matak rolled Hussein off himself. Angie saw where the bullet landed. The Janjaweed commander's good eye was now nothing more than a bloody hole.

Matak stood up, the smoking pistol still in his hand at his side.

"Are you all right?" she asked, reaching down for the pistol.

Matak stared down at the weapon he was holding.

"I'm fine now. We will all be fine now," he said, letting the pistol drop from his grip.

Angie watched as tears formed in the boy's eyes. She put her arms around the teenager and hugged him. It took a moment, but eventually she felt his arms reach up and clasp her back. Then she heard him cry.

44

AS THE FIRST RAYS of the early morning sun broke over the horizon, the train slowly pulled into the small station on the northern corner of Wau of over two hundred thousand souls. Initially established as a base for slave traders centuries ago, the town had grown into a large, diverse commerce center connecting North and South Sudan.

"How's your head?" Angie asked, dabbing the blood still oozing from Jason's forehead.

"It's okay. How long was I out?" he asked.

"Probably half an hour or so. After Matak shot Hussein, we went looking for you. Halima found you propped up in the bathroom."

"I remember seeing Hussein's face in the mirror. Then everything went dark."

"He must have shut the door after leaving you for dead, trying to keep anyone from finding you," she continued.

Matak and Halima returned to their seats, carrying paper cups filled with water. "This was all we could find," Matak said, handing Jason one cup.

"Thanks, Matak. You guys saved my life," Jason said, his back resting on the window.

"Matak saved us all," Angie said, putting a hand on the boy's cheek.

Matak flashed a rare smile. It was one of the few times Angie had seen him express any positive emotion.

"He's brave. Like our father," Halima said, holding her brother's arm closely.

"You both are brave," Jason said, wondering what the long-term effects of the past twenty-four hours would be for the children. "But we're not done yet. We've got to find this UN team and let them know what's going on up north."

"You've got to get to a doctor," Angie said. "You took quite a hit to the head."

"I will. But we have to get through immigration first. If Steve's contact doesn't show up with our passports, we might all need a doctor. Let's go."

The train had come to a stop at the station and the passengers were disembarking. Jason waited until the car had emptied before leading Angie, Matak, and Halima off the train so he could survey the station while the immigration officials were busy with the other passengers.

"I don't see anyone who looks American," Angie said as they walked into the immigration hall. Jason hesitated getting in the immigration line, and the four of them waited near the entrance. "What do we do now if the person from the embassy doesn't arrive?"

Before Jason could answer, an immigration official with sergeant stripes on his sleeves spotted them and walked over.

Jason scanned the room one last time, looking for help from any direction.

"Passports," the sergeant demanded in accented English.

"The U.S. embassy has our passports," Jason answered. "Someone from the consulate should be here any minute."

"No passports?" the man asked angrily.

"They'll be here in just a few minutes. We're waiting for them," Angie added.

"It is illegal to enter South Sudan without passports" came the reply. "You must come with me."

"Technically, we haven't entered South Sudan until we go through immigration," Jason replied, knowing that the ploy would fall on deaf ears.

"You come with me," the sergeant repeated, this time putting his hand on the grip of his holstered pistol.

"I'm from the U.S. embassy in Juba, Sergeant," called a woman's voice from behind the immigration official.

The man turned to face the tall, dark-skinned woman. She was impeccably dressed in a pantsuit, despite the heat. "My name is Karen Brenner," she continued. "Jason Russo and Angie Bryant are U.S. citizens. Here are their diplomatic passports. You'll see everything is in order."

The sergeant looked at the passports carefully. "Wait here," he said, disappearing into a side office with the passports.

"We're so happy to see you, Ms. Brenner," Angie said.

"Steve called me and told me you'd be arriving this morning. It was no easy task getting you these passports last minute."

"Diplomatic passports?" Jason asked.

"You need visas for South Sudan if arriving on a tourist passport. There are fewer questions or hassles if you arrive on a diplomatic passport. I had to pull quite a few favors to get those, so they'd better work."

"Thank you for all you're doing for us," replied Angie.

"No, the U.S. government thanks you for all you've done. Steve told me what you guys went through up in the North. The folks at the embassy are anxious to hear what you have to say," Karen said.

"But I thought you're with the embassy," Angie replied.

"Sort of," Karen said with a smile. "I work with Steve."

"Of course you do," Angie said, smiling back. "Everyone does."

"Steve has a lot of friends. He's very good at what he does."

"He saved our lives more than once," added Jason. "So, what now?"

"First, we get you through immigration, then I'll take you to the conference center where the UN is holding a meeting on human rights in Africa. The ambassador is there and he wants to speak with all of you about what you experienced in Darfur."

"Baba?" Halima asked. "Will Baba be there?"

"One of the SLM commanders is Halima and Matak's father. He said he'd meet them here," Jason told Karen.

"Actually," Karen said, leaning down to speak with Halima directly, "Steve and your father are on their way to Wau. They should be here in a few hours, so don't you worry, little one."

Halima smiled broadly at the good news.

"And," Karen added, "they're bringing us a present."

"What's that?" asked Jason.

"They found Yasser. He's willing to corroborate your story. In exchange for leniency, of course," Karen said wryly.

"Leniency? For that traitor?" Jason asked.

"Think of the bigger picture. There's a lot of power in him backing up the story you guys will tell at the conference. Maybe it'll be enough to get the politicians to finally unite and recommend some stronger sanctions against the North."

"It turns my stomach that Yasser won't hang," Jason said.

"I said *leniency*. He'll still be punished for his crimes. But there's been enough killing, don't you think?" Karen asked.

Jason smiled. "You're right. It's time to let go and move on, I guess."

Angie reached over and held Jason's hand. "We can both move on. Together."

"I'd like that," he answered.

The sergeant returned with their passports. "Welcome to South Sudan."

"Thank you," said Karen. "Let's go. There're a lot of people waiting to hear from you."

45

A CARGO SHIP flying the Panamanian flag pulled into the Baltimore harbor just after sunrise. After a few hours of administrative red tape, a tugboat arrived and facilitated the large ship's mooring at the pier. While the ship's crew was thrilled at the prospect of some liberty on the streets of Baltimore, there was one man even more excited about the arrival of the vessel as he watched the crane lower the red shipping container onto the dock.

Although Edgar had worked with and purchased from the Russians before, this was his first shipment from Africa. Quite a few buyers were waiting up and down the East Coast, and his budding MS-13 clique would profit quite heavily from this sale alone.

"Come on, man, open it up," he said to Sergey impatiently. Edgar had two of his clique with him while Sergey was accompanied only by his driver, whose massive size suggested he was all Sergey needed.

"Please," Sergey said with a smile, handing the key to Edgar.

The Salvadorian snatched it from the Russian's hand and walked over to the shipping container. The key easily opened the lock, and Edgar removed the heavy chain from the large metal doors.

"Sergey, if these girls are half as good quality as you say, we're gonna make a lot of money, you and I," Edgar said, unlatching the door to the container and swinging it open.

"ICE!" cried a woman dressed in an olive-green Nomex flight suit, wearing a helmet and bulletproof vest as she led a Special Response Team out of the container. The law enforcement operators fanned out onto the tarmac, quickly surrounding their five targets. Before Edgar even knew what hit him and his men, they were on the ground getting their hands zip-tied behind them.

Sergey pulled his pistol and got off a few shots on the SRT agents as he sped off down the dock.

"Man down!" shouted the SRT team leader, bending down to care for one of her men.

▼ ▼ ▼

The Russian zigzagged around the large shipping containers stacked on the tarmac as numerous rounds from the SRT's M4 rifles ricocheted around him. Turning a corner, he noticed a small forklift and ducked behind it. He didn't have to wait long before two SRT agents turned around the corner he had just passed a moment before. The two men failed to notice Sergey crouched low behind the forklift, and hurried by, exposing their backs to the experienced Russian mafia killer. Quietly Sergey stepped out from his hiding spot and raised his weapon, aiming for two men.

"Not so fast" came a voice from behind him.

Before the Russian could react, two muscular arms reached around him and lifted him off the ground. Thrown over the forklift, Sergey slammed hard into the steel wall of a shipping container.

▼ ▼ ▼

Lee Jansen, undersecretary with the Department of Homeland Security and head of the Commonwealth Fusion Center in Massachusetts, walked over to the unconscious Russian mobster. He stepped on the man's right hand and kicked his pistol away.

The two SRT agents Lee had just saved ran over and zip-tied Sergey's hands. Lee noticed the unnatural way the Russian's arms twisted as they were pulled behind his body. *Probably a couple of broken bones,* Lee thought, heading back to where the MS-13 gangbanger was in custody.

"Everything all right back there?" Erik Kaiser, DHS special agent out of Homeland Security headquarters in DC, asked.

"For me? Sure," Lee replied casually. "Not so sure our friend Sergey is doing as well, though. I think he might need a doctor."

The two men walked back to the empty container. "Okay, Lee, now that we have these dirtbags in custody, will you tell me how you knew about this shipment?" Erik asked.

Lee looked up at the big cargo ship in front of him. Just over an hour ago, this very same ICE Special Response Team had boarded the vessel and found the Sudanese seaman who had one of the keys for the shipping container. After rescuing the Sudanese girls from inside the container, the SRT climbed into it and waited to be offloaded to surprise whoever had the other key.

"You remember Steve Connors?" Lee asked.

"The CIA guy who tipped us off on the weapons coming in from Mexico awhile back?"

"Yep. He called me yesterday with the ship's name, arrival time and port, and the name of the Sudanese contact aboard who was taking care of the girls during transit."

"How did he get that intel?" Erik asked.

Lee chuckled. "I don't know how well you know Steve, but I've learned not to ask him too many questions. He did tell me that one of the local Darfur rebel leaders helped him get the info. His daughter was one of the girls we rescued from inside the container. Her name's Fatima. There's been so much death in Darfur, at least there's consolation that a few families will be reunited with their daughters. Make sure you work with State on this, Erik. After the girls are checked out by the doctor, I want them on the next flight home to their families. In the meantime, get me a list of their names. Steve said he'd help us inform their families in Darfur that they're alive and well."

"Will do, Lee," Erik replied, happy to comply.

A woman wearing cargo pants, a bulletproof vest, and an ICE cap walked up to the two men.

"Undersecretary Jansen, the suspects have been contained. Officer Figueroa's leg will be fine. Small caliber, went right through the thigh. Didn't hit the bone or any major vessels," she reported. "Another just nicked the skin."

"Great work, Grace," Erik said to the SRT leader.

"Yeah. I can't thank you enough," added Lee. "I know I didn't give you much time to put your team together. You run a tight ship, Agent Forrester."

"Thank you, sir," the head of the capital-region ICE SRT replied.

"From the looks of it, we nailed some MS-13 thugs and maybe even a Russian mafia supplier who traffics women. Not a bad day's work, and it isn't even noon yet," Erik said.

"That means that our work has only just begun," Lee said. "Agent Forrester, how are the girls doing?"

"Good," she said. "No life-threatening injuries or illnesses, although they've been through a lot, as you can imagine. I have a second SRT escorting them ashore. They're on the tugboat, should be here in about fifteen minutes or so. I have a bus with some armed escorts ready to take them to the hospital to get looked at."

"Great. I'll want to talk with them when the doctors think they're ready," Lee said. "We still have a lot of work to do. This is far from over. These dirtbags are only the foot soldiers. Those ultimately responsible are still out there. And we need to find them."

46

"THEY TOOK THE GIRLS and the women. Dragged them away after killing the men in the village. I watched as the Janjaweed killed my neighbor Nadifa's husband. They were just married the day before. The decorations from the wedding were still hanging over the hut behind where they shot him. Nadifa was there. She was crying, begging them not to kill her husband. I saw them laughing at her. They hit her with their rifle then took her away," Halima said, wiping a tear from her eye.

Angie sat beside the young girl, her arm around her the entire time, while Matak sat stoically on the other side of his sister.

"Thank you, Halima," said Serrena Binachi, conference director for the UN Refugee Agency's forum on human rights.

"There is certainly enough here for us to launch a full investigation into this matter," said Eduardo Maldonado, president of the International Criminal Court at The Hague. The Argentinian diplomat and career barrister had been invited to the UNHCR conference to give a lecture on international law as it pertains to refugees.

The closed-door interview with select senior leaders of the international community involved in combating human rights violations had been set up by Dr. Binachi and Michelle Kalakona, the U.S. Ambassador to the United Nations, at the request of Karen Brenner. Judge Maldonado stood from the table in the front of the conference room and walked over to the CIA agent. "Ms. Brenner," he said. "Thank you for bringing this matter to our attention."

"What will happen next?" Jason asked.

"When I get back to the Hague tomorrow, I'll discuss it with Vice Presidents of the Court and we'll launch an official inquiry. In the meantime, I'll type up my report and send it over to the UN Secretary-General this evening. I'm sure he'll have some serious conversations with the heads of the nations involved."

Secretary-General Gautam Mahajan was very popular and influential. Karen and Jason were glad that this was being elevated to his level and that he would be personally involved in fighting for the Darfur people.

"Thank you, sir," Karen said. "It's time the international community stops talking and starts taking action in Sudan."

Judge Maldonado nodded his head and left the room with his entourage of lawyers.

"That little girl never ceases to amaze me," Jason said as he stood in the corner of the room. Angie, Matak, and Halima were still conversing with Dr. Binachi at the head table while dozens of others listened intently in their seats.

"I'm glad Ambassador Kalakona was able to pull enough strings to allow Halima and her brother to speak to the International Criminal Court today," Karen replied.

"I appreciate you increasing security," Jason said, looking at the exits guarded by armed UN Peacekeepers. Ever since word of the Fur children's arrival at the Human Rights Conference became public, international tensions between the two Sudans had risen to a threatening level. "Do you think the accusations from Shao Mining Corporation had any impact?"

"None whatsoever. No one will believe that you and Angie sought to destroy their mine. In fact, given the choice between believing the company's attorney who spoke this morning to an empty press conference and the powerful testimony from Halima and her brother today, I think the public will be in our favor. Besides, Angie's story is already running in all the U.S. media outlets. The Chinese government is supporting us both in the UN on resolutions against Sudan and in the investigation. The Chinese Ambassador to the UN told Ambassador Kalakona that they'll look into the Shao Mining Corporation as well as other rogue Chinese companies operating outside of China. They're cracking down on human trafficking, too."

"I want to thank all of the participants at this important human rights forum," Dr. Binachi said aloud after standing at the head table. "It has been an emotional conference, to be sure, but one that was also productive in its efforts to increase awareness of human rights violations in the region. I would like to take this opportunity to announce that the Secretary-General of the United Nations, moved by the firsthand accounts of the atrocities in Darfur, has agreed to double the number of peacekeepers in Sudan. Additionally, donor nations have pledged financial support at unprecedented levels to continue the fight against human rights violations. Interpol has also announced new collaborative efforts with the Ministry of Public Security in China and the American Federal Bureau of Investigation and Department of Homeland Security to investigate and prosecute those behind the heinous crimes of human trafficking, slavery, and the exploitation of children, especially in war-torn regions of Africa. I want to thank all of the participants here today, and a special thank you to Halima and Matak, whose courage and resilience is an example for all of us."

The select group of influential humanitarians stood up and applauded loudly for the two children. Halima smiled broadly and Angie noticed a smile come across Matak's face as well. Perhaps his healing had already begun.

EPILOGUE

I T WAS GOOD to be back home, despite the circumstances. Feng Wu was from a small village just north of this mountainous city in central China. He walked through the snow and entered the famous public garden where, almost a century ago, the seeds of modern Communist China had been planted in this bloody soil.

Sitting on a bench, dressed in black and accompanied only by her fierce bodyguard, Shao Ying waited.

"Things did not go as planned in the Sudan, did they, Feng?" she asked as he sat down beside her.

Feng Wu had known Ying since she was a little girl. He was certain that he was alive today, despite the events in Sudan, solely because he had been a loyal and faithful servant to her father for many decades.

"Our friends in Khartoum don't want us to rebuild the mine. They said there's too much pressure right now. Too many international eyes on them after the Fur children testified to the UN."

"Not to mention the pressure being put on me by the government here," Ying said, looking at him sternly. "What about the research?"

"All evidence destroyed. There's nothing for anyone to find there," replied Feng. But he had one burning question. "Why did the scientists have to die? They had learned so much to advance the project. It would have been helpful to bring them back here to complete their work."

"You are not in my position, Feng. I had information that you did not. The scientists would most assuredly have been taken by the rebels. I couldn't risk them being exposed or captured. I have enough pressure on me right now from the government in Beijing, thanks to this mess. I can't risk anything jeopardizing this project. Nothing and no one," she said.

"But what is to become of the project now?" Feng asked, clearing his throat at the not-so-veiled threat. He had no idea how Ying would know the SLM leader was going to take the scientists but knew better than to ask.

"We would be ahead of schedule were it not for your miscalculation in the Sudan," Ying chided. "But I have another site in mind to continue the research."

"We'll need more test subjects."

"I'll take care of that myself," Ying answered, looking out over the frozen landscape.

"We had the Janjaweed commander and his men trapped in the mine. If the Americans and their SLM allies had not interfered, everything would have ended peacefully," Feng said.

"I'm not so sure of that," she said, glancing over at her disgraced subordinate. "I saw the footage. Why did you feel it necessary to have a conversation with Hussein? I told you to get rid of him and see if Tawfik could gain control of his Janjaweed army. You wasted valuable time."

"Hussein was inconsequential. Abdullah al-Harbi was instigating Hussein's insolence," Feng said, pulling his smartphone out of his overcoat pocket. "Listen." He pushed some buttons until a recorded conversation began playing over the speaker.

"It's time, my new emir in the Sudan, for us to make our mark on the world. Prove to me that I can trust you as my new prince in Africa. Show me what you can do against the infidels."

Feng pressed another button and the recording ended. "You see, al-Harbi was inciting Hussein the whole time."

"Are you sure this is al-Harbi?" she asked.

"Positive. Our friend in the U.S. government confirmed it using voice recognition. It *is* Abdullah al-Harbi."

"So, the new *khalifah* created all of this trouble for us in Sudan?" she said, leaning back on the bench.

"It appears so. He was behind Hussein going after the Americans and maybe even the attack on us at the mine."

"I have misjudged al-Harbi," Ying mused. She stood up and walked through the empty garden. Feng and her bodyguard followed closely, awaiting her instructions.

"Feng Wu, you were friends with my father for many years."

"Yes. I was one of his first employees and confidants," he replied with a slight bow in deference to his friend.

"You know that he was a master of *wei qi*," she said. The ancient Chinese game of Go was arguably the oldest board game still in existence.

"Of course. We used to play for hours, but I never could beat him. Shao Jun was a brilliant strategist."

"Yes, he was. You know, of course, that *wei qi* is a game of encirclement. Unlike chess, where one seeks to remove the opponent's pieces to capture the king, *wei qi* is much more elegant and relies on strategy to surround and eventually choke out one's opponent. It's not just a game of skill but rather a test of each player's character. In the end, the player who masters his or her own strengths and weaknesses will emerge victorious."

"You have learned much from your father," Feng replied.

"More than you know. I believe it's time for us to make our next move. Tell me about Faisal."

"Faisal Saddiq? He's a Saudi Salafi who moved to Yemen when he was a child. He joined up with al-Harbi soon after that. He's al-Harbi's right-hand man at the UIC. Very trusted, very loyal."

"Yes. But he's Sufi," Ying said.

Feng was taken back. "Faisal? A mystical Sufi? No, I'm sure he's a dedicated Salafi extremist, like Abdullah al-Harbi. Sufism is a relatively peaceful sect of Sunni Islam. I doubt very much he'd be in the UIC terror organization if he were a Sufi."

"Faisal Idris Saddiq is from 'Asir, Saudi Arabia. He was born into a devout Sufi family. They were persecuted by the Wahhabis in Saudi, and many of his relatives were killed. That's when Faisal denounced his Sufi roots, became a Salafi, and joined al-Harbi. But you are correct, he is devoted to his *khalifah*."

Feng was surprised at how much intelligence Ying had at her disposal.

"I make it my business to know all I can about those I deal with," Ying continued with a smile. "Another lesson from my father. Set up a meeting with Abdullah al-Harbi. Just him. Tell him to come alone. It's time for us to make our next move."

ACKNOWLEDGMENTS

I AM BEYOND THRILLED to see *Evil Winds,* the third title in my Tradecraft series, come to life. I could not have accomplished this endeavor without the help and expertise of a team of publishing professionals who worked tirelessly to make it happen. A big thank-you to Leigh Camp, the production manager of the series; Philip Athans, my developmental editor; Debra Manette, copy editor; John Reinhardt, interior designer and typesetter; James Fraleigh, proofreader; and Ty Nowicki, cover designer.

A special thanks also goes out to Joe Andes for the public affairs support. I would not be holding this book in my hands right now if not for your efforts. Thank you all for your excellent work.

And finally, thank you to my wife, my partner, and my dearest friend, Julie—and to my boys, Alex, Sam, and John: I love you all beyond measure.

ABOUT THE AUTHOR

MICHAEL SHUSKO, MD, MPH, FAAFP, FACOEM, was raised in Long Branch, NJ. He enlisted in the Marine Corps in 1985 after graduating high school.

Dr. Shusko cut his teeth in the military in the mid-1980s and early 1990s. As his first assignment, he attended the Defense Language Institute Foreign Language Center in Monterey, CA, where he studied Arabic. Upon completing his language training, he worked on intelligence missions across the globe. He spent time in Liberia, served as a Marine during the first Gulf War, and worked for several years with the Defense Attaché's office at the U.S. Embassy in Kuwait.

After returning to the States in 1995, Dr. Shusko focused his attention on earning his bachelor's degree in Middle Eastern studies from Rutgers University while studying Persian-Farsi at Princeton. He then transferred to the Navy Medical Corps and enrolled in medical school at Wake Forest University,

267

obtaining his medical degree in 2002. He also studied at Harvard University, earning a Master's of Public Health degree in 2013.

Dr. Shusko is a family medicine physician, an occupational medicine physician, and a preventive medicine physician. His Middle Eastern experience and language skills coupled with his background in special operations and intelligence keep him busy deploying around the world. He has traveled extensively throughout the Middle East, Africa, Europe, and Asia and has been awarded the Bronze Star twice for service in Iraq and Afghanistan.

He currently lives in Japan with his wife and eighteen-year-old triplet sons.

TRADECRAFT

I HOPE YOU ENJOYED this most recent installment of the Tradecraft series. If so, please take a look at *Vector* and *Shifting Sands*, books one and two in the series, on Amazon. The fourth book in the six-book series, *The Fifth Column*, is slated to come out soon.

Vector: Tradecraft Phase Zero
Shifting Sands: Tradecraft Phase One
Evil Winds: Tradecraft Phase Two

(Coming Soon!)
The Fifth Column: Tradecraft Phase Three

If you have the opportunity, please take a minute to leave a review of *Evil Winds* on Amazon. I read every review and would love to hear your thoughts!

Thanks,

Mike

P.S. The very first title I'm publishing independently from the Tradecraft series, *The Gardener's Daughter*, is on the docket for my next release.

Sign up to be the first to hear news about all upcoming titles at MichaelShusko.com.